A Harlequin Christmas Carol

BETINA KRAHN · JACQUIE D'ALESSANDRO
HOPE TARR

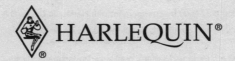

TORONTO • NEW YORK • LONDON
AMSTERDAM • PARIS • SYDNEY • HAMBURG
STOCKHOLM • ATHENS • TOKYO • MILAN • MADRID
PRAGUE • WARSAW • BUDAPEST • AUCKLAND

ISBN-13: 978-0-373-83742-7

A HARLEQUIN CHRISTMAS CAROL

Copyright © 2010 by Harlequin Books S.A.

The publisher acknowledges the copyright holders of the individual works as follows:

YESTERDAY'S BRIDE
Copyright © 2010 by Betina Krahn

TODAY'S LONGING
Copyright © 2010 by Jacquie D'Alessandro

TOMORROW'S DESTINY
Copyright © 2010 by Hope Tarr

Recycling programs
for this product may
not exist in your area.

This edition published by arrangement with Harlequin Books S.A.

For questions and comments about the quality of this book please contact us at Customer_eCare@Harlequin.ca.

® and TM are trademarks of the publisher. Trademarks indicated with ® are registered in the United States Patent and Trademark Office, the Canadian Trade Marks Office and in other countries.

www.eHarlequin.com

Printed in U.S.A.

CONTENTS

"I am here to-night to warn you,
that you have yet a chance and hope of
escaping my fate...you will be haunted,"
resumed the Ghost, "by three spirits."

—*A Christmas Carol:
Being a Ghost Story of Christmas*
by Charles Dickens

YESTERDAY'S BRIDE

Betina Krahn

* * *

"Who, and what are you?" Scrooge demanded.
"I am the Ghost of Christmas Past."
"Long past?" inquired Scrooge.
"No. Your past."

—*A Christmas Carol:*
Being a Ghost Story of Christmas
by Charles Dickens

For my little girls, Kate and Sarah.
May you grow up strong and learn to love well.

PROLOGUE

MacPherson and Daughter Booksellers
Covent Garden, London
December 23, 1890, 3:00 p.m.

APPRENTICE ANGEL PERIWINKLE smiled with relief as she recognized two other apprentices atop one of the dusty bookcases that lined MacPherson and Daughter Booksellers in Covent Garden. Fern and Rose were focused on watching three young women gathering around a tea table at the rear of the cozy shop. Periwinkle joined the two on their perch and, after hugs of greeting, settled in to watch the women with them.

"So, they meet here every month?" she asked. The others had been with their mortals for some time, Periwinkle had learned, but she—a new apprentice—had been assigned to Claire Halliday for just over three weeks and was finding her assignment a bit overwhelming.

"Like clockwork. For nearly two years now," plump and pleasant Rose said with a nod.

"My Fiona brought them together, you know. Book lovers, every one," tall, authoritative Fern declared. "And fast friends now, through thick and thin."

"Well, Claire Halliday can certainly use some friendship," Periwinkle said with a wince. "You should see what she has to put up with at home."

"Ahh. The relatives." Rose nodded again in sympathy.

"We've heard about them." Fern rustled with disapproval, creating a small shower of green and gold sparkles.

"Are they as bad as she makes them out to be?" Rose asked.

"Worse." Periwinkle sighed. "I don't know how the poor thing gets through Christmas at all. If only our charges lived nearer each other and met socially..."

But they didn't; outside of their book discussions, their lives lay in separate spheres. And Claire Halliday's social life was nonexistent, which made Periwinkle's task of helping Claire find True Love within the next week all but impossible. If anything ordained by The Powers That Be could be said to be *impossible*.

"I wish the ladies would pick something else to read." Periwinkle frowned at the discussion underway. "Dickens. It's always that Dickens at Christmas."

"I'm just glad they *can* read," Fern folded her arms. "In my day, books were just for rich men and monks."

"Chain rattling, midnight manifestations and yanking people back and forth through time—" Rose rolled her eyes "—as if any of that were allowed."

Angel work, they knew full well, was done mostly by nudges, whispers and dream work...subtle influences meant to draw people toward good choices and soul-ripening opportunities. Flashy "Lo I bring you great tidings" revelations were forbidden to apprentices, which made their assignments—and Periwinkle's current dilemma—all the more difficult.

"I don't know how I can be expected to help her

find True Love without at least a peek at the future," Periwinkle said with a hint of desperation.

"You don't know who her One True Love is?" Rose asked, shocked.

"Not really. She's supposed to already know him, but she might as well be a nun, for all her contact with eligible males. I haven't heard a single male name in any of her thoughts or dreams." Periwinkle sagged as she studied her auburn-haired assignment, whom she had accompanied now through three stifling weeks of life. Claire was dressed in a simple, stylish navy woolen suit that displayed her womanly curves and good taste in equal measure. She was lovely. Sweet-natured. Kind to a fault. And from what Periwinkle could tell, destined to spend decades crocheting tea cozies and tending crotchety relatives. "Barrellin' straight toward spinsterhood, that one."

"And dragging you with her—straight into another hundred years of apprenticeship," Rose said with a shiver that sent a shower of lovely pink-and-fuchsia-colored sparkles onto the shelf around her. "Unless you can help her find True Love by the stroke of midnight on December 31, you'll be stuck without wings for another hundred years."

"We all will." Fern scowled, obviously thinking of their common deadline.

The three glanced over their shoulders, imagining the long, beautiful wings that would mark their transcendence to full angel status and a new level of connection and empowerment.

"The worst of it is, I *know* who Fiona's True Love

is," Fern said, her mouth tightening with regret. "I've known for several years."

"As do I." Rose sighed, looking at her Adelaide fondly. "Not that it makes the task any easier. He's all but married to her sister. To have a happily-ever-after, you have to believe happiness is possible. I fear my Addie no longer does."

"Claire certainly seems to have given up on it." Periwinkle sighed.

They watched for a while in silence.

"Say—" Fern leaned closer to the others and lowered her voice "—have you tried doing something physical? If you really work at it, you can move things, you know. Like a lamp or a book. Have you ever tried writing something out on a frosty window? Perhaps giving your charge a little push?"

"Yes," Periwinkle confessed. It wasn't like The Powers That Be didn't already *know* about her attempts. "I did. But every time I manifest in the physical plane, my blue sparkles look like dust to her. The poor thing takes a sneezing fit and then gets all stuffy and heads for the Mentholatum ointment."

"Dreams are the most effective tool I've found," Rose said, giving Periwinkle a sympathetic pat. "With a little practice, you can influence your girl's dreams and even speak to her in them."

"I suppose. Just look at old Scrooge, there," Periwinkle said wryly. "A couple of strange dreams and he changed forev— Aay!" She sat straighter, her eyes and thoughts darting. "They're so impressed with that book—why don't we use it? Dreams…past, present and future. It's a natural fit. Claire is a near-widow, stuck in remnants of the past. Perhaps I could use her story to reach her and give her some hope."

Rose perked up. "And Addie can't see what's before her nose in the here and now. I could take the present."

"My Fiona's always worrying about the future," Fern declared. "The 'future' suits me just fine."

Just then the bell on the shop door jingled as a customer entered and all three looked around with a shiver of excitement. That blessed sound! The ring of that bell signaled that somewhere, another apprentice angel had just been granted wings. Their faces brightened. Looking at each other, minds buzzing, the three of them nodded and then turned their gazes to their assignments with renewed determination.

CHAPTER ONE

December 23, 1890, 4:30 p.m.

"PUSHY KNOW-IT-ALLS, those Christmas spirits," Claire Halliday said tartly as she and her friends rose from the tea table at the rear of the book shop. "I feel sorry for Scrooge. I mean, the man was as miserable as he was mean-spirited. His life was as cold as a well-digger's ankle—inside and out. And they came along and practically scared him to death."

"I believe that was the point," Fiona, the shop's proprietress, said with a wry smile. "His life was so barren and desolate that the usual channels of change wouldn't work. It took something supernatural to shake him out of his rut."

"Hmm," Claire said with a look of exaggerated cunning, "I wonder how one would go about suggesting people to receive such visits."

That drew laughter from Lady Adelaide Kendall and Fiona MacPherson. The women had been meeting in Fiona's shop for tea and book discussions long enough for the others to know Claire's circumstances.

"No wassail or Yule log at the Mayhew house, I'm guessing," Adelaide said as they donned their coats.

Claire paused in the middle of fastening her coat buttons. "Stephen died four years ago last week. Every year at this time, it's like it happens all over again. Mother Mayhew weeps and haunts the drawing room like a wraith. Uncle Abner stays late at the factory and comes home potted and morose. Aunt Eloise drags out the black yarn and crochets *more* mourning accessories. Cousin Halbert locks himself in his workshop and Cousin Tillie plays the most god-awful dirges on the spinet."

"Sounds dreadful." Adelaide radiated sympathy.

"And you?" Fiona asked, frowning. "What do you do?"

Claire shook off a somber thought and lifted the brown-paper-wrapped package of books she had just purchased from Fiona.

"I closet myself in my room and read. Thank heaven you were able to find the books I wanted, Fiona. Hot cocoa and a good book—I'll be all right. Christmas lasts only a few days. Perhaps on Boxing Day I'll go to the factory and do some cleaning and organizing in Uncle Abner's office."

"Cleaning? Good Lord—tell me you're not that desperate," Fiona said in mock horror, looking around at the dusty edges of her shop. "Let me lend you a cat for a few days or something."

They laughed and hugged and several minutes later Claire was out on the pavement, coat collar raised and chin tucked against the wind, striding toward the omnibus stand. The weather was changing fast; the light rain was thickening and becoming clingy—true sleet. Perfect, she thought, with a scowl at the leaden sky; it matched her dismal expectations for the evening ahead.

Hugging her package tightly, she struggled to hold on to the warmth of the afternoon's camaraderie and not allow the deepening chill to invade. But by the time she reached the omnibus that would take her all the way to Breton Cross, a village at the very edge of London, she was already cold. The walk from the final stop to her home would probably chill her to the bone.

The word *home* stuck in her mind as she climbed into the vehicle, paid her fare, and took a seat. Her home wasn't really hers, it was the Mayhews'. The house, the fortune and—she hated to admit—the grief were more rightly theirs than hers. An orphan from a good family with whom the Mayhews had often done business, she had been taken in at the age of twelve by them and had been grafted into the Mayhew family tree by virtue of her impending marriage to the family scion, Stephen.

Then Stephen died in a carriage accident, just days before their Christmas wedding four years ago, and the Mayhews insisted she stay on with them. She was family, they said. "Our dear Stephen's poor bride."

But she wasn't really a bride, or a widow or any longer a young girl with a head full of dreams. She was something uncomfortably outside all of those, stuck in an ambiguous nether-land between maid and woman, bride and wife, spinster and widow. She had adored Stephen, but after four long years, she was beginning to forget his broad, pleasant face and the sound of his calm, steady voice. Was that because her heart was going numb from these annual resurrections of pain or because she was finally getting past the tragedy?

The omnibus route took them past the cemetery at St John's Church where Stephen had been laid to rest, and for the first time in four long years, she didn't turn away from the sight. The stately, barren trees and forest of stones and monuments no longer tugged at her heart or caused a constriction in her throat. It was simply a quiet, hallowed place that served as comfort to those who needed to remember. With equal measures of relief and regret, she realized that she no longer needed that comfort.

What she needed was a life of her own, one not borrowed or dependent on someone else's family traditions. It was time she took matters into her own hands and began to realize some of the dreams that had made her life bearable these past four years. She looked down at the wrapped package on her lap and ran a gloved hand over the outlines of the books it contained. She wanted to travel and see some of the wonders she'd read about…taste the world's different foods, hear the music of other languages and see sunsets untainted by London fog and chimney smoke. And perhaps somewhere in her wanderings she might meet a tall, dark stranger who could make her feel excitement and hope and a sense of intimate connection once again.

It was growing dark by the time she reached Mayhew House, which was nestled in an enclave of sizeable homes built with gardens in the front. A brick-and-wrought-iron fence surrounded the entry garden and rose to a wide arch over the front walkway. The golden glow coming from the windows and the elegant approach spoke of comfort and the trappings of a pleasant life. Unfortunately, behind those impressive black lacquered doors, life was anything but comfortable just now.

Claire paused under the gate arch, looking at the doors, half expecting mourning wreaths would have reappeared in her absence. Inhaling the icy air, bracing for the gloom that was about to descend, she headed for the doors.

"Here she is!" Mother Mayhew's penetrating voice rang out over a large pile of boxes and crates stacked in the entry hall. "Claire is home!"

Claire halted just inside the door, staring at imposing Mother Mayhew's muslin mobcap and dirt-streaked apron. From behind the stack of dusty boxes, Cousin Tillie's birdlike form appeared, swathed in similar protection. Ample, pink-faced Aunt Eloise bustled out of the dining room, wearing an apron and dust guards over her sleeves. Dust was a long-standing Mayhew obsession.

"What is all of this?" Claire asked as they rushed to close the door behind her and draw her into the warmth.

"Look at you—you're half frozen." Mother Mayhew brushed at the moisture on Claire's shoulders and felt her cold cheeks. "You insisted on going out to that 'book group' of yours in the worst possible weather. Let us get you out of those wet clothes before you come down with pneumonia!"

As they divested her of her package and coat—which, in truth, *was* damp and cold—she returned to her question.

"What is in all the boxes? Where did they come from?"

"The attic and cellars," Uncle Abner called from the stairs as he descended with another sizeable pasteboard box that was yellowed with age and covered in dust. For the first time in years, he smiled, softening his long, somber face. "Storage, don't you know. Got things tucked all over."

She scowled, trying to make sense of that non-answer, and Mother Mayhew took her by the hand and pulled her into the drawing room, where the remnants of afternoon tea waited. As Claire settled on a chair near the fire, Aunt Eloise pulled Claire's gloves from her hands and Cousin Tillie threw a crocheted coverlet around her, tucking it in as if she were a child. Cousin Tillie had unfulfilled "mothering" impulses.

"Have some tea, dear, to warm you up." Mother Mayhew felt the side of the silver teapot and, judging it to be acceptable, poured Claire a cup. As Claire sipped and wrapped her cold fingers around the delicate china, Mother Mayhew, Aunt Eloise and Cousin Tillie jammed themselves into the settee across from her, leaving Uncle Abner to perch on its arm. Claire closed her eyes for a second to savor the warmth and opened them a moment later to four faces staring intently at her.

"What is it?" She braced herself. "Has something happened?"

Three of them answered all at once:

"We've had a bit of news."

"We're going to have a Christmas."

"We're about to receive a guest."

She gaped at them, unable to merge three separate trains of thought into one coherent picture. Mother Mayhew scooted forward on her seat, taking the lead.

"You recall Cousin Ralph Hutton...posted in India?" she asked.

"Of course I remember," Claire responded, looking from face to face. How could she forget? With every letter or package from their estimable cousin-twice-removed, the Mayhews had launched into a recitation of the man's virtues. Cousin Ralph was clever with figures and finance, was born with ledger ink running in his veins. Cousin Ralph could walk around the block with a penny and come back with a pound. Cousin Ralph was as solid as the Bank of England and as sensible as woolen socks. Cousin Ralph was loyal, dutiful, trustworthy and diligent—which, Claire had always thought to herself, made him sound suspiciously like a sheepdog.

But, however virtuous Cousin Ralph might be, his writing was nothing short of snore-worthy. The half-dozen letters that had sent the Mayhews into raptures had all the charm of a counting-house ledger sheet. Then there were the *things* he sent. The strange statues and carvings, she learned after some research, were objects of reverence and worship in India and the Far East. Idols, actually. Odd things indeed to send a clutch of aging English gentlefolk mired hopelessly in grief.

Worse yet, it didn't take a mind reader to see that the Mayhews sang his praises *in her direction*. She didn't want to think about the implications of that.

"We had a letter this morning," Uncle Abner said with more zest than Claire had seen him display in years. "It seems he left the Merchant-Holmes Company a month back. Resigned. He's on his way home to England."

"To *us*," Mother Mayhew added, touching her heart, clearly transported.

"To this very house," Cousin Tillie added as if she hardly dared hope.

"Arriving Christmas Eve." Aunt Eloise always injected a practical note.

Claire glanced through the open drawing-room doors to the crates and boxes piled in the hallway. Cousin Ralph's announcement that he was coming to visit had somehow snapped them out of their grief and persuaded them to rejoin the rest of the human race—all in the space of a day? As a miracle, it ranked right up there with the parting of the Red Sea!

"How...wonderful," she said, stuffing a tea biscuit into her mouth to keep from saying anything that might dampen their enthusiasm.

"I never thought to see such a happy day again." Mother Mayhew's gaze fixed on some fair and distant vision. "Our dear Ralph is coming home."

"And at Christmas," Cousin Tillie said, dabbing her eyes.

"By George," Uncle Abner said, punctuating his determination with the swoop of a fist, "we must give the boy a proper welcome."

"All those years away from home, stuck in that awful foreign place, surrounded by heathens." Aunt Eloise's mouth pursed with righteous fervor. "Our dear Ralph deserves a proper *English* holiday."

And just like that, the house was plunged into producing the most idyllic "English" Christmas possible. The kitchen was set to cooking mincemeat tarts, sugary biscuits and sticky pudding, and the housemaids were ordered to freshen Stephen's old room and see that the fireplaces and bathing rooms were given extra attention.

Uncle Abner hauled Cousin Halbert out of his workshop to assist, and they were soon opening boxes and unpacking festive decorations, serving ware and Christmas linens.

The cleaning, polishing and arranging seemed to go on forever. The grim, black antimacassars and table leg skirts had to be replaced by more cheerful white ones and space had to be made for the crèche display. Then the drawing room had to be reconfigured to accommodate a Christmas tree…although everyone seemed to have a different notion of where the tree and decorations always used to be. By midnight it seemed that the entire main level lay dismantled like a giant puzzle waiting to be reassembled.

Through it all came a renewed litany of Cousin Ralph's somber virtues, accompanied by not-so-subtle glances her way. It wasn't lost on Claire that "our dear Ralph" was now spoken of with the same reverence and affection as "our dear Stephen." But by the time she dragged herself up the stairs to her room that night, she was so tired that she no longer cared about their behavior.

She could have sworn she heard someone say her name in the upstairs hallway, but when she turned to look, she was alone. The dust from the crates and boxes must have wafted up the stairs, because at that moment she took a sneezing fit and hurried into her room to get away from it.

Later, as she lay nestled in her bed, she seemed to hear a faint whisper. Perhaps just a stray thought of her own—something about mistletoe…

Periwinkle sat on the bed beside Claire, waiting for that magic moment when her charge's quiet mind stirred anew with dreams. She had tried before to search Claire's memories for someone who might serve as a True Love candidate, and had been frustrated by Claire's dearth of interest in men. Left to her own devices, she'd dream about ships and caravans and spice bazaars...not a handsome sea captain or romantic sheik in the lot.

Hours later, Periwinkle sprawled on the floor with her back against a bedpost, feeling drained and dispirited. She had whispered to the dreaming Claire of Stephen and their sweet intimacies, hoping to pull some useful longing out of the pleasures of the past. All she got was a hazy, insubstantial figure who remained stubbornly distant in every scene she resurrected. Even the kisses Claire recalled seemed to have been stripped of passion and emotional weight. The poor girl was in worse condition than Periwinkle had realized; even in Claire's dreams her well of desire was bone dry!

In desperation, Periwinkle tried searching for memories of this "Ralph" who was coming to visit. There were only two or three, and in all of them Claire was quite young. Her glimpses of him had been so incidental that she couldn't actively recall him. He had left Oxford well before Stephen and had gone straight to a post in India.

Periwinkle sighed. What were the odds that he'd be tall, dark and charming enough to melt a frozen heart? Ralph. What kind of name was that for a True Love, anyway?

DARKNESS AND FREEZING RAIN shrouded the landscape around the train, which was crowded with holiday travelers and stopped dead on the tracks forty miles from Greater London. Heavy rains of late had undermined some of the rails ahead and the conductor had announced that they were stuck for the night. Rafe Hutton thought of the old cousins waiting for him, watching the door on Christmas Eve and growing worried when he didn't arrive. He had promised them, and he was a man who kept his promises. With a road-weary sigh, he turned his back on his first-class cabin with its freshly made-up sleeping berth, called the porter and asked for his bags.

Fortunately, the nearest village had a tavern that was open late and he was able to get directions to the local livery. Banging on the cottage door, he roused the owner and convinced him to open the stable.

"That little gig," the stable man said, pointing to an aged one-seater that was little more than a wooden buck cart. "She ain't much, but she's all I got."

Rafe winced, looked out at the icy rain still pelting down and nodded.

"I'll take it."

CHAPTER TWO

HALFWAY THROUGH Christmas Eve day, the obvious finally struck Claire. She sat in the drawing room, making garlands and staring at the fir tree leaning in the corner, trying to imagine it upright and filled with glowing candles, and overheard Mother Mayhew speaking to Uncle Abner.

"We simply have to have oranges," Mother Mayhew said, standing in the doorway. "It's just not Christmas without oranges and beeswax candles."

"Well, I can't pull oranges out of a hat, Hortense," Abner groused. "And he's not going to be persuaded to stay by some fruit floating in a punch bowl."

"Our dear Ralph, of course he'll stay," Mother Mayhew said with enough force to lay bare her fears that he might not. "He'll see how much we need him at the factory and—" she caught sight of Claire watching them "—there is so much to keep him here."

So *that* was what was behind their transformation, Claire realized. In their minds Cousin Ralph, who had no other family, was coming to take over the Mayhew cutlery factory. It had been Stephen's familial duty before the accident, and that mantle was being transferred to Cousin Ralph. It made sense, she supposed, from their self-absorbed point of view.

She just hated to see them get their hopes up about something so—

The odd look Mother Mayhew had given her registered. *There is so much to keep him here.* Claire dropped the roll of wire she was using to fasten the boughs together. The comment knitted together nuances in her mind. Ralph wasn't just expected to take Stephen's place at the factory, he was expected to take Stephen's place with *her!*

"It will be good to have some youth and energy in the fork works again," Uncle Abner said. "I can't wait to show him our new stamping machines—"

"Abner." Mother Mayhew frowned. "Promise me you will postpone all talk of business until after the holiday. He will need time to get to know us again. We're all the family he has left." She glanced fondly at Claire. "Much like our Claire. You see, they have something in common already."

She watched Mother Mayhew head for the kitchen and Uncle Abner reach for his coat to join Cousin Halbert in fastening a garland around the front doors. Caught between the effrontery and the absurdity of their assumptions, she rose and headed for the stairs.

With each step, she grew more outraged. After all of the love and care and consideration she'd shown them… after all of the wailing she'd endured and the weeping she'd comforted…the meddlesome old trots were hoping to yoke her to a perfect stranger to benefit the family business!

Her dismay enlarged to include herself as she paced her room. She should have seen this coming. It wasn't like there hadn't been hints. With every letter and package they received, they sang his praises—to her. With every recitation of Stephen's early life, "dear Cousin Ralph" was portrayed as his upright and salutary companion—for her sake. She had sensed that more than family pride motivated such glowing accounts, but how could she have taken any of it seriously? Cousin Ralph was half a world away!

She saw now where she had gone wrong. Out of consideration for them, she had delayed implementing her plans to leave and take suitable lodgings of her own. She had withheld from them her growing desire to travel and see the wonders of the world that she had so often read about. In trying to spare them, she had contributed to their intolerable expectations.

She had a comfortable income from her parents' estate and she was of a respectable age for living independently. She had to talk to them before this went any further and make it clear that she had plans of her own.

But halfway down the upstairs hall, she was revisited by memories of luminous pain in Mother Mayhew's eyes, the stoic misery of Uncle Abner's clenched jaw and the heartbreaking quiver of Cousin Tillie's chin. Her footsteps slowed. It was almost Christmas Eve, for heaven's sake. They were working so hard to make it perfect, and not just for Cousin Ralph. *They* needed a wonderful Christmas, too.

Wavering, she surrendered to her higher impulses yet again, and postponed that difficult talk. After all, they would soon see for themselves just how mismatched she and snore-worthy Cousin Ralph were.

In the middle of the main stairs, she stopped dead.

Uncle Abner and Cousin Halbert were hanging a large, beribboned ball of mistletoe from the entry-hall chandelier. They caught sight of her on the stairs and shot her beaming smiles. Sailing past them, she headed for the drawing room and found mistletoe hanging above the doorway...more above the settees, still more above the arched doorway leading into the dining room. She looked around in horror. It was all over the blessed house!

Mother Mayhew caught her glaring up at a clump installed at the rear of the main hallway and gave her what could only be called a suggestive wink.

Claire's eyes narrowed and her shoulders squared. If they thought that cursed stuff was going to have any effect, they were wrong. Her thoughts began to race. She intended to see that Cousin Ralph found her every bit as unsuitable and unappealing as she found him.

DAYLIGHT WAS DISSOLVED IN banks of dark, frigid clouds that afternoon. Rain started to fall again, and the servants lighting the entry lamps reported that the streets, pavements and even the front steps were encased in a layer of ice. The Mayhews glanced uneasily at each other, but continued to trim the tree and talk emphatically of celebrations past, while Cousin Tillie doggedly plunked away on the spinet trying to resurrect a Christmas carol or two. The Mayhews enthused that there would be carol singing and sticky pudding eating and even a Dickens reading...once Cousin Ralph arrived.

Just as the servants brought in tea and an assortment of Christmas sweets and savories, a fierce banging burst against the front doors. Male voices exploded into the entry hall, and Uncle Abner and Cousin Halbert rushed to see what was the matter. The words *accident* and *icy bridge* galvanized the women into abandoning their tea cups and hurrying into the hall.

A stooped and unsteady figure swathed in tattered blankets was being trundled through the front doors by several roughly clad men.

"Went right off th' stone bridge into th' river. Lucky fer him it was still daylight," one rescuer said. "A dairyman out feedin' cows seen it happen."

"Took a knock on the head, he did," said another, struggling to support the crumpling figure. "We had to fish 'im outta the water."

"Took a while to figger out where to bring 'im," offered a third.

"Cousin Ralph?" Emerging from shock, Mother Mayhew rushed to his side, pushed the blankets back from his head to confirm his identity. With a gasp, she began issuing orders for the servants to build a fire in Stephen's old room and bring her medicine chest. Ralph mumbled something incoherent and sank to his knees.

In short order, the rescuers were thudding up the stairs, ferrying the icy, unresponsive Ralph to a sickbed. When they reached Stephen's old room and heaved him into the four-poster bed, Aunt Eloise and Cousin Tillie pushed through the group to join Mother Mayhew at his bedside. She put a hand to his cold, gray cheek. "Poor, dear boy. You're home now. Don't you worry."

As they unwrapped their shivering patient, his grizzled rescuers reclaimed their tattered blankets and offered advice on warming a frozen body. Mother Mayhew shot her brother a commanding look.

"Abner, take these gentlemen downstairs for some mulled wine and hot food. And see to it they have something by way of a reward."

Claire, who had lagged behind, backed out of the doorway to let the men exit and stood for a moment in the hall, staring between the group lumbering down the stairs and the flurry of activity around the sickbed.

It was so much like four years ago, she could barely catch her breath. Another carriage accident. Another Mayhew family member in peril.

When she entered the sick room to see if she could help, Aunt Eloise intercepted her and shooed her back out into the hall, insisting that it wasn't proper for her to be there as they stripped a man of his clothes. Nursing, she said sternly, was for older, more experienced women.

Two hours of hot-water-carrying, tincture-brewing and blanket-ferrying passed before Cousin Tillie emerged to announce that Ralph would most likely live. Another hour passed before Aunt Eloise appeared to say that Ralph was feverish and talking nonsense, but wasn't actually *frozen* anywhere.

Claire kept a vigil with Uncle Abner and Cousin Halbert in the drawing room. It was almost midnight when Mother Mayhew came downstairs looking exhausted and announced that her patient was past the worst. With her careful tending, he would make a full recovery. Claire climbed the stairs to her room with a twinge of guilt for having felt such antipathy toward him and said a penitential prayer for poor Ralph.

Christmas, Mother Mayhew decreed with great relief the next morning, would be celebrated in traditional style after all. Cousin Ralph was sleeping, but by evening should be well enough to join them in the drawing room for some carol singing and the postponed lighting of the Christmas tree.

As twilight fell, after an early Christmas supper, Mother Mayhew and Uncle Abner pushed a creaky wooden wheeled chair into the drawing room. It was piled thickly with blankets, atop which sat a head with a newfangled rubber hot-water bottle tied to it.

This was the fabled Cousin Ralph? Claire bit her lip to keep from laughing at the parboiled countenance surveying the drawing room in disbelief.

Periwinkle toppled from her perch on the mantel where she had been overseeing the manger scene display, and righted herself with a gasp. A shiver of prescience that she understood came straight from The Powers themselves, announced that this *was the one. In spite of herself, her first reaction was doubt. He looked ninety years old and half drowned to boot. Surely the powers could have found someone more suitable for poor, poor Claire. After all, it was supposed to be "True Love."*

THE REST OF THE FAMILY gathered around to welcome him, each introducing him or herself with a moldy memory or familial descriptor that only seemed to make the hapless Ralph shrink even further into the blankets. When the others finished, Mother Mayhew rolled the creaking chair straight over to Claire.

"And this lovely young lady is our Claire Halliday.

Surely you remember—she came to live with us after her parents passed away."

Ralph blinked several times and squinted, making Claire wonder if his vision or perhaps his wits had been impaired by the accident.

"Good to meet you, Cousin Ralph. I've heard so much about you." She bent down into his line of sight, but quickly pulled back and reached for her scented handkerchief. They'd slathered him with one of Mother Mayhew's poultices. Petroleum, mustard, sulfur and God knew what else… The poor thing smelled like he'd just crawled out of a tannery vat.

"As you can see, we've saved lighting the tree so you can enjoy it with us," Mother Mayhew broke in, fussing with the chair and retucking her patient's blankets. "Abner, we need some oil on these wheels. I don't know how dear, departed Aunt Delia stood it—all this screeching." Then she turned to Claire. "Do be an angel, dear, and begin lighting the candles."

Claire leaned near Ralph and muttered, as she grabbed the brass candle lighter, "If something catches fire, head for the snow bank in the front garden. But mind the steps. They're covered with ice."

She looked back as she climbed the ladder to begin lighting the upper candles, and found his gaze fixed on her. She fancied there was misery and pleading in them—especially when Cousin Tillie opened the spinet and began to play what sounded uncannily like Good King Wenceslaus's funeral music.

CHAPTER THREE

Rafe Hutton couldn't take his eyes from Claire Halliday. Everything about her sparkled—hair, eyes, skin— she was aglow with what looked like starlight. Clearly, he was hallucinating, which meant he was worse off than he'd realized. His nose and sinuses were swollen shut, making breathing difficult, but his foremost discomfort was the heat. He was so damn hot; he was sweating like a racehorse and his chest was on fire.

He attempted to shed some of the blankets over him, but Cousin Hortense chided him and covered him up once more. He would have yanked that damned hottie off his head, but each time he tried to remove it, he felt like his skull might explode. Seeking a distraction, he fastened his gaze on the curvaceous angel climbing to the top of the Christmas tree.

Everything she touched burst into heavenly golden light as she floated downward, weaving a glowing spell over that massive evergreen. Soon the entire thing was alight with her special magic and she was coming toward him... settling on a chair beside him.

She was lovely. A face to climb mountains and cross oceans for. Big, bright eyes the color of sea glass, luminous skin and lips like plump, luscious cherries. If she was a dream, he wasn't sure he ever wanted to wake up.

He managed to sit a little straighter.

That music…that damnable off-key plinking…if he could just stop *that,* he'd feel a lot more normal. When he located the source, it turned out to be a pianoforte played by a frizzled wisp of a woman wearing spectacles. And then Cousin Hortense was back, shoving a book in front of him and insisting that the angel hold it for him.

Singing began. He knew it was singing, because the angel beside him opened the book to printed lines of music and produced a melodious string of sounds. The rest was an awful caterwauling that made him want to rip the hot-water bottle from his head and just let his skull explode.

But then he had to wonder if he weren't just hallucinating after all, for the words the angel sang bore no resemblance to any carols he knew.

"God help ye, merry gentlemen
You're going to need the rest.
Remember you're hip-deep in debt
And can't afford a fest…
The landlord's barking at the door
The grocer must be paid.
It will be a lean holiday, I fear—rock soup and beer—
Yes, it's going to be a thin Yuletide this year."

He shook his head to clear it. There was a look in her eye that made him think he might have heard every word correctly. Could she really be singing:

"Here we come acaroling
Among the weeds so green
Lots of poison ivy,

With stinkweed in between.
Rash and boils come to you
And to you fierce itching, too" ?

It was nothing short of surreal…the tree, the angel, the odd glow about her, the bizarre lyrics. A dream— that was what this was, he decided. A fever dream that distorted ordinary perception. How else could it be explained? He was suffering the combined aftereffects of the accident and those god-awful potions they had been pouring down his throat.

They halted the caterwauling long enough to serve what looked like mulled wine in punch cups. He was dying of thirst. The angel brought him some, but Cousin Hortense intercepted it before he could take a sip. The interfering old trout insisted he have barley water instead. At least the angel—what was her name again?— stayed to help him drink it. When he looked up, she was staring at him a bit too intently and he remembered her gleefully wicked song lyrics. His thirst evaporated.

Shortly, Cousin Abner called for their attention, positioned himself beside the glowing hearth and opened a book.

"'Marley was dead…'" he proclaimed with a stentorian flourish, then launched full bore into a reading of the story that had seized the English imagination decades ago and had now become a perennial part of the British Christmas. A groan came from the angel seated beside Ralph, and it was a moment before he realized she was expressing an opinion and not just providing theatrical effects.

When she added a quietly vehement "hear, hear" to Scrooge's demands to be left alone to keep Christmas or not as his conscience dictated, Ralph roused a bit and turned to stare at her in dismay. What kind of angel was this, who sided with Ebenezer Scrooge rather than the devotees of Christmas?

"Well, he has a point," she said, seeming to read his mind, or at least his expression. "No one should be forced to celebrate when they're miserable. You, for instance. Surely you can understand his point of view. Wouldn't you rather be in a nice, quiet bed, resting and recovering, instead of having to listen to an ill-tuned piano, tone-deaf old warblers and a lot of moralistic claptrap?"

"Whooo—" His throat was so parched that his voice came out a scratchy whisper. "Who *are* you?"

"Claire Halliday. Poor Stephen's *almost* bride." She leaned closer and lowered her voice. "He died at Christmas, you know. In a carriage accident." Her sea-green gaze narrowed, driving home her point. *"Just like yours."*

He couldn't seem to tear his eyes from her. What the devil was she implying? That he was at death's door?

Oh, God. His heart skipped a beat. He wasn't, was he?

She studied his dismay and then gestured to his face with a covert swirl of a finger. "Are the whites of your eyes always that yellow?"

He blinked and looked around at the others, who seemed totally absorbed in Cousin Abner's reading. His gaze settled on Cousin Hortense and he thought of her appallingly thorough approach to nursing. She seemed to think he was recovering.

He looked back at Claire Halliday and found her

suppressing a wicked hint of amusement that said she was probably teasing. A frisson of unexpected and irrepressible interest raced down his spine.

Suddenly, it was as if a fog lifted. He felt more clearheaded and alert than he had in days. He turned to focus on her and, though it hurt his head to think, made himself pull together the scant information he had about her.

Claire…an orphan, taken in…Stephen's *almost* bride…who sang strange lyrics and thought Scrooge was badly used by everyone, especially the Spirits of Christmas. She was fiercely lovely…clear-eyed and statuesque, with a complexion like fine porcelain and features so classical that they looked like they belonged in a Pears soap advertisement. But there was a hint of fire in her glossy hair and brilliant aqua gaze; a spark of heat that warned she wasn't to be trifled with. She wasn't an angel, Claire Halliday; she was something a good bit more complicated. And more interesting.

"Personally, I think—" she leaned closer to murmur when Scrooge's romantic failure was revealed "—he was better off not marrying. I mean, wives require attention and, as the saying goes, 'time is money.' He probably would never have gotten rich if he had married and been saddled with half a dozen mouths to feed." She paused for a moment to sip her wassail. "But I'm sure you know all about such trade-offs, being a man of commerce yourself."

He did indeed know about such trade-offs. He'd gone to India with the prestigious Merchant-Holmes Company to learn the foreign end of the business and had stayed to make political and economic connections that would further his career. And while he was gone he'd lost his boyhood companion, Stephen, and found himself alone in the world—always a stranger in a foreign land—and often personally at odds with the company practices and policies he'd been sent to implement.

The angelic Claire got up to refill her cup.

She returned and put it to his lips, pressing a finger to her own to indicate that it would be their secret that she was helping him sample the wassail. The warmth of the richly spiced brew felt cool by comparison as it invaded his limbs. When she rose for yet another cup, he wondered briefly if getting him soused counted as a kindness or some kind of rebellion on her part.

By the fourth cup, each a bit fuller than the last, he was feeling rather relaxed. He no longer cared about her motives and he was starting not to mind the incessant sweating so much. As the story wound toward the dramatic finish in which Scrooge was miraculously transformed, Claire sighed.

"Three visits from those celestial bullies, and he is a changed man," she whispered with a hint of disgust. "Where's the free will in that?"

Rafe was surprised to find himself sharing her annoyance at the moral tidiness of it. But before he could voice his agreement, Cousin Tillie was back at the spinet playing another of her off-key carols, her modest musical skill not exactly enhanced by the mulled wine she had consumed. This time, however, he was heat-crazed and inebriated enough to spool out a few lyrics of his own.

"We three kings of orient are

Eager to belly up to the bar.

Give us some beer, some whiskey or rum

And let us drink until we are numb…"

When the song finished, he looked up to find Claire staring at him in surprise. Then she leaned close to utter in a husky tone that made his toes tingle, "Bah, humbug to you, too."

He began to laugh; first a chuckle, then a guffaw and then a roaring belly laugh that went on and on. His ribs, bruised from the accident and tenderized by Cousin Hortense's heat plasters, were killing him, but he couldn't seem to stop laughing.

MOTHER MAYHEW SHOT to her feet, alarmed. "Oh, dear—we've overdone it. We must get him upstairs to bed and give him a strong draught to settle his nerves." She turned frantically to her brother. "Call the servants and then help me get this wretched chair to the bottom of the steps." Then Ralph started to throw off those smothering blankets, and she tried desperately to restore them.

"Abner, do something!" Mother Mayhew said, trying ineffectually to keep Ralph in the wheeled chair.

But Abner was not inclined to interfere with a man attempting to stand on his own two feet, no matter how much his sister disapproved. He did, however, grab a blanket to throw over Ralph's shoulders. Then he rolled the wheeled chair back out of the way as the patient rose…and rose…and rose.

Cousin Ralph stood a good head taller than Uncle Abner even in bare feet. Shocked, Claire focused on those feet and followed the sight of naked calves all the way up to his knees. More shocking still, the nightshirt hanging above them was sweat-soaked and clinging to his body like a second skin.

All Claire could think was that she'd never seen a man's bare feet and legs before, much less a lurid outline of a man's naked thighs and buttocks. It was strangely...stimulating. And how depraved of her to be thinking such things about a man who was ill and clearly irrational.

But then, he moved with surprising vigor and determination for a man who, only twenty-four hours ago, had lain at death's door. He waved off Cousin Halbert's help and lumbered barefoot across the cold floor of the entry hall, trailing a blanket, with the hot-water bottle still strapped to his head.

Mother Mayhew hurried after him, wringing her hands and predicting deadly bouts of catarrh and even consumption if he didn't heed her advice. Responding with a boisterous "Bah! Humbug!" to each of her pronouncements, he continued to pull himself hand over hand up the railing.

By the time they disappeared down the upstairs hallway, Claire was awash in unwelcome feelings. The sight of Ralph's naked feet lingered in her mind as she helped Tillie and the servants tidy up. That brief glimpse had stirred something curious and potent and long-buried in her.

By the time she reached her bedchamber, a flood of memories came crashing through the barriers she'd built around her heart. The memory of Stephen's manly presence, the warmth of his hands on her waist, the scent of his shaving soap when he came down to breakfast, the shivers his chaste pecks on her cheek sent through her body and the intimate tingling she felt when he pulled her into an empty stairwell for a very different kind of kiss... With the blithe innocence of youth, she had taken it all for granted. And in a single moment on a dark, wintry road it all had been taken from her.

She didn't ever want to be that vulnerable again, didn't ever want to need something or someone so much that she ached inside. She spent the next hour trying unsuccessfully to stuff all of those painful memories and traitorous yearnings back into the deepest, strongest chamber of her heart.

Finally. A breakthrough, Periwinkle thought as she whispered and nudged and steered Claire's turbulent dreams into sweet, steamy remembrances that roused desires and potent longings. Toward the end of Claire's dreams were long, lurid glimpses of bare feet and legs and the outline of male buttocks. It didn't take an archangel to figure out who they belonged to. By the last dream of the night, Periwinkle had withdrawn with reddened cheeks from vivid impressions of hands sliding over Claire's eager body and settling in places... Well, in places angels didn't wish to contemplate.

This was progress, she told herself desperately. Human passions were critical in developing a bond between a man and a woman. She bit her lip nervously. Passions were also tricky things to manage. To be healthy and helpful in building True Love, they had to be attached to worthy people and higher emotions. How could she get Claire's unleashed and free-floating desires to settle on this poor, wretched "Ralph" creature when Periwinkle still had doubts about the rightness of it, herself?

CHAPTER FOUR

THE NEXT MORNING CLAIRE rose much later than usual and dawdled over her toilette, unsettled by the vivid and shocking nature of her dreams. They seemed to linger in every burning curve and crevice of her body, just waiting for the chance to seize her thoughts and bloom into longings.

Turning firmly toward other matters, she was soon wrestling with the thought that—Christmas or not—she should seize the first opportunity to tell the Mayhews her plans. She even worked out a strategy, which began with mentioning it to Cousin Halbert and then shepherding it up the family chain of command to Mother Mayhew. But her determination evaporated the moment she reached the breakfast room and spotted Cousin Ralph at the table attacking a plate of ham and eggs.

What was he doing out of bed, in the breakfast room, eating regular food? Mother Mayhew always required at least a week of sops before allowing her patients back at the table. Claire paused just outside the door, trying to get a grip on her reaction.

He had apparently bathed and shaved and managed to find a proper suit of clothes to fit his strapping frame. Without a hot-water bottle strapped to his head, he was actually something of a looker. His eyes were a soft russet brown and thickly lashed, his features were neatly carved and his dark hair fell into place without the aid of any pungent macassar oil. Just now his memorably curved lips glistened with butter from the scone he was eating. She caught herself watching the muscles of his jaw as he chewed, and licking her lip. Dull and snore-worthy might not be so bad if it looked this good at breakfast every morning.

Out of nowhere, a shower of dust started her sneezing and she delved in her pocket for a handkerchief. Everyone looked up from the table and Mother Mayhew sprang up and came to usher Claire into the room.

"Here is our Claire, now. Look who insisted on joining us for breakfast, Claire. Can you believe the luck—the men who rescued him found his trunk and bags and brought them to the house first thing this morning!"

"It's a miracle," Claire said, teetering between sarcasm and amazement.

"It's Hortense's chest plaster, that's what it is," Aunt Eloise declared. "I'm always telling her she ought to bottle and sell it. It burns the poisons right out of a body."

"*Incinerates* is more like it," Ralph muttered, sending a hand to his chest.

"Were your ears tingling, dear?" Mother Mayhew gave an uncharacteristic giggle as she drew Claire to the chair across from Ralph.

"We were talking about you," Uncle Abner said with a chuckle.

"Telling Cousin Ralph how you always have your nose stuck in a book," Aunt Eloise said, folding her hands primly. "And how remarkable it is that all that reading doesn't seem to have harmed your eyesight a bit."

"How you help Abner with his figures, down at the factory," Mother Mayhew said, adding in Ralph's direction, "She's a regular adding machine."

"And how you love spring cleaning and say you prefer the smell of beeswax and turpentine to stinky old French perfume," Tillie put in eagerly.

Claire closed her eyes. The Mayhews, bless them, had to be the most socially oblivious people on the face of the earth. In singing her praises, they had managed to make her sound about as appealing as a bucket of wet rags. Which, she realized with chagrin, was exactly what *she* had intended to do. Ralph was now looking at her as if she might sprout a second head at any minute.

"Then you're acquainted with all my best qualities," she said, feeling her face heat. "Stubbornly healthy eyes, the ability to calculate long sums in my head and a great passion for turpentine vapors."

The Mayhews chuckled as she picked up her plate and headed for the food laid out on the sideboard. She felt Ralph watching, so she piled the food higher and higher, all but cleaning out the serving dishes.

"I do love breakfast. A healthy appetite is a great blessing. Right, Aunt Eloise?" She sat down, smiled and proceeded to fill her cheeks with food. "Mmm. The ham is lovely. The oatcakes…divine." She looked up to find Ralph watching. "Would you be so kind as to pass the syrup?"

"Cousin Ralph, tell us about your journey from India," Uncle Abner asked, clearly hoping to distract him from her display of gluttony. "Did you pass through the Suez Canal? How long did it take?"

"The whole trip took a little over a month by sea," Ralph said after handing Claire the syrup pitcher. "The Suez passage required five days."

"What is the canal like?" Cousin Halbert perked up with interest.

"Oddly unremarkable. A narrow ribbon of blue in an unending sea of sand." He paused for a sip of coffee. "Run with admirable British efficiency."

"Unlike the post," Aunt Eloise put in with a frown. "Your letter arrived just two days ahead of you, you know."

"For which I must apologize. I gave it to my clerk to post weeks before. He went back to his home village to be married, and while he was gone I found it mislaid on his desk and posted it myself. By then my passage had already been booked." He looked to Claire. "If you would pass the butter, please."

"Did you buy a lot of tea for the company?" Tillie asked.

"Not directly. Most of my time was spent traveling, contracting with planters to supply tea and coffee and other commodities."

"Other commodities?" Uncle Abner said. "Like what?"

"Silk, coffee, pepper, nutmeg, cardamom, cinnamon…"

"Spices?" Tillie clasped her hands. "You were a spice buyer?"

"One could say that." He returned to eating.

Claire swallowed hard and gripped her fork, knowing

she shouldn't be staring at him but unable to help herself. *A spice buyer.* Cinnamon and nutmeg and cardamom… Into her mind blew a sultry Mediterranean breeze laden with exotic scents that she could almost *taste* on the air.

He had traveled all over the East, buying tea and spices and no doubt seeing all the things she had read about…the golden pagodas of Rangoon, the tea plantations of Ceylon and that breathtaking monument to love, the Taj Mahal. He glanced up from his plate and their gazes met. She was shocked to see images of graceful eastern minarets reflected in the depths of his eyes.

She looked quickly away and told herself it was just the reflection of the salt cellar. And possibly her own overactive imagination. This was Cousin Ralph… sober and salutary Ralph…who reportedly still had the first penny he had ever earned and was as sensible as woolen socks.

Who also has long, muscular legs and broad shoulders to match.

Where did *that* thought come from? she wondered. Feeling her cheeks flush, she couldn't resist the urge to glance at his big, neatly shaped hands…imagining those long, muscular fingers sifting through bags of fragrant cloves and saffron and nutmegs…imagining that traces of those delectable scents lingered on his skin…

Lord, was she impressionable. Mention the words *spice* and *Suez* in the same breath and her wits melted into puddles. She shook herself and sat straighter. Apparently an aura of adventure had the power to make men seem more desirable than they truly were.

"Tell us about your travels," Uncle Abner entreated. "Did you visit any rich pashas in palaces?"

Looking a bit uncomfortable, Ralph nonetheless squared his shoulders and nodded. "I did. Though most of my dealings were with people of far less exalted rank. At first, I was given a number of plantations to call on in India. But as time went on, I was sent further afield, to Ceylon, Jakarta, Rangoon, Bangkok. However, I managed to visit a number of great palaces when conducting business with the local rajas."

Palaces and plantations. Claire experienced vivid visions of him striding commandingly along rows of tea-producing camellias one day and bowing gracefully as he was received by Indian royalty the next.

"So you actually spent time on plantations where the tea is grown?" Mother Mayhew asked, giving a sigh of wonder when he nodded.

"Did you actually see them worshipping cows?" Aunt Eloise asked with a pursed mouth and a frown to match.

"Frequently. Although *worship* may be a bit strong. They believe that the souls of their ancestors are reincarnated in cows, as well as in other animals."

Aunt Eloise clasped her heart, scandalized. "Well, never you mind. You're back home in England now, safe and sound, for Christmas. And there is nothing more English than Christmas, you know."

At that, his eyes widened. "I completely forgot. I brought some things for you. If you'll excuse me." He rose and headed for his room.

"He brought gifts?" Mother Mayhew looked stricken. "But we have nothing for him." Then she looked around at Claire and the others. "For anyone. We haven't kept Christmas that way in years."

"Well, I have something I can give him." Cousin Halbert rose and headed for his workshop, inciting a scramble from the breakfast room.

Claire watched them depart, relieved not to have to finish that monstrous plate of food, and drank her coffee in peace. As she entered the drawing room later, she paused in the doorway to appreciate the fragrance of the evergreens and the sweetness of the beeswax candles.

She was grateful beyond words for the change Cousin Ralph had caused in the family, but was far less pleased about the changes happening in her. These unsettling things she felt, these womanly and stimulated things—surely they would not be for the good.

The family gathered in the drawing room a short while later and Ralph soon appeared with several packages wrapped in brown paper and presented each member of the family with one to open. Abner's contained a carved rosewood pipe; Halbert opened a book on Indian architecture; and Mother Mayhew, Cousin Tillie and Aunt Eloise each discovered in their packages lengths of vibrantly colored silk that Ralph called "saris." Ralph proceeded to show them how Indian women pleated and wrapped the flowing panels around them to form a graceful and functional garment.

Claire watched their delight, admired the beautiful fabrics and relished the sound of their rusty laughter breaking free as they tried on the garments. She had longed to see them like this again—happy and filled with lively interest. When he came to her with an irregular, oblong package, she was surprised.

"I am sorry to say that I had forgotten your age," he said as he offered it to her. "I wasn't even certain that you still lived here. But I think this may be rather appropriate."

Inside the wrapping she found a statue of a portly man with the head of an elephant who appeared to be dancing. Startled, she looked up at him.

"Ganesh," he said, amused by her reaction. "A much revered figure in the Hindu religion. He is the god of beginnings and of obstacles." His voice lowered and softened. "Rather fitting, I think."

A smile transformed him into the most handsome man she'd ever seen, and, for a moment, time stood still. Her defenses slipped and suddenly she felt that he could see all the way into her heart and could read her doubts, disappointments and desires. But the worrisome part was that she had not the slightest impulse to pull away. Apparently, part of her wanted to be seen, to be known, to be touched in that alarmingly intimate way.

Heat swirled through her and bubbled up as nervous laughter when she looked back at the statue's genial elephant face and bulging belly.

"So, are you implying I have obstacles or I am one?"

"I would never presume to judge, Miss Halliday. Nor, I believe, would Ganesh."

"Claire, please," she said on impulse.

"Claire," he repeated, sending a shiver of pleasure through her.

In his beautiful cinnamon-dusted eyes, she suddenly saw her own image reflected, smiling, happy. The sight stirred a sweet ache in the middle of her chest. How long had it been since she felt herself on the brink of possibilities of any kind? And what irony that the source of this decadent new sense of hope was the heretofore dull Cousin Ralph.

She set the statue she found herself hugging down on the tea table and turned to watch the Mayhews present him with their gifts.

THE LAST THING RAFE HUTTON had expected upon arriving in cold, dreary old England was to experience sultry tropical heat fanning through his body. This long-delayed duty visit to the family oldsters was intended as time for him to make peace with Stephen's death and to console Stephen's mother and uncle…not to plunge into a fascination with Stephen's "almost" bride.

And yet, he *was* fascinated. As he watched Claire studying the carving of Ganesh, he could see her mind working, her quixotic wit rallying, her emotions rising. A strange tightness enveloped his chest. Moments ago, when he slipped into her big Mediterranean-blue eyes, he had glimpsed fear, strength, compassion and long-suppressed desires. And—heaven help him—he wanted to see more.

Rattled by that thought, he managed to respond graciously to the walking stick, experimental egg spoon, monogrammed handkerchiefs and hand-knitted scarf he received from the family. He dutifully tried on the scarf and tucked a handkerchief in his breast pocket and tried out the walking stick. But the whole time he was thinking of Claire Halliday's delicious curves, the sweet slope of her lips and the challenging tilt of her heart-shaped face.

He all but cheered as the rest of the family found excuses to abandon the drawing room...except Aunt Eloise, who lingered a bit.

He rose and strolled over to where Claire had begun to replace the candles on the Christmas tree with fresh tapers. He was so caught up in watching her that he didn't pay attention to the tree itself at first. Then it struck him that most of the ornaments on the tree were made of silver flatware. Spoons, forks and knives had been recrafted into snowflakes, gingerbread people and geometric shapes, while retaining vestiges of their former shapes.

"These ornaments," he said to Claire in surprise. "They're all cutlery."

"What else would you expect on a Mayhew tree?" she responded with a grin. "Actually, it's something of a pastime for Cousin Halbert. He's an inventor. But there are only so many ways to make spoons and forks, so he decided to try making spoons and forks into something else."

There was something heartwarming about that eccentric bit of ingenuity. He adjusted an ornament on a bough here and there, then stepped back to assess the tree from a different angle and caught sight of Aunt Eloise contemplating the statue of Ganesh with a grave expression.

He watched her for a moment, then approached Claire.

"What is she doing?" he said quietly, tossing a look over his shoulder.

She turned, saw Eloise and sighed. "She's trying to decide if he's naked or not."

"What?" He straightened as Aunt Eloise tucked Ganesh under her arm and hurried out of the drawing room.

"She can't abide nakedness, not even the suggestion of it. Haven't you noticed the table legs all wear crocheted skirts?"

"You're joking." But he looked around the room and, sure enough, every table leg was swathed in a dainty crocheted skirt. Every blessed one.

"She's quite the crusader. Take a look at the baby in the crèche."

He spotted the manger scene on the mantel and strode over for a look. His eyes widened at the little figure of Baby Jesus…who, instead of swaddling clothes, wore a delicately crocheted and beribboned dress. He choked back a shocked laugh as Claire joined him.

"The figure was mostly naked and she said it was wrong to see the blessed baby displayed so." She looked up, assessing his reaction and fighting back a grin. "You should see what she did to— Come with me."

She led him to a cabinet in the far corner, where a number of Staffordshire figurines were displayed behind glass doors. Reaching into the back, she pulled out a bulky figure in a pair of crocheted trousers, a smock with a ribbon bow and a starched straw-colored hat.

His jaw dropped at the familiar face smiling broadly at him from under the hat. It took a moment for him to realize he was looking at the carved Buddha he had sent them a couple of years back. It hit him like a hammer: the old girl had crocheted clothes to cover up the half-naked Buddha!

CHAPTER FIVE

HE GAVE A STARTLED chuckle as he turned it over and over, coming back each time to its joyful face and letting the humor it embodied infect him. The laughing Buddha's lesson of finding joy in even the most adverse conditions was somehow enhanced, not diminished, by the statue's sad circumstance.

"If you think that is bad—" She stooped to liberate a large piece from the back of the lowest shelf. A great bronze circle decorated with stylized flames, in which a figure with four arms was suspended…wearing an incongruous crocheted skirt and a frilly, crocheted blouse.

"She worked on it for weeks. The four sleeves nearly drove her crazy."

He burst into laughter and found himself unable to stop. He set the statue down to grasp his aching ribs and she took it as the sign of pain that it was and helped him over to the sofa. For a while they both laughed, setting each other off anew whenever one of them started to sober. He used his new handkerchief to wipe his eyes, and when he could speak again he said, "My fault, I suppose. I should never have sent them a dancing Shiva."

"Why on earth did you?" she asked, studying him.

He looked into her glistening eyes and knew the truth was safe with her.

"I thought the ideas behind the images might somehow comfort them. The hope of joy in adversity, symbolized by the laughing Buddha. The circle of life and death and rebirth to a life beyond…the way each life is a part of the great dance of creation, symbolized by the dancing Shiva…"

"Without you here to tell them all that, they rather missed the point," she said quietly, drawing his gaze into hers. There was no blame, no bitterness in her words, nothing to fuel the guilt and anger he felt toward himself for failing to be there to share and help them through their grief.

"Stephen and I were very close as boys." Tangled emotions welled in him as he allowed himself to finally open bittersweet memories. "We went off to school together and then on to Oxford together. We were more like brothers than cousins. Now, being back in England, I feel his loss even more."

"We all miss him," she said, reaching out to touch his hand. A shiver ran through him. "Every year at this time the family sinks into despair over his death. Your coming has given them back their Christmas. Thank you for that." Then she looked toward the tree and smiled. "They so wanted to give you a proper 'English' celebration, complete with a Yule log and plum puddings and a Dickens reading and a Christmas tree."

"Which is German, by the way," he said as she rose and pulled him up with her to continue replacing the tree candles.

"Don't let Aunt Eloise and Uncle Abner hear you say that." She handed him some new beeswax candles to replace the melted ones. "To them, the Christmas tree is as English as the queen's bunions."

"You know, of course, that the queen is four parts German, too," he said, hoping it would elicit a laugh. It did, and they worked together for some time to resupply the huge tree with candles. He pulled out the ladder and held it for her while she climbed to reach the holders near the top.

Glowing with exertion, she paused to smile down at him. Small wonder he had thought he was looking at an angel the previous night, he realized. Her every movement was grace personified and made him want to touch her, to explore her and these unprecedented feelings. His body was warming dangerously and no doubt affecting his judgment…which was his only excuse for refusing to move from the bottom of the ladder as she descended.

He was standing so close to it that there was no room for her to step down. When she turned with a questioning look, he could only guess what she saw in his face. And he didn't move. Couldn't move. To reach the floor, she would have to share space intimately with him.

"Cousin Ralph—"

"It's pronounced 'Rafe' actually. Only the Mayhews call me 'Ralph.' "

"Rafe." She tried it out, her voice a little breathless. "That fits you."

A moment later she stepped down off the last rung, letting her body come to rest against his as she settled to the floor. He drank in the feel of her curves pressed against his tender skin, the sweet scent of her hair filling his head and the luminous depths of her dark-centered eyes.

He lowered his head, reading in her tension the same questioning desire he was feeling. He ached to wrap his arms around her, but he settled for cupping her face between his hands and pressing his lips to hers.

The jarring sound of the front bell ringing and the rush of feet on the marble floor of the hall shattered that fragile moment.

BOISTEROUS VOICES BURST through the entry hall, and she hurried to see what was happening, her face on fire. A motley crowd of locals were invading, shouting "Merry Christmas" and "We've a tale to tell for you!"

Several ruddy-faced villagers in homemade costumes stepped to the front of the group and took bows that were somewhat unsteady…owing to the performances they had already given that day and the liquid gratuity they received from their audiences. With exaggerated courtliness, they requested the permission of the good lady of the house to perform.

"Play on." Mother Mayhew called from her place on the stairs. "And if your tale rings true, you'll have a fine reward for your effort."

The family and servants lined the steps and crowded around to watch the tale of Flautus and Mephistopheles, the latter of whom was mispronounced as "Met-he-aw-ful-fleas." One of the mummers narrated the tale of a poor unhappy fellow—Flautus, in their version—who was beset by money troubles and unlucky in love. The desperate fellow swore he would sell his soul to the devil to better his lot, and the devil—Mephistopheles, played by a grizzled old tavern hound—took him up on the offer.

For a while, Flautus strutted, swaggered and abused his good fortune, unaware that the payment on his debt drew ever closer. He married a succession of unlucky women, built a great and wicked fortune and spent his days counting his money and being horrible to people. On the day the devil returned to claim his soul, the misused townspeople refused to help him.

Then in a Christmastide twist, a young girl—played by a feisty boy with a squeaky falsetto—stepped forward to beg the devil to spare Mr. Flautus, claiming he had once given her a crust of bread. She went on to list his begrudging, less-than-helpful charities to various townspeople present and to cast his actions in a benevolent light. The townspeople were shamed into giving the devil a beating and sending him packing.

The beating degenerated into a free-for-all that ended with "Met-he-awful-fleas" rushing out the front door and the villagers collapsing into a merry heap on the hall floor. Enthusiastic applause ensued. The troop collected for a bow and then followed the family into the dining room, where the cook had hastily assembled a spread of fragrant wassail, beer and sweet treats.

As the drink-merry mummers filled their pockets with sweets and filed out, the fellow who had narrated the play paused in the entry hall to look up at the mistletoe hanging from the chandelier.

"That's the biggest kissin' ball I ever seen. Must be yours, eh?" He winked at Claire, who escorted them to the door. "A pretty lady like you."

"No, actually. Not mine." She tucked her hands

behind her back, fiercely aware of Rafe's eyes on her and horrified by the heat that flooded her face at the memory of their brief, tantalizing kiss. The narrator's leer made her add, "A-anyway, it's defective. It doesn't work. It's bad mistletoe."

"Yeah? Well, we'll jus' see about that." He was so quick to pull her under it with him that she had no chance to protest. Wiping his mouth on his sleeve, he leaned in for a royal bussing—only to be shouldered out of the way and replaced by a tall, dark form that wrenched a quick "ahh" from her as he pulled her against him and claimed her lips.

Modesty and propriety all but disappeared the instant they touched.

She was oblivious to the family's elbowing and only dimly aware of the titters, "ooh's" and encouragements from the villagers.

Pleasure rolled through her senses and spread through her body to damp in exquisite tingles along her nerves. It was all she could do not to slide her arms around him and embarrass them both with her eagerness. His lips were so velvety and supple against hers and tasted of spiced wine. By the time the kiss ended, she was breathless and barely able to stand upright.

"Naw," the narrator roared good-naturedly, "there's naught wrong with *that* kissin' ball!" Laughter broke out all around and the mummers tramped out the front doors into the cold, calling "Merry Christmas to all."

Frantic to collect herself, Claire escaped into the drawing room and went to a far window to stare out at the dusky front garden. Her face was on fire; she wanted to press her burning cheeks against the frost-rimmed windowpane.

He'd kissed her roundly in front of the family and an entry hall full of tipsy village folk. What must the family—

"The nerve of that Willie Makepeace." Aunt Eloise's indignation resonated through the drawing room as she and the rest of the family entered moments later. "Getting fresh with our Claire."

"Thank heaven, Ralph was there to intervene," Mother Mayhew said.

"Indeed. Quite gallant of you, dear boy," Uncle Abner added staunchly.

Claire froze with disbelief. They had eyes in their heads. Did they not see how he kissed her and she had responded—in front of God and everybody?

"My pleasure." Rafe's voice was calm and unruffled.

She turned back to the room to find them settling into chairs...the men with newspapers, the women with stitchery and a ladies' journal...behaving as if watching Rafe kiss her witless were as ordinary as overcooked porridge.

"I had forgotten about the mummers on Boxing Day," Tillie said with a giggle. "They're so much worse than they used to be."

"Disgraceful, I say," Aunt Eloise opined, though there was a suspicious curl at the corners of her mouth. "That scamp playing the little girl..." She came out with a chuckle. "I'll bet he gets his ears cuffed on a regular basis."

"It was a rowdy bunch," Mother Mayhew said, pulling out her stitchery hoop with a sigh. "But it *is* only one day a year. And it is tradition."

A ROBUST CHRISTMAS TEA replaced their dinner at five o'clock, after which they called in the servants, lighted the tree and read the Christmas story, as was the duty of the masters of large houses. Each servant then received a holiday bonus, as well as the balance of the evening and the next day off.

The house quieted as the servants quickly banked the fires and prepared the lamps, then hurried off to their annual Boxing Day party.

Claire played a few hands of cards with Eloise and Tillie, who then insisted Rafe join them as a fourth for "whist." It was torture, watching his relaxed, companionable manner while she felt like a locomotive boiler that was building steam. Where was the eager, passionate man who had seized her earlier and kissed her until he all but melted her bones? Her mind kept wandering from her cards to his incredibly kissable lips. Was she was the only one wondering if—*when*—it might happen again?

When the elders began to yawn and nod, Mother Mayhew rubbed her eyes and suggested they retire. The family exited to douse hall lamps and check doors, leaving Claire and Rafe alone in the drawing room.

As Rafe folded the chessboard, boxed the pieces and carried them to her, every nerve in her body came alert. His hand brushed hers in the transfer and she drew a sharp breath. Seeming as if he hadn't heard, he went to douse the candles on the mantel while she stowed the games in the cabinet.

When she turned back, he was standing beside a settee, staring up at the mistletoe hung from the drawing-room chandelier.

"This stuff is all over the blessed house," he said, pushing his coat back and propping his hands on his waist. Then he caught her looking at him and cocked an eyebrow. "Who do you suppose Cousin Abner and Cousin Hortense intend to kiss?"

CHAPTER SIX

CLAIRE FLUSHED AS HER heart started to pound.

"It is not for them," she said, surprising herself. "It's for you."

"Me?" A smile toyed with the corners of his mouth.

"You cannot tell me—after their behavior today— that you don't know what they're up to." When he merely frowned, she crossed her arms and told herself that she must be mad to speak to him so frankly. "They're playing matchmaker."

"I can't say that hasn't occurred to me." He scanned the other sprigs hung about the room and glanced out into the entry hall, as if estimating their determination from the amount of mistletoe on display. But he gave not a single indication of whether the idea pleased or infuriated him.

"Well, you needn't worry," she said, hoping it sounded as casual and impersonal as he did, curse his hide. "As I said earlier— It's bad mistletoe."

"Yes, and I wondered about that. How can mistletoe be 'bad'?"

It was hard to shrug nonchalantly when every muscle in her body was coiled like a steel bedspring.

"Whatever power mistletoe normally has, this lot

hasn't. It produces no throbbing pulse or shortened breath or giddy thrill. It simply doesn't work."

Finally a reaction. The narrowing of his gaze was satisfying.

She blew out the lamp on the card table and strode out into the darkened entry hall, where a pair of lighted candles sat on the sideboard, waiting to see them to their rooms.

Before she could pick up a candlestick, he grabbed her waist from behind and propelled her ahead of him to the mistletoe they had kissed under.

"Whaaat are you—"

"I think you're wrong, Claire Halliday. And there's only one way to prove it." He turned her, wrapped her in his arms and kissed her again.

This must be what it was like to fall down a well, she thought disjointedly. Minus the disagreeable splat at the bottom. As he bent to kiss her she was too stunned to react, to even *breathe*.

His lips were soft and entreating at first, then firm and demanding; a calming salve for her stinging pride and then a challenge to her most powerful feelings. He was relentlessly gentle and undeterred by her initial lack of response. He knew what he wanted and he was willing to wait for it.

There was no room for half measures, no way to remain aloof or unmoved. His kiss demanded a decision as deliberate as any she had ever made in her life. Did she or did she not want this?

Sweet heat and lush pleasure with the most handsome man she'd seen in years? What was there to think about?

Stop thinking for once—and just feel.

She melted into him, hungry for sensations half remembered and, until now, relegated to forbidden areas of her being. Everything about him seemed exotic: the scent of sandalwood in his hair, the cinnamon taste of his mouth, the surprising hardness of his body against hers, the shocking skill with which he traced sensual patterns through her clothes onto her very skin.

But everything about him was inexplicably familiar, as well: his size, his cleanly carved features and the bone-melting warmth he radiated. She felt like she'd known him all her life, and yet every part of him was a fresh, enthralling discovery.

He moved his hands over places that made her tense and hold her breath, while making her want to move against him in response. Heat migrated to the underside of her skin as his tongue slipped between her lips and coaxed hers to return the exquisite sensations it produced in kind. Never had she imagined, much less experienced, the delicious decadence of such kissing—with open mouths and tongues meeting and stroking. It was as if he had found the key to her body and was throwing it open to irresistible new possibilities.

She ran her hands inside his coat and over his lean, muscular back, wishing she could get even closer... dispense with her wretched corset—with clothes altogether—and feel him directly against her tingling breasts, her bare belly, her naked thighs. It was the wild and reckless impulse to make that happen—right here, right now—that finally blew the steam from her head and brought her back to her senses.

She found herself air-starved and weak-kneed and wrapped around his body like a mustard plaster.

"You still think the mistletoe's defective?" he asked, his breathing fast and his voice thick.

When Claire peeled herself away enough to look at Rafe, his hair was ruffled—*had she done that?*—and his eyes were brindled dark and luminous.

"Perhaps it's just a variety I haven't seen before." She struggled to catch her breath and take control of her reeling senses. "A slow-acting mistletoe."

"Umm. To be certain, we should do more experiments." His eyes twinkled as he pulled her to the rear of the entry hall and beneath another clump of mistletoe.

This time when he pulled her against him, she wove her arms around his neck and rose onto her toes to meet his kiss. His hair was soft and thick as she dragged her fingers through it. He trailed kisses across her face and down the side of her neck, nuzzling, nibbling and sending chills through her. She might have groaned aloud. Or was that him? It was strangely difficult to tell where she ended and he began. If only she could bare more of her skin to that ravishing attention...

Heat again spiraled downward through her, igniting every sensitive inch along the way. Her breasts burned and her loins grew taut with anticipation.

This was desire, she realized, giving herself over to it. This was the primal, bone-deep longing that poets and artists had struggled to portray and despaired of capturing. It was powerful and beguiling and utterly unexpected, coming now and with this man. She had never felt so alive as she did in the grip of that new and compelling feeling.

He lifted his head to gaze down into her eyes and she glimpsed the same need, the same wonder in his expression. It was only then that she realized that her back was against the wall at the side of the steps and that his knee was wedged between hers. The shocking part was that she wanted to part her thighs farther and rub her aching flesh against that muscular leg—

He straightened and looked around, then took a deep breath and backed up a half-step, giving her room and time to recover. Disappointment and relief battled in her as he took her hand and kissed the back of it…banking the passion in him, recalling honor and restraint. She suddenly had new respect for "sober, sensible and salutary." And his version of "dutiful" and "trustworthy" was anything but collie-like.

Warmed by that insight, she drew him toward the stairs with her, pausing just long enough to pick up a candlestick. Halfway up the stairs, she stopped under a sprig of mistletoe and swirled onto the step above him to kiss him. He grinned and then took the lead and pulled her farther up the steps. At the top, he pulled her against him for a brief, playful buss. And when they reached the door to her room, she leaned into him and savored the feel of his big body sheltering hers for a longer, more leisurely kiss.

Periwinkle danced around them, showering the rug with iridescent blue sparkles that formed a luminous crescent in her wake. Her heart and hopes soared at the certainty that her work here was almost finished.

The glow the couple produced as they kissed confirmed that they were developing a True Love bond.

"*Rafe Hutton is the man for you, Claire Halliday,*" *she sang out giddily, forgetting for a moment the strength of her connection to Claire's thoughts and moods.* "*Who else could kiss you like that? I say, get busy and marry the man and have a dozen babies with him!*"

Claire's eyes flew open. Marriage? Babies? Where did *that* thought come from? A vague feeling of alarm seized her as she slipped out of his arms.

"Good night," she whispered, darting into her room.

"Good mistletoe," he responded, with a wicked chuckle.

Leaning back against the closed door, she felt her racing heart skip a beat. Marriage and babies and a future with a man were things she hadn't thought about in a very long time. Was that where this was going? Certainly, it was if the Mayhews had anything to do with it. But what if this was just an enjoyable dalliance in his mind? And what of her plans to travel and take lodgings and make a life of her own? Could she abandon the travel dreams that had sustained her over the past four years and change—yet again—the course of her life?

Committing to a lifetime with someone meant counting on them to be there and trusting them with the whole of your being. It meant taking a risk on the trueness of another's heart. By all accounts—and now even her own experience—he was trustworthy and sincere and honorable. But that didn't mean he wanted the same things or thought of her as more than just a holiday diversion.

Kisses too easily became promises of pleasure owed and emotion due, and she had lived too long with unsought obligations not to recognize the trap that conforming to another's desires and expectations could pose. If they were to make something of this start, it would have to be for the right reasons, not because of the manipulations of a few dotty old relatives. All of that would take time. Right now, with her skin hot with pleasure and her body aching with need, she was in no condition to decide if she wanted to go down that path again…with him or with anyone.

PERIWINKLE STOOD OUTSIDE in the hall, staring at Claire's door and reading her charge's suddenly chaotic emotions with a sinking feeling. She turned to watch Rafe head for his room and found him frowning in a way that suggested second thoughts.

"You can't make water run uphill, Periwinkle."

The voice was not Periwinkle's own. It belonged to one of the archangels who supervised the apprentices. The truth of the great angel's words resonated in her heart. Periwinkle sagged at the realization that her outburst hadn't convinced Claire, it had confused her. The poor girl might be further than ever from True Love, and it was all Periwinkle's fault.

"You're too eager to get the task done. And not for their benefit—for your own." The voice chided her gently, but wielded a power that resonated in the apprentice. *"Their lives, their very destinies are being decided here. Loving changes the course of peoples'*

lives. They each must make the decision for themselves. You once had to make that decision, Periwinkle. Would you have wanted to be pushed into it?"

The compassion in the angel's voice brought tears to Periwinkle's eyes and the burn of conviction to her heart.

"You would do well to remember—" the voice gentled *"—that angel whispers can be more powerful in a human heart than the loudest shout."*

THE NEXT MORNING, THE festive holiday spirit remained as the family gathered in the brick-lined kitchen for the annual adventure of preparing their own breakfasts. Cousin Halbert lighted the gas-warming oven and fired the stove and the hot-water boiler. Mother Mayhew put on the coffee while Uncle Abner carved a ham and Aunt Eloise sliced bread for toasting. Cousin Tillie set plates, napkins and cutlery on one end of the long central table that served as both a preparation surface and the servants' dining table.

Claire raided the ice box for butter, milk and cheese, and found a bowl of eggs. She was standing on a stool, pulling a pot down from the overhead rack when Ralph strolled in, looking hale and handsome and hungry.

"What can I do?" He came to stand by Claire's stool, looking up at her and making her blush. He looked good enough to eat.

"I don't know," she said, flustered. "What *can* you do?"

Mother Mayhew gasped and Aunt Eloise snapped upright in dismay…until Ralph grinned and began to roll up his sleeves.

"Eggs," he said, gesturing to the bowl of them on the table. "I can cook eggs that will make your mouth water."

"You cook?" She accepted his help in stepping down from the stool.

"When alone in a foreign country," he said, holding on to her hand longer than was necessary, "a man learns to do things for himself."

Rafe explored the shelves and larder and came up with a large iron skillet, some onions, bacon and dried herbs. Soon he had cooked and crumbled the bacon and added the onions. He set Claire to watching and stirring them while he sliced some of the cheddar and then seized a whisk and beat a dozen eggs in a bowl with some light cream.

Everyone strained to see as he poured the eggs into the warm skillet with a flourish and then moved it about on the burner to find just the right heat. The omelet rose slowly. Just before he folded it and slid it onto a platter, he laid in more bacon, onion and strips of golden cheese to create a savory filling inside. Then he set the plate in the middle of the places Tillie had laid at the table.

For a moment everyone just stared at it.

"Well, I can see I'll have to prove it's not poison. Come, Claire, be my taster." He pulled her to a seat at the table and cut her a piece of the omelet. Everyone watched with baited breath as she took a bite and her eyes closed. Next came a groan that made them exchange worried glances.

"It's wonderful." Her eyes flew open to focus on Rafe with unabashed awe. "The cheese, the bacon, the herbs—they're all so perfectly blended."

Excitement filled each of the chairs as Rafe sliced and served his creation, and soon the others were stuffing themselves and singing the omelet's praises. Coffee, toast with butter and fruit preserves, and slabs of cold ham supplemented what was generally acclaimed to be the best servants' holiday breakfast ever.

They sat for a while after eating, sipping second cups of coffee and quizzing Rafe on his travels and how he learned to cook. He said he'd been taught by a quirky Frenchman who had stayed on in India after the failure of a commercial venture. The fellow believed that a gentleman should be able to feed himself in style, no matter what his circumstances. Since that lesson, Rafe revealed, he had sometimes cooked for himself and added to his skill.

"But surely you could afford a cook." Aunt Eloise was a bit unsettled by the thought of a gentlemen setting a hand to something so menial.

"Afford one? Yes. English money can buy anything in India. And *has* over the years," Rafe answered with a rueful smile. "It was just that…after years of being overrun with servants, I felt the need to do things for myself again. Which was one indication to me that it was time to make a change."

"You mean, that's why you resigned and came home?" Uncle Abner said looking thoughtful. Rafe hesitated a moment and then nodded.

"One of the reasons."

"You didn't like India?" Mother Mayhew asked. "We thought from your letters you were settled in over there."

"I liked it very much." He toyed with his coffee cup.

"The people are warm and gracious and the culture is fascinating…rich in art and ideas."

"But, they do worship idols," Aunt Eloise said emphatically.

His laugh was a surprise. "Not any more than Englishmen worship the pictures of Jesus and the Virgin Mary found in their homes. They understand that their carvings and images represent things beyond this world."

"If you liked it so much, why did you resign?" Claire asked, propping her chin on her hand, thinking of him in those magnificent plantations and palaces.

A subtle tension developed in his face, and he shifted in his chair.

"I grew restless and felt it was time to—" He halted, took a deep breath and started again. "The truth is, I no longer wanted to be responsible for Merchant-Holmes's practices in India."

Uncle Abner sat forward, puzzled. "But you were fortunate to have landed such a prestigious post. Merchant-Holmes has a vast reputation in the world of commerce."

"So it does." Rafe looked intently at Claire, as if seeking something in her face. After a moment, he blew out a breath and said what was on his mind. "Do you have any idea who picks the tea you enjoy every afternoon?"

The question surprised them all.

"Why, I suppose farm workers do," Uncle Abner said. "They do the planting and harvesting in every country."

"Well, in Ceylon and many parts of India, African slaves do the work."

"What?" Aunt Eloise was aghast.

"Slaves?" Cousin Tillie echoed in disbelief.

CHAPTER SEVEN

"BUT INDIA IS PART of the Empire. Slavery is outlawed throughout the Commonwealth," Mother Mayhew insisted, frowning.

"On paper, perhaps. But as is often the case in the East, there is a great discrepancy between law and practice. African slaves were imported by the hundreds of thousands under the old East India Company. They were settled on plantations and their descendents remain there to this day, working for meager food, unable to leave or refuse labor and traded like property. If that is not slavery, I don't know what is."

"And you saw this yourself?" Claire asked, glimpsing in the control with which he spoke how much the practice had affected him.

"Not every tea planter uses such labor, but many in India and Ceylon do. And it is Merchant-Holmes's policy to ship tea from planters with the lowest costs…who use the cheapest workers. I visited plantation after plantation and saw firsthand the situation. I wrote reports to the company, but was told repeatedly that Merchant-Holmes would never be a party to such practices and was given larger quotas of tea to secure. I finally realized I was only helping to perpetuate the situation. That was when I decided to resign."

Claire studied his tensed jaw, conjuring a very

different image now as she imagined him walking those tea fields. From the looks on their faces, the rest of the family were having similar thoughts.

"Merchant-Holmes... It's so hard to believe," Cousin Tillie murmured.

"Which is also what makes it so hard to change," Rafe said.

Silence settled over them as each considered and dealt privately with Rafe's revelation. His darkened eyes contained wariness as he waited for their response. It was all Claire could do not to reach for his hand.

"Well, you're home now, my boy." Uncle Abner announced his opinion and hauled the conversation back to more productive venues. "I can't wait for you to see the fork works. We pay our workers a decent wage, you know. Always have. And don't hire under fourteen years."

"We've installed the latest machinery in the foundry," Cousin Halbert added proudly. "Electrified the factory, too. Healthful lighting all around."

"I would love to see the changes you've made," Rafe said, relief flooding his expression. "I remember Stephen and I climbing up into the rafters and walking them like tightropes while the workers egged us on and the poor foreman—Mr. Hampstead, I think—roared at us to get down."

"You boys nearly gave him heart failure with your antics," Cousin Halbert said without thinking, then glanced at Mother Mayhew with a wince.

At the mention of her son, she had tensed and her eyes began to fill. But, seeing the others' troubled gazes on her, she blinked back the tears.

"Awful scamps they were." She produced a determined smile. "Don't know how we put up with them." She dabbed the corners of her eyes with a handkerchief. "But they turned out well, in the end. Good men, the both of them."

And she reached out to squeeze Rafe's hand.

IT WAS THAT IMAGE THAT stayed with Claire throughout the morning: Mother Mayhew's hand touching Rafe's, drawing comfort and strength from his presence. There seemed to be something about him that fortified and grounded others. She couldn't decide if it was his big, solid presence; his easy, accepting manner; or that knowledgeable twinkle in his eyes. In the end, she gave up trying to give it a name. It was just *him.*

The sun came out late that afternoon, and the weather warmed enough to permit a stroll in the private gardens across the square. They encountered neighbors also out for an airing on their servantless day, and the Mayhews introduced Rafe with the pride they would have shown in a visiting son. Everyone sensed something good in him and responded, even the children. While adults talked, two little boys in matching coats raced up to stare at him.

"You're *tall,*" the elder of the two said.

Rafe squatted down to face them. "Do you know how I got this way?"

They shook their heads. When he lowered his voice as if sharing a great secret, Claire was as charmed and fascinated as the boys were.

"I ate plenty of meat and all the vegetables I could get my hands on. Lettuce, greens, cucumbers, cabbage, beans, peas, leeks…anything green. It works like a top. Eat your greens and ask for more, and you'll grow to be wicked-fast cricket bowlers. Think you can remember that?"

Their eyes widened and they nodded as he gave them a wink and rose.

Claire laughed softly as the boys went racing back to their parents, whispering about his secret formula. "Poor things, they'll be grazing the front lawn come spring."

He chuckled and offered her his arm to continue their walk.

"Children…they're the same the world over."

"The same how?" She threaded her arm through his, surprised.

"They're curious and open to new ideas and eager to learn and experience new things… Qualities that education and society usually manage to drum out of us by the time we reach adulthood."

"Dangerously libertarian sentiments, Rafe Hutton," she teased. "Have you never heard that, if you spare the rod, you spoil the child?"

"I've heard it all my life. But, I'm convinced there are more humane and effective ways to raise children."

She was a little stunned. He had views on raising children?

"So are you a 'wicked-fast' cricket bowler, yourself?" she asked.

"Absolutely. Played on championship teams three out of five years in New Delhi. It's a great way to work off steam."

A quick and steamy vision of him in cricket whites—

hair tousled, shirt wet with sweat and clinging to his muscular back—bloomed in her mind. She paused on the path and he halted to look down at her quizzical expression.

"Every time I think I know who you are," she said, "you come up with something unexpected and I have to tear up the puzzle and start again."

"I'm not all that complicated." He urged her on with him, holding her so close against his side that his every step moved her skirts. The slide of her petticoats against her legs stirred a delicious tension inside her. She was suddenly aware of his maleness and her femininity in a new way.

"I have a few principles and I try to live by them," he went on. "Honesty, fairness and respect for others... Pretty basic stuff."

Pretty extraordinary stuff, she thought. He was one of a kind.

Her self-consciousness—knowing that the May-hews were watching—faded into a curious feeling of belonging beside him. Her every step, every smile, every comment took on new meaning as the walk proceeded. She had never—not even with Stephen—experienced such a profound and intimate sense of connection with someone.

IT MIGHT HAVE BEEN the children. Or perhaps the way Claire Halliday listened and teased and made him feel valued, included. Rafe found himself thinking of his family and his mother and wondering where the May-hews had stored the family keepsakes he had entrusted to them when he went overseas.

After their walk, he asked Cousin Hortense about it, and it took her a moment to recall. "The attic. We put your trunks up there." She smiled. "I can have the servants— Oh, no, I can't—the servants aren't here. If you want them today, Ralph dear, I'm afraid you'll have to go up to the attic and find them yourself." Then inspiration struck. "Perhaps Claire will help you search."

That was how he and Claire came to be trudging up the stairs to the fourth floor, pausing at every landing to let Cousin Tillie catch her breath.

Tillie bore a key from Mother Mayhew's sizeable household ring, and had orders to open the attic door and help them locate Rafe's things. She babbled anxiously about how the cold and the dust always made her wheeze and apologized in advance for the neglected state of the attic. By the time they opened the door— which was swollen and somewhat difficult to move— she had worked herself into an asthmatic episode. Rafe offered to escort her back downstairs, but she declined, insisting that they go on without her.

THEY WERE MAKING PROGRESS. Periwinkle watched them climb the final few steps into the attic proper, and thought again of her deadline. Mere days from now they had to be fully and irrevocably in True Love, or—

Or Rafe might just climb back into a carriage and head off to who-knew-where without ever declaring himself to Claire. They were so close, and yet they still might decide to be "sensible" or begin to worry too much about "tomorrow" and draw back into their lonely, protective shells.

What if the door just happened to shut and the key

just happened to turn? They would be trapped up there together...out of sight, out of mind...for who knew how long. They probably wouldn't be missed for *hours*.

Interference was frowned upon. Hugely frowned upon. Angels were agents of influence, not prime movers of situations. She had limits. Then she thought of the strain and sadness that often marked Claire's lovely face and of the pain her charge would feel when Rafe climbed into a carriage and rode away after the holidays. Given the isolation and deprivation of the last four years, this might be her last chance for real love and partnership.

The heck with limits!

The door scraped the floor and groaned as Periwinkle shoved it closed. It took every ounce of strength she possessed to exert such physical force. By the time she heard the soft click of the latch, iridescent blue sparkles lay piled on the floor like snow. Panting, weak from the effort, she managed to turn the key and slid limply down to sit with her back against the planks.

It was for their own good, she told herself. And she prayed that it was her higher nature talking.

CLAIRE PRIVATELY BLESSED Cousin Tillie's asthma and followed Rafe up the final few steps. He stopped at the top to take in the size of the place and the astonishing jumble it contained—furniture, crates, lamps, wardrobes and outdated curtains and clothes, dish barrels, paintings, trunks, hat racks, a cheval mirror, surplus kitchen crockery and well-worn rug beaters.

"Good Lord, it hasn't changed a bit. There's still

enough stuff up here to stock a dry-goods store." He rested his hands on his waist, surveying the lot.

"The Mayhews do have a quirk about saving," she said. "Similar to the one they have about dirt. This is the one place in the house where you'll find a speck of dust." She shivered as the chill of the unheated space penetrated her jacket. "I should have worn a coat. There is usually some warmth up here from the chimney stacks." She eyed his generous frame, remembering the delicious heat it radiated and wishing— "But it's been colder than usual."

Off to one side, he spotted an open area containing a bed and mattress, a gentlemen's chest, a washstand with a pitcher and bowl and a braided rug.

"I remember this. Temporary quarters for the servants of visitors. We used to sneak up here on rainy days to play and explore." He strode over to the back-to-back brick chimneys that created a makeshift wall behind the bed, and searched for something. When he found it, he smiled. "It's still here."

"What?" She joined him and found him looking at initials carved roughly into the brick. *SM* in one place and *RH* in another.

"We did that when Stephen was ten and I was twelve years old." He smiled ruefully. "We'd just gotten our first penknives and all but ruined them gouging our initials there." He leaned a hand against the chimney and found it pleasantly warm to the touch. "Here." He took her by the shoulders and set her back against the warm bricks. "This will keep you warm."

She relaxed back against the unexpected warmth and moistened her lips.

"If you really want me to be warm, you can—" kiss me sounded so brazen that she hastily substituted "—find me a blanket."

To her profound disappointment, he did just that: took a quilt off the foot of the bed, unfolded it and wrapped it around her.

She sighed privately at that missed opportunity.

"You can stay here and keep warm while I look," he said, stroking her cheek as if committing the curve of it to memory.

"Don't be silly. I want to help," she said, holding the quilt wrapped around her as she followed him. "So, what are we looking for?"

"Two large trunks—one brassbound, the other leather—and a crate or two." He drew her along with him as they threaded their way through the stacks of surplus household goods. "I'll know them when I see them."

She pulled the quilt tighter and shivered. Never mind trunks and keepsakes, she thought. Right now, all she could think about was how warm and pleasurable his lips, his breath and his chest would be against hers.

"What the devil are these?" He stopped beside some boxes filled with odd-looking metal pieces that resembled cutlery.

"Cousin Halbert's inventions," she said, lifting piece after piece from the box. "These are fish forks…self-draining egg spoons…collapsible forks…food pushers… oyster pickers…scissorlike lettuce tongs. And this is his most treasured idea—all-in-ones. Forks with detachable spoon bowls."

He shook his head in bemusement, fingering the

odd implements. "He needs to direct his efforts toward something besides eating utensils."

That gave Claire pause. "What's wrong with manufacturing cutlery?"

"Not a thing." As he looked around, he spotted something of interest nearby and headed for it. "It's just that he's stuck away in the cellar, trying to reinvent something that doesn't need reinventing. Imagine what he could do if he put his mind to something the world really needs. He's still young enough—he should get out in the world and see what is happening."

Get out in the world. Words that went straight to her heart. And how would he feel about a woman wanting to do that very thing? When Claire returned from the flight her thoughts were taking, Rafe had already moved on.

She joined him by a crate of books. *"The Seven Wonders of the Modern World. A Voyage to Rangoon. Pistols and Petticoats, Adventures in the American West."* He read off several titles and then dipped back into the box for another. *"An English Lady's Travels in Africa."* He looked up with a raised eyebrow. "These can't be Cousin Eloise's."

"They're mine," she confessed, looking down into the box. "I read a lot, remember? History, geography and accounts of expeditions…but travel journals are my favorite. Someday I'm going to travel to every city and see the cultures and natural wonders I've read about in books."

"That might prove expensive." He folded his arms and studied her.

"Growing up orphaned doesn't mean I'm penniless.

I actually have money of my own. I'll find a way to travel, someday."

"And where would you start this epic journey of yours?"

"All right— But don't you laugh. I want to see the Sahara Desert."

He did laugh, but then grabbed her hands by way of apology. "I'll be good, I promise. Why the desert? There's nothing there but sand."

Relenting, she let herself be drawn toward him. "I just can't imagine a place so huge without *any* rain."

"You are *so* English." He chuckled. "Aren't you afraid that if you go to all these places you've read about, you'll be disappointed?"

She squared her shoulders.

"I know I may sound naïve to you, but I'm not a green young thing. And I'm not afraid of disappointment. I've already had some of the worst disappointments life can throw at a person, and I survived. So what if the Taj Mahal isn't pink at sunset or elephants are mean and smelly or the Kasbahs are full of pickpockets? For every disappointment, I'll find something interesting and unexpected to compensate."

He studied her for a moment and nodded. "Something tells me you didn't learn that in books."

"Reading saved my sanity these past four years. But I know enough to realize that the most important lessons in life aren't found in print."

He laid the books back in the box and regarded her thoughtfully.

"It's been hard for you, here, without Stephen," he said.

She sensed he meant more than just living with the Mayhews. He was asking about her relationship with Stephen.

"It's taken four years—" her throat tightened around the words "—but I've come to terms with his death. I wish I could say the same for the others."

When she looked up, his eyes were glowing with intensity.

"Did you love him?"

CHAPTER EIGHT

Now was not the time to be coy or clever, Claire realized.

"I did. I still do." Her heart began to pound as she felt him searching her eyes for the truth about her feelings. "He was good and kind to me when I came to live here. He went away to Oxford soon after, but always returned for holidays and gradually became my dearest friend. It seemed only natural, later, that we should marry.

"After the accident, there were days I couldn't imagine life without him." She paused, hoping Ralph would understand and not think her callous. "But I had to develop new dreams and new things to look forward to, new reasons to live. I believe Stephen would have wanted me and the rest of the family to get on with our lives."

"Lucky Stephen."

"Lucky?"

He ran his knuckles down the side of her cheek. "To have had you to come home to. Small wonder he insisted on going home on holidays from Oxford instead of kicking about the continent with me. I never understood."

As he moved toward her, she raised her chin and closed her eyes. He managed to veer at the last minute so that the kiss landed on her forehead instead of her mouth. Claire's eyes flew open.

With a guilty flush, he turned away. It seemed wrong suddenly to make advances on Stephen's bride, especially when she'd just admitted to loving him still. Confused by conflicting ethics and impulses—she sure as hell didn't kiss like she was still pining for his cousin!—he stalked through the attic, determined to find what he came for and leave quickly.

"There they are." Relieved to be able to focus on the task at hand, he unloaded some boxes and a pair of old carriage lanterns from the top of a brassbound trunk and dragged it out into a clear space on the floor. He went down on one knee, produced a key and opened the trunk.

The smell of cedar laced with memories wafted up from the contents. There were stacks of letters bound with ribbon, a venerable old greatcoat, a child's christening gown, an antique silk opera hat, a dried nosegay... bittersweet echoes of lives long past.

He knelt fully by the chest, remembering, seeing his parents' tragically short lives in the meager mementos they'd left behind. They'd barely had time to settle and start a family when his physician father had been caught up in a typhoid outbreak and died. Delving past the garments on top, he uncovered tintypes of a newly wedded couple and a child of two or three years wearing long curls, a pinafore and a glower.

"Who was that?" Claire asked quietly, peering over his shoulder.

"Me." His voice sounded a bit thick in his own ears as he set the pictures aside and continued to look for a flat mahogany box.

"You were adorable," she said, her voice low and laced with feeling.

"I looked like a little girl," he said gruffly.

"Everyone looks like a little girl at that age. The important thing is, you don't look like one anymore."

The trace of seductive humor woven through those words brought his head up. She had knelt beside the trunk, facing him, and her big turquoise eyes were glowing softly. When he looked back into the trunk, the sight of those eyes came with him. He took a ragged breath, sensing that they would haunt him from now on unless he said what was on his mind.

"You still love him," he said, quieting his clamoring pride to listen.

"Ahh." She sat back on her heels with a look of understanding. "Of course I do. Don't you?"

He felt like he'd been sucker punched. Him? Of course he loved Stephen. Then he realized that with two little words she had turned his thinking upside down and laid the logic of it out for him like a road map.

"He was a formative part of my life, just as he was yours," she continued. "With him, I learned how to give and to receive, how to honor another's strengths and understand another's weaknesses." She inched closer so that her knees were almost touching his. "Love doesn't die just because people do. And loving him doesn't mean there is no room in my heart for anyone else." She paused, took a breath and seemed to force herself to say, "For *you*."

His hands trembled as he reached for her shoulders and drew her up and against him for a long, steamy kiss. It was a damn good thing they were both on their knees on a dusty floor in the unheated attic, otherwise the kiss might have turned into a great deal more. When they finally parted, she sank back onto her heels and fanned her rosy face with both hands.

"Now, that's the way to keep a girl warm."

After rummaging around in the trunk, he located the wooden box he sought and opened it to reveal several pieces of jewelry. He removed a delicately carved cameo set in gold filigree and cradled it in his big palm.

"My mother wore this nearly every day. It was her favorite." He held it for a minute, feeling a sweet ache of remembrance flooding his chest, then closed his fingers around it. Claire somehow read the state of his emotions just then and reached out to cover his hand with hers. He felt that gentle caress all the way to his heart.

He looked into her shimmering eyes and saw with fierce clarity the longing in his own reflection. She was right; love lived on, even when people didn't. How grateful he was that her heart was as wise as it was loyal.

He gathered the mahogany jewelry box and some leather-bound journals decorated with gold leaf, and then closed the trunk. He helped her to her feet and soon they were headed for the stairs and the attic door.

"I'm a mess," she declared, pausing at the top of the steps to brush dust from her skirts while he continued down to the door.

He was surprised to find that the door didn't yield to a push when he reached it. He didn't recall shutting it behind them, but it was clearly closed tight. Giving it a smack with the side of his fist, he tried again. Using his shoulder produced only a jarring *thud* and a shooting pain up his collarbone and down his arm.

"What are you doing?" Claire's voice came from nearby and he glanced back to find her standing two steps from the bottom, frowning.

"It's stuck. I don't see how it could have blown shut— but it seems to have done so. I can't get it to budge." He turned the knob to its limit and rammed his shoulder into the planks again, rattling both the door and the surrounding wall. In frustration, he pounded on the door panels and yelled, "Hullo there—open up! Anyone out there? Can you hear me?"

"No one comes up to the fourth floor but the servants. And they're not due back until late tonight." She sighed. "Unless the others miss us at tea and look for us, I think we're stuck."

CLAIRE'S HEART THUDDED WITH anticipation as she watched him close his eyes and lean his head back as if summoning his strength. It was hard to be too upset about being locked in the attic with a man who kissed like a magician. When he started back up the steps, his foot caught on something at the bottom and he yanked hard to free it. Stumbling upward with surprising force, he fell straight into her, knocking her back on the steps. A dazed second later, she found herself on her back with him sprawled atop her.

"Are you all right?" He pushed up on an elbow to look at her.

"I'm fine. I think." Better than fine, actually.

"I don't know what happened. I think I tripped, but I don't know on what. It felt like there was something holding my foot." He rose, testing his limbs, then helped her to her feet and supported her with an arm around the waist while she checked for injuries. They were both more shaken than hurt. They climbed the stairs again to the attic.

"It's getting dark," she said, running her hands up her arms. "And cold."

He went for the quilt she had abandoned moments ago, while she looked for a lamp or a candle to light. It took some doing, in the gathering dusk, but she finally located some candles in a box of old brass wall sconces and some ancient sulfur matches in the washstand near the bed.

The only source of heat was the chimney stack by the bed.

In a few minutes, they were huddled together on the bed, under a quilt and a wool blanket, with their backs against the warm brick wall.

"Sweet heavens above," she said with exaggerated breathiness, "I'm locked in the attic with a man. Whatever will my family say?"

"The same family who larded the house with mistletoe and have been throwing us together for days? My guess is, 'congratulations!'"

Claire giggled. "They probably would, the old things." She looked up at him and could have sworn there was a fine layer of something sparkling in his hair and on his shoulders. She blinked several times, but when she opened her eyes, it was still there. "You know, they could have saved themselves a lot of trouble if they had just told me you're the handsomest man alive."

He laughed and the vibrations migrated from his body into hers wherever they touched. "They probably didn't want to get your hopes up."

"Either that or they seriously underestimated how shallow I am."

"You are a pure vixen, Claire Halliday." He grinned at her and she grinned back, feeling a little shivery and expectant. "I'm crazy about you, you know. Which shouldn't be confused with you making me crazy—which has happened, too."

"You!" She pushed him away with ineffectual outrage.

"Wait," he said, pulling her back into his arms. "There's more."

"Oh." She turned to face him, setting across his lap. "I like *more*."

"Where was I? Oh." He took her face between his hands. "You make me happy that I resigned my post… happy to be back in England…and even happy to be related to those scheming old trouts downstairs." His voice lowered to a velvety scrape. "But most of all, you make me deliriously happy that God made mistletoe."

"A pity we don't have any right now." She bit her lip, staring at his.

"We can improvise." He leaned down and kissed her with enough sweetness to make sugarcane jealous. Her eyes shone and her breath came faster by the time that kiss ended.

"You're a brave man, Rafe Hutton. And amazingly durable. To have faced down both the medicinals and the manipulations of the Mayhews. I'm impressed." She took a deep breath and came right out with it. "I'm also falling in love with you."

When he didn't respond immediately, she thought of trying to dilute her declaration by adding… "and with saltwater taffy, yellow flowers, Beagle puppies and warm woolen socks." But she didn't have the chance.

He pulled her into his arms and kissed her long and passionately. It probably would have gone on all night if she hadn't had to breathe.

"Does this mean you're happy about it?" she said, panting with as much decorum as she could muster.

"I've never been happier in my life," he said, laughing, kissing her cheeks, her chin, her eyelids and the tip of her nose. "Say it again."

"I love you." She softened against him, her eyes glistening in the candlelight. After a pause, she looked expectantly at him.

"I love you, too, Claire Halliday." He pushed a strand of hair back from her face. "You're the most unconventional, unpredictable and desirable woman I've ever known. And I can't wait to make you mine."

"Then don't wait," she said with a come-hither look that made him stammer. "You kiss like a magician... so make my virtue disappear."

"N-now?"

"Unless you have other plans."

With a strangled laugh, he pulled her against him and kissed her within an inch of her sanity. She responded by removing his tie and loosening his collar. He unbuttoned her jacket and the fastening of her skirt. Her kisses drifted down the side of his neck and slid beneath the buttons of his shirt; his rolled back the shoulder of her blouse and bared her corset cover.

His lips wove a spell over her exposed skin as he loosened her clothing piece by piece...leaving her in a swirl of half-dispatched clothes that made her seem more naked and alluring than if she were completely bare. By the time her shoes and hairpins lay scattered on the floor, his braces and cufflinks had joined them. He paused, holding himself above her to better appreciate the disheveled glory of her charms.

"You are so very beautiful. You make me want to write sonnets to your hair and those dazzling eyes. Except, I'm not particularly good at writing."

"I know. I read your letters." She stretched her arms above her head, baring one breast in invitation. "Stick to what you do best, Englishman. Kiss me. Nibble me. Thrill me."

A laugh came from deep in his throat and set her skin tingling as he kissed, nibbled and thrilled his way across her breasts and then up her neck to her lips. The rest of her body ached for that same attention, but had to be satisfied with feverish touches and hungry caresses…until he parted her thighs with his knee and slid his hot body intimately against hers. Then the balance of sensation shifted and her lower body gloried in the steamy possession of his weight and rhythmic movements against her.

She responded like the veriest of hoydens, seeking the heat of his sex to relieve the burn in hers. But he delayed and toyed with her until she could no longer breathe or think, until her senses were stuffed to gluttonous levels and simply exploded.

When reality returned, she found him watching her with eyes like hot coals.

"Oh, my."

"Oh, yes." His voice was smoky velvet. "And there's more to come."

How could she crave more when she'd already had so much? But, she did, shameless creature that she was. When he joined their bodies, she found pleasure of a shocking sort—a hot, well-filled delight that coaxed her to meet his movements with her own and brought her to the brink of sanity once more. This time, he came with her, comingled with her pleasures and sharing her response. For one stunning and irreplaceable moment she was at one with him, with her whole self and with the rest of the cosmos.

Blankets had been cast aside and clothes were at least half shed, but the cold didn't seem to touch them as they lay in each other's arms. She was exhausted, but had never felt less like sleeping in her life. She wanted to memorize every moment of this and to learn his body and explore the way he looked and felt against her. Fortunately, he didn't seem very sleepy, either.

"You know, of course, that you can't just introduce me to things like this and not expect me to want them again." She rubbed his leg with her foot.

"I was sort of counting on that, actually." He ran a finger down her nose and over her lips. "We should open negotiations for exclusive rights to said consortium…with all legal rights and appurtenances to be included."

"What?" She was baffled.

"I want you to marry me," he interpreted. "I know this may not be the most romantic proposal in the world, but it is the sincerest. I want to marry you and live with you and travel with you. And if I'm lucky, someday make babies with you." His heart was visible in his eyes. "What do you think?"

"You want to marry me? Really?"

"Really." He kissed her fingertips, drawing each into his mouth for a nibble. She shivered and pulled her hand back so she could concentrate.

"And we can travel?"

"You said travel was a dream of yours. Well, I'm your dream man. I've been to dozens of countries and seen wonders and sights you wouldn't believe. I never expected to have someone to share them with."

"Yes. Just, *yes!*" She sat up, threw her arms around his neck and peppered his face with kisses. "I'll marry you and travel with you and...*oh.*"

"Don't stop," he said with a laugh, nudging her to continue.

"The family will be ecstatic," she said, beaming. "This is just what they wanted." Could it honestly be that simple? Then she remembered. "You know, don't you, that the family expects you to take over the business, now that you're back."

"Cousin Hortense has been dropping hints the size of an elephant."

"Not the most subtle of folks, the Mayhews," she said watching his reaction. "What do you think? Could you be happy manufacturing and selling cutlery for the rest of your days?"

"A good question," he said, nuzzling her bare shoulder and rubbing his palm in distracting circles over her tingling nipple, "for another day."

CHAPTER NINE

LATER THAT EVENING, the lock clicked and the attic door opened with a series of dry, incremental rasps against floorboards. Mother Mayhew, Uncle Abner and Cousin Tillie crept up the steps, keeping to the edges of the treads to avoid creaks. They spotted the candle guttering on the washstand and ventured farther. Seeing Rafe and Claire fully dressed, curled around each other beneath some blankets on the bed, they quickly backed down the steps the way they had come, grinning at each other.

Periwinkle stood, glowing in the darkness, gazing fondly at the pair. This was it. The real thing. True Love accomplished. Then why was she still there? Shouldn't she have been recalled to the heavenly precincts? Unless…oh, unless there was still more to do.

A groan awakened Rafe, something like the sound of wind moaning about the corner of the house. His heart pounded as he sat up and listened. It was probably nothing. Still, he ought to check. When he crept to the stairs, he found a dim glow coming from the hallway beyond. The door miraculously had been opened—they were free.

He awakened Claire and, arm in arm, they swayed down the stairs and hallways until they reached her room where they kissed and then parted to their separate beds and shared dreams.

IT WAS LATE THE NEXT morning when Claire, freshly bathed and glowing with contentment, arrived in the breakfast room to find the family already gone. Only Aunt Eloise sat at the table, crocheting furiously. She answered a bit crossly when asked if Rafe had been down to breakfast yet.

"*Ralph,* you mean? He was up at the crack of dawn, preparing to go into the city for some 'meeting' or other. I told him he should wait until Cook had a chance to prepare him a decent breakfast, but he wouldn't hear of it."

"I don't recall him mentioning a meeting," Claire said as she rang the kitchen and had a plate and some coffee sent up for her breakfast.

It was a huge disappointment to find him gone. As she prepared for the day, she had anticipated the pleasure of making the announcement of their upcoming marriage with him. She couldn't wait to see Mother Mayhew's and Uncle Abner's faces. Not to mention that such a happy prospect would eclipse the necessity for an explanation of where she and Rafe had been until the wee hours of the morning. Now, without him to help her announce it, she was stuck explaining how she and Rafe had been stuck in the attic for hours.

When she could postpone it no longer, she went into the drawing room and found Mother Mayhew, Uncle Abner and Cousin Tillie taking the ornaments and candleholders off the Christmas tree.

"There she is!" Mother Mayhew hurried to embrace

her. "We were so worried last night when you and Ralph missed dinner. Where did you go?"

"A strange thing… Remember we went up to the attic with Tillie? Well, somehow the door swung shut and locked. We were stuck up there for hours and hours in the cold and dark." She was gratified by Tillie's gasp of horror. "One of the servants must have unlocked the door when they returned from their holiday, because in the middle of the night we awoke and found it open."

"Goodness." Mother Mayhew looked genuinely concerned. "I had no idea. Abner, you must have the servants look at that door straight away."

"You could have frozen to death up there." Tillie's eyes were wide and anxious.

"We found some blankets and a candle or two. We made do. Rafe is quite resourceful." Claire hoped she wouldn't be struck by lightning for that misleading bit of understatement.

"Rafe?" Mother Mayhew said in a way that managed to sound both puzzled and judgmental.

"That is the way he prefers to hear his name pronounced."

"He does, does he? Well, he's always been plain Ralph to us."

"Well, it is *his* name, Hortense," Abner said, tucking some newspaper around the candleholders and ornaments that were headed for storage. "The boy can pronounce it however he wants…I guess." Then he asked Claire, "When's he coming home, this 'Rafe' of yours?"

She was so surprised by their prickly attitude toward

his preferred pronunciation that she failed to notice the way he had assigned ownership of Rafe to her.

"He didn't say," she answered, feeling oddly unsettled by that fact.

Hers was the last word on the subject until tea that afternoon. She had managed to keep busy with the household linen inventory and doing some work on ledgers Uncle Abner had brought home for her from the factory. But with each passing hour, she grew more anxious. Rafe might have told her he had an appointment and would be gone most of the day. What if he was avoiding her? What if—*stop*—that way lay madness.

The hall clock was striking five when Rafe returned with a broad smile and a bouquet of flowers. The minute she saw the twinkle in his eyes, all doubt about what had happened between them melted away. When he dropped a kiss on her cheek while presenting her with the flowers, everyone in the drawing room sat up and took notice.

Tea was trundled in on a linen-draped cart just then, and Claire asked for a vase and water for the flowers. The whole family was soon assembled, and Claire began arranging, Mother Mayhew began pouring and Uncle Abner began quizzing.

"You seem pleased," Abner addressed Rafe. "I take it your business in the city went well."

"Quite well," Rafe said, smiling at Claire. "In fact, it couldn't have gone better. But I couldn't wait to get back here to see Claire." He went to stand beside her at the table, where she was clipping and arranging flowers, and lifted her hand to his lips. Eyebrows hit the ceiling at his behavior.

Claire began to feel nervous. The old things would be happy, wouldn't they, when they learned their plan was a success?

"I would like you to know," Rafe said, pulling her against his side, "that I have asked Claire to marry me. And now, since you are her closest kin, I humbly ask your permission to wed her as soon as it can be arranged."

Mother Mayhew sprang from her chair with a squeal to embrace Claire, and Uncle Abner rushed to pump Rafe's hand and call him "my boy." Tillie, Cousin Halbert and Aunt Eloise weren't far behind, hugging and patting and welcoming Rafe to—well, back to the family. Everyone was genuinely delighted with the news.

Claire's eyes moistened as Rafe got down on one knee to present her with a lovely ruby-and-diamond ring he had purchased while in the city. She accepted all over again and he kissed her warmly beneath the mistletoe.

Spirits were high, almost giddy, as they made their way into dinner at eight o'clock. The wedding was already half planned—each woman had different ideas to offer about what Claire should wear and who should officiate and the size of the guest list for the wedding breakfast. The one thing they all agreed on was the date…six weeks away…Valentine's Day.

Claire was sailing in such a blissful fog that she didn't see the cannonball plowing through the side of her nuptial ship of dreams…until Uncle Abner's face became a thundercloud and Rafe stiffened sharply.

She'd been listening to Tillie on the other side of her

when the exchange occurred. It took a moment for her to reconstruct the conversation.

"So, my boy, I assume you'll be wanting to come to the factory with me tomorrow…start getting a feel for things. Turning out matched sets of cutlery ain't as easy as it seems, you know."

"No, I don't think so," Rafe had answered with subtle tension.

"What, you have plans for tomorrow? Claire can spare you for a day or two. After all, it's your future."

"No, I'm afraid it isn't."

"Isn't what? What are you talking about? You're coming into the business…training in to take over Mayhew Cutlery in a couple of years."

"I'm afraid I have other plans." Rafe's clear, resonant voice carried to the far corners of the room. But it was Uncle Abner's raised voice that halted all other conversation at the table.

"What plans? What the hell could be more important than the top chair at Mayhew Cutlery?" Abner's fists were clenched around his napkin and Halbert was suddenly so tightly wound that he looked like a jack-in-the-box.

Rafe turned to Claire with an apology. "I'm sorry. I should have spoken with you first, but I've just this day entered into an agreement with three men I knew in India to charter a new company. Our aim is to develop a business that will allow small farmers and independent planters to grow crops and sell them at a fair price without corruption or exploitive labor practices. It's been my goal for some time now and we've just acquired the funding for it."

"What does that mean?" Mother Mayhew looked around frantically. "Abner, what does it mean?"

"It means he's going back to that heathen place," Eloise snapped.

"With our Claire," Tillie said with an ill-suppressed moan. "He's taking our Claire away with him."

Silence reigned as Tillie's words sank in.

"The devil he is." Uncle Abner shot to his feet. "How dare you, sir! To come into our home, accept our hospitality, steal our Claire and carry her half a world away from us…it's unthinkable…unconscionable!"

"You're abandoning us again and taking our Claire away from us?" Mother Mayhew practically strangled on the words.

"Over my dead body," Halbert declared, leaning pugnaciously across the table while shoving his owlish spectacles back up his nose.

"Who said anything about dying?" Tillie squeaked.

"But we've counted on you, Ralph." Mother Mayhew—always such a formidable presence—seemed to crumple inward. "It's too much…just too much… losing Stephen…and now Ralph and our dear, dear Claaaire!"

Tears began to roll.

The sight of Mother Mayhew in such distress horrified Claire. She rushed to her foster mother's side and tried hugging and comforting her while Abner and Aunt Eloise began to lecture Rafe. Cousin Halbert ran for a broom handle and set about knocking down the balls of mistletoe in the dining room, the entry hall, the morning room and the drawing room. Tillie turned white, made horrible asthmatic gasps and ran for the bathing room to hang over a pan of Mentholatum salve and boiling water.

This was madness!

Claire could see Rafe trying to be reasonable, trying to talk it out and explain and remind her family that he'd made no promises in coming to visit. But she also saw Abner's and Mother Mayhew's pain at the prospect of losing yet another family member when they had expected to finally *gain* one. Cousin Halbert seemed to have snapped; he was turning into a dervish with a broom handle, battering the chandelier as much as the kissing ball that was still hanging by a thread. And through it all, Mother Mayhew wailed and rocked, keeping up a steady stream of disbelief and pleas for divine intervention.

It was all her fault, Claire thought desperately. If she had only…

The din and craziness pressed in on all sides. Where was a foothold in sanity or reason? Her family was tearing itself apart and she— Then a voice sounded in her head, as clear as a church bell.

Quiet—make them be quiet. Take charge and tell them what you really think, for a change.

Where that voice came from she couldn't imagine, but it seemed so calm and familiar that she instinctively trusted it. Collecting her powerful emotions, she stuffed them into her spine and into her voice.

"Silence!" she roared, shocking even herself with the volume she was able to muster. "Stop it! Right now!" She let the echoes die before continuing. "I want you all to shut your mouths and sit down and listen to me for a change!"

The three in the dining room turned to her with stunned expressions. Halbert, in the hall, didn't seem to hear and continued flailing away at the now ruined globs of mistletoe. The others' mouths dropped open as she strode into the hall, grabbed him by the shirt collar and dragged him into the dining room. Wrenching the broom handle from him, she ordered him into a chair.

When Halbert, seeming dazed by his own outburst, sank to a seat, the others copied him and soon were seated and staring at her in disbelief.

"I'm shocked. And saddened. And horrified. You're my family. I asked you to celebrate with me my promise to marry the man I love. And you're behaving like—like...

Spoiled brats came that bolstering voice in her head.

"Spoiled brats," she declared. "You should hear yourselves...talking about me as if I were a possession, not a person. Your Claire. You know, you've done that for four bloody long years and, frankly, I'm sick of it."

You have hopes and dreams of your own, the voice prompted.

"I'm a person, you know. With feelings and hopes and dreams of my own. Most of which you know nothing about. You roll your eyes at my books and treat my passion for learning as if it is a sad little eccentricity. Did you ever once ask me what I was reading or show any interest in my thoughts or feelings or hopes? In the few days he's been here, Rafe has learned more about me than you have in twelve years. He cared enough to ask, to seek, to encourage me to share my thoughts and feelings."

She sought out their gazes, one by one, glimpsing shock and irritation in some, recognition and guilt in others.

You put up with their tears and their sniveling...

"For the past four years, I've comforted your tears and put up with your self-pity and hang-dog expressions. I thought I was helping you—but in truth I was only helping you prolong the agony of losing Stephen. It's time you let go of your loss and make the most of the good things that are left in your lives. Stephen would have hated what his death has done to you—to all of us."

"Ungrateful child," Aunt Eloise ground out, but it came out more hurt than angry.

"We've always loved you like a daughter," Mother Mayhew wailed, her chin quivering and her eyes almost as red as her nose.

"You were our little sprite, our sweet little pumpkin," Abner moaned.

"Who read me stories while I worked in my workshop," Halbert mumbled, unable to look at her just now.

"And look at how you treat us. You abandon us and run off with the first smooth-talking dandy that comes along." Mother Mayhew buried her face in her hands and let the heaving of her ample shoulders speak for her.

Rafe's eyes were now nearly as big as his fists. He would have shoved to his feet just then, but she stayed him with a hand on his shoulder.

"I am *not* running off with a dandy. I'm marrying Cousin Ralph. Remember him? Ralph, who could go around the block with a penny and come back with a pound. Ralph, who is as loyal and dutiful and faithful as a sheepdog and as sensible as good wool socks."

"No, you're not," Mother Mayhew charged with petulance, waving at him with her soppy handkerchief. "You're marrying this 'Rafe' fellow."

They were acting like children, she thought, spurred to true irritation. But her very next thought undercut her indignation. They were slipping into second childhoods, the lot of them. Aging and cranky and crotchety—they had been isolated with their grief for too long. Crossing her arms, she thought fiercely of the longing and loss and the love they had shared. They were her family. And, damn it, she was not going to be forced to choose between them and the man she loved. There had to be a way, and she was going to find it.

A heartbeat later, she turned to Rafe with a stern look in her eye.

"So. Do you think you could bear to be called 'Ralph' and only 'Ralph' while you're under this roof? It seems to be a sticking point."

He scowled, looked at her quizzically and then nodded.

"Quite reasonable of you, dear." Giving his shoulder a squeeze, she then turned to her family. "Fine, you can call him Ralph. He's back to Ralph…everywhere but in my room."

"He's going to take you away where we'll never get to see you," Halbert charged. She turned to Rafe.

"Are you?"

He met her eyes and for a moment they gazed into

each other's hearts. Nothing was held back. Nothing was more important than the trust being shaped right here, right now between them. She was stunned to see that he seemed to understand how important this was to her and that he supported her in it. That love, that generous sense of connection, gave her the courage to ask him the question that burned in every heart present.

"Where are we going?"

"Nowhere for the time being," he said, his spice-colored eyes full of warmth and care for her and whatever mattered to her. "Except to our own lodgings in London. I've agreed to handle this end of the business and let my Indian partners do the contracting and acquisitions on the other end. There will of course be occasional trips to India and the East. And we'll have to forge connections on the continent. But all of that can wait until we get back from our wedding trip. I was thinking Paris, or maybe Rome."

She smiled at him with all the love in her heart. He rose and pulled her into his arms and the sight of them together—so happy and hopeful—drained every last bit of rancor and contention from the family.

"But, wait!" Uncle Abner, ever one to seize an opportunity, sat forward and tugged his vest down. "If you're staying in London, why go to the expense of setting up your own house? Why not stay here with us? We could move things around a bit… and make you a suite of rooms. And you'd be with family, Claire, when Ralph has to travel."

She looked at Rafe, who gave her a private wink, then turned back with a canny look.

"Which rooms?"

THERE WAS QUITE A little bit of negotiating that evening…some hard bargaining on both sides. Fortunately Claire's clever and insightful turns-of-phrase kept things from getting out of hand. Through it all, grievances were aired, old hurts were resolved and a new and more enlightened regimen was established for Mayhew House.

It helped that plans for the wedding and the remodeling of a suite of rooms for the newlyweds proceeded simultaneously…giving everyone something to do and something to make decisions on. And on the wedding day, everything was perfect…the bride's ivory gown, the groom's impeccable morning coat…the cascades of spring flowers that Tillie chose…and the ring that Cousin Halbert helped Rafe design, cast and polish.

That night, the bride and groom entered their very own suite of rooms for the first time, holding their breaths and finding it all…*perfect*.

Rafe took Claire into his arms. "At last. We're legal and alone and I can't wait to test that bed."

"Have you even looked around? Did you see what they've done for us?"

"I saw it." He planted his lips in the curve of her neck and kissed her until her toes curled. Then he raised his head and turned her to face a table on which sat an incongruously happy statue with crocheted clothes.

"First thing tomorrow, those clothes come off that poor Buddha." He turned her back so she could see his wickedly desirous look. "But first thing tonight, the clothes come off my wife."

As Rafe lifted her against him and swung her around, she sensed a curious presence in the joy filling her heart. And for a brief moment it felt like something soft brushed her face…something light and ethereal… like a feather…like a wing. And when she looked up at Rafe, she could have sworn she caught a glimpse of an angel reflected in the depths of his eye.

* * * * *

TODAY'S LONGING

Jacquie D'Alessandro

* * *

"I am the Ghost of Christmas Present,"
said the Spirit.
"Look upon me...
You have never seen the like of me before!"

—*A Christmas Carol:
Being a Ghost Story of Christmas*
by Charles Dickens

This book is dedicated to my dear friend
and colleague Kathleen Givens. Kath,
you were taken away much too soon, but your
reminder that "life is short" lives in my heart.
Everyone who had the honor and pleasure of
knowing you is heartbroken that you were right.
I love you, kiddo. Xox, Jac.

And to Richard Dugas, Michael Bottoms,
Jason Byham, Claire Bowie and Eddie Moss for
their help and kindness. You all are
always welcome at Casa D'Alessandro.

And, as always, to my wonderful husband,
Joe, who goes Above and Beyond every day
and is my very best BFF, and our terrific son,
Christopher, BFF, Jr.

PROLOGUE

"I'M GOING TO PARIS to study art," Lady Adelaide Kendall announced to the pair of friends with whom she sat drinking tea near the bookstore's fireplace, where cheerful flames snapped. "I depart five days from now, and I'll be gone several months."

Rose, guardian angel to Addie, stared down at her charge in horror from her vantage point on a wooden rafter set high in the bookstore's vaulted ceiling. "Good heavens, did you hear that?" she asked the two apprentice angels hovering near her. "My Addie is leaving England—for several months!" Rose's face puckered into the anxious frown that, over the years, had creased a deep wrinkle between her brows. She wrung her plump hands together, spilling a wave of pink sparkles into the shadows. "How can I possibly hope to accomplish the already daunting task of joining her with her One True Love if she isn't even in the same country with him? Oh, dear!"

"That will certainly make things more difficult," agreed angel Periwinkle, her voice filled with sympathy. "I thought my assignment with Claire was difficult," she added, nodding toward her auburn-haired charge below, "but yours is—"

"Impossible," Rose wailed. "I simply *cannot* contemplate another century as an apprentice angel without wings, should I fail to bring Addie and her One True Love together before the New Year's Eve deadline imposed upon us. I'm too old and too tired for such a fate."

"You wouldn't be so old and tired if you hadn't failed in all your previous attempts to bring them together," angel Fern pointed out in her forthright manner. "Perhaps that's a sign you are mistaken as to who Addie's One True Love is."

Rose bristled, shooting another arc of pink sparkles into the air. "I don't see that you've had any more success matching your Fiona with her One True Love than I've had with Addie. And I am most certainly *not* mistaken." Yet worry shivered through her. *Could* she be wrong? Oh, if only her angel powers allowed her to influence human emotions! But alas, they did not.

"I'm not mistaken," she repeated. Surely if she said it enough—believed it enough—it would be true. "I've been with Addie for years. I know her heart. I know who she loves."

"That doesn't mean he loves her in return," Fern said bluntly.

Everything inside Rose rejected that horrible possibility and she shook her head, sending her spectacles gliding down her nose. "He simply *has to* return her feelings." And quickly. The threat of another century without wings rippled a shiver of dread through her. Such an outcome was simply not to be borne. A sense of profound desperation joined her worry. She pointed to Addie, who was adding a lump of sugar to her teacup. "Look at her. She is beautiful, accomplished, witty and charming. Kind and loving. And from a fine and noble family. What sort of fool wouldn't fall in love with her?"

"Human males are notorious for being fools when it comes to women," Periwinkle intoned, sounding like The Voice of Experience in spite of the fact that she'd been an apprentice angel the shortest amount of time of all of them.

"Surely Claire and Fiona will talk Addie out of going," Rose said, her voice laced with hope. "Why, they can't forego their book club meetings for months."

"If you'd cease chattering, we could listen to what they're saying," said Fern in her tartest tone.

"I hadn't mentioned my travel plans previously as I wasn't certain arrangements could be made." Addie's soft voice drifted upward, and Rose held her breath as she listened. "My aunt Margaret has been helping me work out the details. I received a letter from her just before coming here, confirming that everything is set."

"We'll miss you," said Fiona McPherson, proprietress of the cozy bookstore where the women had met two years earlier. Their mutual love of books forged an otherwise unlikely friendship between them that overlooked their divergent backgrounds and social situations.

Addie smiled. "I'll miss you, too. Our monthly meetings have come to mean a great deal to me. But I'm looking forward to furthering my art studies."

"I've always longed to travel," said Claire Halliday

with a wistful sigh. "Is your sister going with you?" she asked, setting aside her leather-bound copy of Charles Dickens's *A Christmas Carol* with a haste that made it clear all discussion of their latest book selection was temporarily suspended.

Addie shook her head, dislodging one of the chestnut curls she forever fought to tame. "No. Grace will be very busy over the next several months with her own plans."

Claire's eyes lit up. "Has Lord Channing proposed to Grace?"

"Not yet," Addie replied. "Although now that Sebastian's official mourning period for his mother has ended, it will surely happen over the holiday."

Rose yelped as if she'd been jabbed with a hot poker. "Good heavens, did you hear that?" she cried. "I'd completely forgotten about Sebastian's mourning period ending—and now Addie's One True Love is about to become engaged to her sister! How can I fix it when Addie is leaving for Paris? Oh, dear, this is a disaster of *epic* proportions!

"That is indeed a mess," Fern confirmed.

"There's never been a more incompetent guardian angel than I," Rose fretted. "How many times have I attempted to bring Adelaide and Sebastian together? Too many to recall. And now my time is nearly up."
She paced for several seconds, stirring up a blizzard of pink sparkles. Her gaze fell upon Addie's copy of *A Christmas Carol,* which rested on her lap, and Rose halted. The ladies had chosen the book for its holiday theme and the story had thoroughly engaged Addie... Addie, who was stuck in the present—torn between

her feelings for her One True Love and devotion to her beloved sister. Addie would never do anything to hurt Grace, would never think to interfere with her sister's happiness—but Rose would. Surely a visit from the Ghost—or rather, the *Angel*—of Christmas Present would make things right. Wouldn't it?

Rose wasn't sure, but she was desperate enough to do anything…*anything* to bring Addie and her One True Love together—and save herself from another century without wings.

CHAPTER ONE

3:45 p.m.

ADDIE CAREFULLY SET her tea cup in its matching china saucer, proud that her steady hands revealed nothing of her inner turmoil. The last thing she wanted was for Fiona and Claire to suspect how distraught she was. She'd announced her news about going to Paris and now it was time to steer the conversation back to Mr. Dickens's story. She only had to make polite conversation for a little while longer, then she'd have the entire train ride to her family's country estate in the sleepy village of Buntington, in East Hertfordshire to be alone with her thoughts—and not pretend a gaiety she was far from feeling. "My favorite character was—"

"Do you think the betrothal announcement between Grace and Lord Channing will be made tomorrow night at your family's Christmas Eve ball?" broke in Claire, her lovely face glowing with excitement. As much as Addie didn't want to prolong the conversation about Grace and Sebastian's imminent engagement, she was most gratified to see that light in her friend's eyes. This time of year was especially difficult for Claire given her fiancé's tragic death a week before their Christmas wedding four years ago.

"Most likely." Addie's voice cracked on the words,

and she cleared her throat. "And now that I've shared my news, why don't we continue discussing the book? I very much enjoyed Mr. Dickens's use of ghosts to illustrate—"

"But what about Evan?" interrupted Fiona.

Addie had known the question regarding Sebastian's younger brother would come, and had known Fiona would be the one to ask. Part of Addie felt deep sympathy for her friend, who had suffered the loss of her father and now held the heavy responsibility of running the bookstore. But another part of Addie envied Fiona's independence and straightforward manner. Fiona would never find herself in an untenable situation like the one Addie was now up to her neck in. No, her forthright friend would have spoken up years ago. Unfortunately, Addie hadn't done so, and now it was too late. How would it feel to say exactly how she felt? Addie didn't know, and knew she never would. If she ever revealed what was in her heart... A shudder ran through her at the thought of the people she loved the most being hurt.

"Addie? Are you listening?" Fiona's voice yanked Addie from her thoughts. "What about Evan?"

"What do you mean?"

Fiona made an impatient gesture. "Surely he's distraught that you're going to Paris for several months."

"I haven't told him yet. But when I do, I'm sure he'll be happy for me to continue my studies. Now, about those ghosts of Christmases Past, Present and Future—"

"But with his family now officially out of mourning

over his mother's death, surely Evan plans to declare himself your suitor this Christmas," continued Fiona.

Claire smiled and nodded. "Yes, wouldn't that make for a perfect holiday?"

Addie put off answering immediately by taking a sip of tea. Certainly her family would be thrilled if Sebastian's younger brother, Evan, expressed a romantic interest in her. Indeed everyone she knew hoped for a match between them. She took another swallow of tea, then said, "No. For, while I do love Evan, it's in the same way I love my brother. Not in the way a woman should love the man she marries. One wedding to plan will be quite enough." She offered her friends a smile, then said firmly, "Now, about Mr. Dickens's story—"

"And what a wedding it will be," said Claire, heaving a dreamy sigh.

Addie heaved her own inward sigh and braced herself to continue this discussion she clearly couldn't avoid—one she'd be forced to endure many more times over the holiday. *Just five more days until you leave for Paris.* Five more days. She could do it. She'd pretended for years—what were five more days? Forcing a smile, she said, "It will be the event of the season."

"Grace and Lord Channing…they'll certainly be the most beautiful couple in the entire kingdom," remarked Fiona.

Addie nodded, not trusting her voice. Individually, her gorgeous sister and the devastatingly attractive viscount turned heads whenever they entered a room. Together they could stun an entire ballroom into momentary silence. She swallowed, then said softly, "They will be blessed."

Which is the way it should be, she told herself firmly. Grace and Sebastian were meant for each other—their families had informally agreed to the match years ago, even then recognizing how perfectly suited the two were. Ever since then, society had anticipated an engagement announcement from the moment of Grace's coming out two years ago, the inevitable being delayed only by the tragic and unexpected death of Sebastian's mother. Now that his mourning period had ended, and there was nothing to further delay the highly anticipated betrothal, an engagement would thrill everyone.

Everyone except her.

"Their children will surely be equally as beautiful," Fiona said, yanking Addie back to the conversation. Her voice held a whiff of wistful envy, the same note Addie often heard when people spoke of Grace and Sebastian.

"I'm certain they will be," Addie said. A crystal clear image of a gaggle of miniature Graces and Sebastians toddling about flashed through her mind. "I cannot wait to be an aunt."

"You'll be a wonderful aunt," Claire said with a smile. Then she reached out and patted Addie's hand. "And someday a wonderful mother."

Of course the words were meant as a compliment, but still they knifed pain through Addie's heart. "Thank you," she managed to say, aware it was the only answer that wouldn't further prolong a conversation she wished had already ended. At five and twenty, society might not yet consider her on the shelf, but Addie knew spinsterhood awaited her.

The sound of laughter coming from outside drew

Addie's gaze to the window. In spite of the threat of snow hanging heavy in the cold air, the cobblestone street was filled with horse-drawn carriages and pedestrians bundled up against the wintry gusts. Muted voices, the clip clop of horses' hooves, the squeak of carriage wheels and even the distant sound of Christmas carolers drifted into the deliciously warm bookstore. A smiling couple passed beneath the circle of light cast by the shop's lamp, their arms laden with brightly decorated packages, and envy walloped Addie at their obvious happiness. How wonderful it would feel to be half of such a loving couple.

"A wedding to plan," Claire said softly, pulling Addie from her brown study. "How romantic." Her gaze bounced between Fiona and Addie. "Perhaps romance will find you both, as well, this Christmas."

"To steal a quote from *A Christmas Carol,* 'Bah! Humbug!'" said Fiona. "Indeed, I'm exhausted from feigning a gaiety I do not feel at this time every year."

"I think perhaps you're missing the true theme of Mr. Dickens's story," said Claire. Beneath all the 'Bah! Humbug!' *A Christmas Carol* is, at its heart, a story of hope and love. Of redemption and new beginnings. Let us not forget that love can bring about miracles."

"What a bunch of drivel," pronounced Fiona in her usual forthright manner. "What do you think, Addie?"

"Miracles are possible," she answered carefully. But her conscience kicked at her because in her heart she didn't believe her words. What she knew was that, rather than miracles, love brought buckets of heartache. And that she couldn't wait for this holiday to be over so she could escape to Paris and avoid all the upcoming wedding plans. For she couldn't bear to be trapped between the impossible, conflicting vise of profound love for her sister, and her hopeless, unrequited love for Sebastian, the man Grace would marry.

CHAPTER TWO

Kendall Manor
Village of Buntingford
Christmas Eve

SEBASTIAN HARTLEY, Viscount Channing, walked down
the long carpeted corridor leading to the ballroom at
Kendall Manor with the dainty gloved hand of argu-
ably the most beautiful woman in all of England resting
in the curve of his arm. He looked down at the petite
vision that was Lady Grace Kendall and knew he'd be
the envy of every man in the ballroom the instant they
crossed the threshold.

She looked up at him and offered him a dimpling
smile that he'd personally witnessed turn normally intelligent men into love-struck mutes.

"It's lovely to see you, Sebastian," she said, giving
his forearm a light squeeze. "You've been missed."

He returned her smile. "I've missed you, too,
Poppet."

Her smile deepened at his use of the endearment
bestowed on her at birth, when he was a worldly man
of six. He'd known her since the day she was born and
had watched her grow from a gorgeous, sweet-natured
child into a stunning young woman, who, in spite of
her beauty, had remained kind and loving. Dressed in

a frothy turquoise satin-and-lace gown that accentuated her eyes and highlighted her creamy complexion and shiny blond curls, she was the epitome of beauty, charm and elegance. Having Grace on his arm...he was a lucky man indeed.

The melodic sounds of a waltz drifted toward them, increasing in volume as they neared the room. They turned a final corner, and a few steps later paused in the wide arched doorway. The ballroom resembled a winter wonderland, the glow from the dozens of gas lamps and hundreds of candles glinting off the huge crystal snowflakes and icicles hanging from the ceiling. Fragrant boughs of fir and pine, splashed with colorful oranges, berries and pomegranates, draped the walls and mantel, while garlands of glossy holly decorated the long refreshment table where guests could enjoy a mulled cider and an assortment of nuts, candies, fruit and cookies.

By Sebastian's estimation, more than two hundred guests filled the spacious room, not a surprise as the Earl of Gresham's annual Christmas Eve ball was the social event of the year in the village of Buntingford. Not even the snow that had begun falling earlier that afternoon could keep people from attending the soiree. He and Grace stood framed in the doorway for no more than five seconds before stepping over the threshold, but it was enough time for word of their arrival to start spreading through the room with the speed of a flame set to dry kindling. The whispers reached his ears as the crowd parted like the Red Sea for them as they exchanged holiday greetings with friends and made their way toward the dance floor.

"They're here at last!"

"Isn't she stunning?"

"He's so handsome! So dashing!"

"Such a perfect couple!"

"The most beautiful couple in England!"

"Do you think the announcement everyone's waiting for will come tonight?"

"Did you see the way he just looked at her? 'Tis clear he loves her."

"Did you see the way she just looked at him? 'Tis clear she adores him."

"He's the luckiest man in the kingdom."

"She's the most fortunate woman in the world!"

When they reached the edge of the parquet dance floor, the music stopped and, for what seemed an eternity but was surely no more than ten seconds, a hushed silence fell over the ballroom. The weight of more than two hundred stares and what felt like the expectations of an entire nation pressed down on Sebastian. He could actually feel the anticipation hanging in the air. It surrounded him like London's ubiquitous yellow fog. He knew what they all were waiting for. What they all wanted. What they all expected of him. And now that the mourning period for his mother was officially over, there was no longer any reason not to ask Grace the question everyone expected him to ask. No reason not to honor his beloved mother's deathbed request—to marry Grace and forever join the Hartley and Kendall families, who had been friends and neighbors for generations. No reason not to make the betrothal announcement everyone expected—most especially his father, who'd reiterated to Sebastian since he was fourteen years old that a match between Sebastian and Grace was counted upon.

No, there was no reason at all.

Except for the fact that he was in love with someone else.

The string quartet launched into another waltz and the buzz of conversation resumed, granting Sebastian a temporary reprieve, although neither the music nor the chatter in any way lessened the expectations weighing around his neck like an anchor. He turned toward Grace to ask her to dance, but the request died on his lips when he caught sight of Evan making his way toward them. His normally robust brother looked pale and tense and, behind his wire-rimmed spectacles, his eyes appeared troubled.

"Good to see you, Sebastian," Evan said, offering his hand. "Merry Christmas."

"Same to you," Sebastian said. Now that only an arm's length separated them, Evan's distress was even more obvious to Sebastian. Before he could question him, however, Evan said, "I'm looking forward to catching up with you later, but for now—" he turned to Grace "—I believe this is my waltz."

Grace consulted the dance card dangling from her wrist, then nodded. "It is indeed."

"May I steal her away?" Evan asked.

"Of course," Sebastian said. "Enjoy your dance."

Evan extended his arm and with a becoming blush coloring her cheeks, Grace tucked her hand in the crook of his elbow. "I just left Addie by the terrace doors," Evan said to him in a gravelly tone that cemented Sebastian's belief that something had his brother badly unsettled. "She is unclaimed for this dance if you're in the mood to waltz." He then led Grace to join the colorful array of couples circling the dance floor.

Sebastian turned toward the glass-paneled French doors leading to the terrace. And saw her at once, not difficult as Addie's unfashionable height made her easy to locate in a crowd.

His heart tripped over itself and his breathing hitched in that irrational way it did every time he looked at her—as if the mere sight of her sucked all the air from the room, leaving him in a void where only she and his impossible, hopeless love for her existed. He hadn't seen her for months, but as he well knew, time apart did nothing to lessen his feelings or desire for her. Nor did distance, as his years serving in the Royal Navy had proven. He'd done everything he could think of to stop loving her. Stop wanting her. All to no avail. He'd loved her his entire life, and been in love with her since that summer day twelve years ago when they'd shared a kiss in Kendall Manor's garden.

In spite of his mother's deathbed request, in spite of the heavy expectations from everyone for him to marry Grace and a lifetime of honor and duty being drummed into his head, he'd have tossed it all aside in a heartbeat and claimed the woman he loved—except for one thing.

Evan loved Addie. And Sebastian loved Evan—and would never do anything to hurt his younger brother. Still, the temptation to selfishly steal his brother's love away was something Sebastian had to fight every day, a battle he lived in mortal fear of losing. In spite of the gut-wrenching guilt that would follow should he ever

succumb, he still might have given in if not for one irrefutable fact: it was clear Addie loved Evan in return.
And there was nothing Sebastian could do about that.

Except to avoid Addie whenever possible, which with
some effort he was able to accomplish most of the year.
But not at the family Christmas festivities.

So now here he stood, frozen in place, heart pounding, breathing erratic, his hungry gaze locked upon her,
devouring her from across a sea of people, all of whom
faded from his awareness as he greedily drank in every
aspect of her appearance.

Bloody hell, she was beautiful. Society had dubbed
Grace England's Greatest Beauty, and while there was
no denying Grace was stunning, it was Addie—with
her less than perfect features and enchanting smile and
that whiff of mischief that lurked in her eyes—who had
captivated him from the first time they'd met as children. As he stared at her across the ballroom, the years
fell away, and he vividly recalled that early memory of
her.

"Would you like to play with me and my doll?"
Addie asked, holding out a porcelain-faced baby with
a painted cherubic smile.

"Certainly not," Sebastian answered with a haughty
sniff and all the masculine disdain a five-year-old could
muster. "I don't play with dolls."

Addie had regarded him through huge golden-brown
eyes, nodded solemnly and set her doll down. Then she'd
smiled, and it had seemed as if the sun burst through
the clouds, filling him with warmth. "Then let's run in
the garden and climb a tree!" she'd shouted, grabbing
his hand and nearly yanking him off his feet in her

enthusiasm. Unaccustomed to such freedom or such a mischievous playmate, he'd run along with her. And climbed a tree for the first time in his life.

It wasn't until nine years later, when he was fourteen, that his love for her changed into something more. Something deeper. Something filled with an awareness of her that bordered on pain. An aching need to touch her. See her smile. Hear her laugh. Fabricate any excuse to be near her. The desire to kiss her filled every corner of his mind. That summer, on their last day together before he'd left the pastoral beauty of Buntingford to return to Eton, he'd given in to his yearnings and they'd shared a kiss—an instant in time that to this day he recalled with minute clarity. The heart-pounding exhilaration, the sense of utter rightness, as if he'd found a part of himself he'd been missing.

He'd spent the entire school term counting the days until Christmas when he'd see her again, his mind buzzing with questions. Did she miss him? Did she think of him even a fraction of the number of times he thought of her? Did she care for him the way he cared for her? He purchased a special gift for her—something to remind her of that last summer day together—and he couldn't wait to give it to her. He'd never looked forward to Christmas more than that year.

It had turned out to be the worst Christmas of his life.

He and Addie had exchanged gifts, and everything had been perfect. Until his father told him on Boxing Day that he and Addie's father had decided upon a match between Sebastian and Grace. That it was the perfect way to join the two powerful families whose estates bordered each other.

Sebastian had been too shocked to argue, and even if he hadn't been, fighting his father's wishes was something he'd simply never done. Honor and duty to his title, to his family, had been drummed into his head since the cradle, therefore gainsaying his father, especially at the age of fourteen, was not anything he could conceive of doing.

Even worse, Addie had also been apprised that day of their fathers' wishes and an unprecedented awkwardness formed between them. For the next few years, he'd pretended all was well while avoiding her as much as possible during the summer and Christmas holidays. But there was no running away from his feelings for her, which only grew stronger, in spite of his best efforts to exorcise them. Tormented, he'd joined the Royal Navy as soon as he graduated Eton to remove himself from the situation, certain that with enough time and distance his feelings for her would fade.

He could not have been more mistaken.

Instead, his love for her burned like a banked fire in his heart, gaining strength, until he finally realized it was useless to try to extinguish it. His time in the Navy had served him well and he'd returned home a strong, confident man. One who knew what he wanted and had every intention of getting it, filled with resolve to refuse his father's dictate and commence a courtship of the woman he loved. His and Addie's fathers would simply have to understand that he loved her and therefore could not marry Grace—whom he did love, but fondly, as one would a sister. Surely their fathers wouldn't balk, as the families would still be joined. But even if they did object, he'd been determined to have Addie.

However, his plans had gone horribly awry that Christmas, when it had become clear to Sebastian from the easy camaraderie, laughter and obvious closeness he witnessed between Evan and Addie that they loved each other. He'd been too late. He'd lost her. To his own brother. Then last December had brought his mother's deathbed request. He'd spent the year-long mourning period telling himself he would do what was expected of him. He'd tried his damnedest to talk himself out of love with Addie, and in love with Grace. But he'd failed. Therefore, although he'd now have to bear the sting of his father's disappointment, disapproval and anger, he simply couldn't marry Grace. Not when he loved her sister. It wouldn't be fair to himself, or to Grace, who deserved a husband who was arse over heels in love with her. And it certainly wouldn't be difficult to find such a man. He didn't know who that lucky man would be other than to know it wasn't him. There was no magic, no spark between him and Grace, which thanks to a brief interlude in the stables last Christmas, she knew as well as he did. In the interest of not ruining Christmas for his father, he'd wait until after Boxing Day to tell him his decision. Hopefully by then Evan would have proposed to Addie, thus lessening the blow to both fathers' plans to unite the families through marriage.

Evan proposing to Addie…an unpleasant sensation that felt like a brick smashing into his gut seized him. Bloody hell, he couldn't wait for this holiday to be over.

Just then, as if feeling the weight of his regard, Addie

turned toward him and their gazes met. For several seconds it seemed to him as if time stopped. In his mind's eye, he imagined himself striding across the room and, the crowd and propriety be damned, yanking her into his arms and kissing her breathless. Claiming his heart's desire. Never letting her go. And her welcoming his actions.

Then she blinked, breaking the spell. Color flushed her cheeks and something that resembled panic flashed in her eyes. Had his countenance given away his errant thoughts? Before he could decide, her expression cleared and she inclined her head in greeting and offered him a smile.

He crossed the room, drinking in the face that society would never deem classically beautiful but that nonetheless haunted his days and nights, and mentally cursing the fates that made him love a woman he could never—would never—have.

He halted an arm's length in front of her and swallowed the words that rushed into his throat. *You are the most beautiful woman I've ever seen. I want you so badly I ache. I'll love you until the day I die.* "Good evening, Addie," Sebastian said instead, offering her a formal bow.

"Good evening, Sebastian."

Just hearing her say his name shot want and need through him.

"Merry Christmas," they said in unison, then smiled.

"Still saying the same thing at the same time," he murmured. It was something they'd done since childhood.

"Yes, well, you know the proverb about great minds

thinking alike." One corner of her mouth lifted in the lopsided, teasing grin he adored. "Although, you must admit it's not really extraordinary that we'd both say 'Merry Christmas' on this occasion."

"True. If we'd both said, 'Happy Easter'—now, *that* would have been extraordinary."

She laughed, a magical sound that never failed to enchant him, and he actually had to fist his hands to keep from reaching out and snatching her into his arms. Still, the need to touch her was too strong to completely resist. "May I have this dance?"

She hesitated and shifted her gaze to the dance floor. Looking for Evan, no doubt. Jealousy punched him directly in the heart, but out of long habit he stifled the feeling. Before he could remind her that Evan had partnered Grace for this dance, she returned her attention to him and smiled. "I'd be delighted."

They moved to the edge of the dance floor and he settled his hand on her lower back, just above the small bustle of her green-and-white-striped silk gown. A warmth he only experienced with her raced through him, making him feel as if he'd come home after a long, arduous journey. She rested her gloved hand on the exact proper spot on his shoulder, and taking her free hand, he swung them into the swirl of couples circling the floor.

Silence swelled between them and Sebastian allowed himself several seconds to simply savor the sensation of holding her. Of her gloved palm nestled snugly against his. Her gown brushing against his trousers as they moved around the floor. His eyes met hers and he instantly found himself being pulled into their beautiful depths. Bloody hell, he could simply look at her for hours. At those huge topaz-colored eyes that reminded him of toffee, his favorite sweet, and that unfashionable smattering of pale gold freckles that marched across her straight nose, giving testament to her dislike of hats and parasols. Indeed he knew from experience she was much more likely to use a parasol to jab him in the buttocks than to protect her from the sun.

He looked down at her mouth which was far too plump and wide to be fashionable, yet to him was utterly perfect. He'd tasted those luscious lips only once, yet they'd set a standard no other woman had ever come close to matching. The mass of brown curls he longed to touch, and that she considered an untamable, ridiculous mish-mash of muddy colors and the bane of her existence, were artfully arranged in a becoming upswept style that left several shiny spirals brushing her shoulders. A vivid image of Addie as a young girl flashed in his mind, laughing as she ran toward him, her hair flying behind her, the sun bringing out every shade of brown from the palest gold to the deepest mahogany.

"You look lovely, Addie."

A gentle wash of rose colored her cheeks. "Thank you." Her gaze drifted briefly over his black formal attire. "So do you."

"Thank you. Although—" he leaned a bit closer, as if imparting a secret, and inhaled the delicate scent of jasmine that rose from her skin "—I don't believe gentlemen are normally regarded as 'lovely.'"

Her lips twitched. "My apologies. I meant 'hideous,' of course."

He winced. "Ouch. Surely there is something between 'lovely' and 'hideous.'"

"Oh? What would you suggest, Lord Shameless Seeker of Compliments?"

"I'm nothing of the sort. Knowing your penchant for assigning me titles, I'm merely trying to avert being dubbed Lord Lovely."

"You must admit, Lord Lovely has a certain *je ne sais quoi.*"

He shot her a mock glare. "No, it most certainly does not. How about…*debonair?*"

She looked toward the ceiling then heaved out a put-upon sigh. "Oh, very well. You look debonair." Deviltry danced in her eyes. "Lord Lovely."

"Imp."

"Scoundrel."

"Mischief-maker."

She pursed her lips, considered for several seconds, then grinned. "Guilty."

Her smile was impossible to resist, and he found himself grinning back, enjoying their camaraderie that harkened back to the days when they'd talked about anything and everything. Laughed freely. Shared secrets.

Shared a kiss in the garden.

The memory slammed into him and his gaze again dropped to her mouth. To those perfectly formed, plush pink lips that haunted his dreams. So soft…they'd been so soft and had tasted faintly of the apple she'd been eating—

"What have you been doing for the past few months?"

Her voice yanked him from his brown study and

his errant gaze snapped back up to collide with hers. "Doing?"

"Yes—doing," she reiterated, her voice laced with amusement. "Your activities? For the past several months? Since I saw you last?"

Their last meeting… It had been more than several months ago. April fourteenth, actually, outside Gunter's in Berkeley Square, where he'd purchased a box of toffee. He'd been exiting the shop just as she and her aunt Margaret had arrived. They'd done nothing more than exchange brief pleasantries then gone their separate ways, yet the unexpected encounter had brought her racing to the forefront of his mind where she'd remained firmly embedded for more weeks than he cared to recall.

"Mostly continuing my fundraising efforts on behalf of the Royal Brompton Hospital," he said. *And trying to forget about you.* Needless to say, his fundraising endeavors were far more successful. "And you?"

"Painting and drawing. Father kindly allowed me to convert the attic in the London town house into an art studio. Then there are my monthly meetings with the Society for Women's Suffrage and my reading club."

"So, you've stayed mostly in London rather than here in Buntingford?"

"Yes. Aunt Margaret has remained in town with me. She'll be traveling with me to Paris as well."

"Paris?"

"Yes. We leave in four days' time and won't return until summer."

Sebastian's brows hiked upward. "That's quite an extended holiday."

"We're not taking a holiday. I'm planning to study art." Addie's eyes sparkled as they always did whenever she spoke of something about which she was passionate. "The city is filled with exhibitions and countless opportunities to learn. I want very much to improve."

The wave of loss he experienced at the thought of her being so far away puzzled him. Damnation, he should be relieved—with her in Paris, there was no risk of another unexpected meeting between them. And he'd never begrudge her the chance to do something that clearly brought her such joy. "I've always admired your ambition to improve yourself and explore your talents to their fullest. I hope your studies are a great success, although I think you're already a marvelous artist."

A deep flush stained her cheeks. "Thank you, Sebastian. That's a lovely thing to say."

"Well, I'm not called Lord Lovely for no reason, you know."

She smiled at him and he nearly lost his footing from the impact. He covered his misstep with another turn, then said lightly, "I'm well acquainted with your artistic talent, especially as you gave me an early example of your work."

For the space of single heartbeat, something he couldn't decipher flickered in her eyes. Her complexion seemed to pale, then twin flags of scarlet stained her cheeks. "Th...that was a long time ago."

Twelve years. The Christmas after their kiss. The holiday that had begun so hopefully then ended so disastrously. She'd given him a small painting she'd done. Of the garden at Kendall Manor. Where they'd kissed. He'd given her a gold charm of a half-eaten apple. To commemorate the bit of fruit that had led directly to that unforgettable kiss.

"Yes," he agreed softly. "A long time ago." Yet, if he lived to be one hundred, he knew he'd never forget a single detail of that encounter.

Silence swelled between them, one that felt tense and awkward to him, and he cursed his careless words that had damaged their easy rapport.

After what felt like an eternity, she finally said, "I like to think my work has improved since then. And I'm hoping my studies in Paris will result in even more progress."

He nodded and swung them in a wide arc, one which brought them within several feet of Evan and Grace. His brother was smiling at Grace, but the smile didn't reach his eyes and to Sebastian, Evan's entire demeanor seemed stiff and tense. Understanding suddenly dawned.

Clearly Addie's upcoming departure and extended trip to Paris had Evan unsettled. He obviously wouldn't want her gone for such a long time, especially with a wedding to arrange. Why would Addie plan such a lengthy trip? Perhaps Evan would join her and her aunt? He hadn't mentioned it, but then they hadn't spoken at length lately, and even when they did speak, Sebastian tried his utmost to steer the conversation away from any mention of Addie. He was about to question her about the timing of her trip when the song ended. Addie's hand slipped from his shoulder and he slowly released her, then stepped back. And instantly missed the feel of her palm nestled against his. He curled his fingers inward to hold on to the warmth she'd left there for a few more seconds. He then joined the other dancers in a smattering of polite applause before saying, "Addie, why are you—?"

"The next dance is a quadrille, Addie," came Evan's voice. He and Grace joined them on the edge of the dance floor, then Evan heaved a loud sigh. "I'm afraid you're partnered with me. I'll try not to tread upon your toes."

"If you manage not to, it will be the first time," Addie said, her tart tone tempered with her teasing grin. "I believe every pair of dancing slippers I own bears the imprint of your shoes."

Evan nodded solemnly, then extended his elbow. "I am nothing if not consistent. Shall we?"

And Sebastian watched the woman he loved smile at his brother and walk away.

CHAPTER THREE

ADDIE COULDN'T SLEEP.

The last guest had departed an hour ago and now the house was silent. And she was alone. With her thoughts. Which weren't allowing her to rest.

Heaving a sigh, she pushed back the brocade counterpane and slipped from her bed. After donning her slippers and robe, she crossed the thick Turkish carpet to the window and peered through the frosted glass. The moon cast a silvery glow on the snow-covered gardens below, and her gaze was drawn, as it always was, to the elm tree rising majestically in the northwest corner.

She squeezed her eyes shut and Sebastian's words, spoken during their waltz, reverberated through her mind. *I'm well acquainted with your artistic talent, especially as you gave me an early example of your work.*

She reached out a hand that wasn't quite steady to slowly trace with a single fingertip the outline of the distant tree on the windowpane. Twelve years ago, yet the memory remained so fresh in her mind it could have happened yesterday. Sitting on a branch, summer sun warming her face, munching on an apple, smugly proud of herself that she'd climbed higher than ever before.

Then spying Sebastian walking below, holding the reins to his old mare that most likely wouldn't live to see another summer. She'd always loved how competent, gentle and compassionate he was with animals, but that summer she'd just been so *aware* of him. The mere sight of him had made her breath hitch and her heart stumble. Watching him stroke the old horse's flanks, feeding her a carrot, his obvious affection for the animal, touched something deep inside her. When his shoulders had slumped and he'd rested his forehead against the mare's velvety neck, he'd looked so uncharacteristically vulnerable, so alone and somehow defeated that Addie's heart had slipped from its moorings.

As if he'd sensed her watching him, Sebastian had raised his head and seen her sitting high in the tree. He'd started climbing, obviously convinced she'd required rescuing in spite of her assurances she didn't. He'd kept coming…and then he had been so close…and so handsome, and had smelled so clean and delicious, and all the affection she'd felt for him over the years that had suddenly shifted into something deeper that summer, had rendered her helpless with a yearning she didn't understand.

Confused at the whirlwind of emotions—and annoyed at him for confusing her—she'd stiffly insisted she was fine and had told him to leave. Then looking as annoyed as she'd felt, he'd climbed down. For some reason the fact that he'd left her there had unreasonably irritated her further and she'd descended right after him. Unfortunately her gown had caught on the bottom branch, trapping her. By then Sebastian had been stalking away from the tree. When he'd ignored her shout to him, her temper had snapped. She'd grabbed her half-eaten apple from her gown pocket and hurled it at him.

Her aim had been true and her missile had struck him in the back of his head.

For several seconds, he'd stood rooted to the spot, then he'd slowly turned to face her. Even now, all these years later, her lips twitched in amusement as she recalled his thunderstruck expression. The glare he'd shot her had obviously been meant to incinerate her on the spot. Tightlipped, he'd stomped back toward the tree, clearly intent on issuing her a severe dressing down. Determined to meet him face-to-face, she'd given her gown one final, mighty tug. The fabric had ripped suddenly and she'd lost her balance. With a cry, she'd tumbled toward the ground.

But instead of landing in an ignominious heap in the dirt, she'd ended up in Sebastian's arms. For several stunned seconds she'd simply stared into his beautiful eyes that reminded her of twilight—when late afternoon melted into early evening and dark azure painted the sky. He'd asked if she was all right, and she'd answered yes, but that had been a blatant lie. The way he'd looked at her…as if she were a slice of cake and he'd harbored a sudden craving for sugar, had halted her breath and set her heart to beating so rapidly she'd feared it would jump from her body.

He'd slowly set her on her feet, but his hands had remained on her waist and hers continued to rest on his shoulders. *"Addie."* He'd said her name so softly, so reverently it sounded like a prayer. Then he'd lowered his head.

Never could she have imagined the heart-stopping sensation of Sebastian's mouth on hers. His hands had tightened on her waist and her fingers had curled around the lapels of his riding jacket, which had been fortunate for she otherwise would have melted into a puddle at his feet. And then it had ended, as slowly as it had begun. And she'd never been the same.

With a sigh, Addie now slid her hand from the icy window and moved away. For Christmas that year she'd painted him a small picture of the tree with a half-eaten apple resting beneath it. And he'd given her a gold charm. It had been so perfect...until her father had told her on Boxing Day that he and Sebastian's father had decided that Sebastian and Grace were a perfect match, and that as soon as Grace was old enough, a couple years after her come-out, they would marry, thus joining by a most advantageous marriage the two families that had been friends for years.

What would have happened if she'd spoken up then? Told Sebastian she cared for him? Would knowing she loved him have made any difference? She'd never know. And it was too late now.

She glided her fingers over the fine gold chain around her neck and pulled the charm attached to its length from beneath her nightgown. A gold charm of a half-eaten apple rested in her palm, still warm from her skin where it rested between her breasts. Sebastian's gift to her that Christmas after their kiss. She'd worn it every day since. Which was ridiculous. Especially as an engagement announcement would surely come tomorrow or Boxing Day—indeed she was surprised, as were most of the guests, that it hadn't come during tonight's ball. Yet even though she knew it was silly to still wear his gift after all these years, she couldn't bring herself to stop. Even though Sebastian loved Grace. And Grace loved Sebastian. If she'd ever harbored any doubts about that, they were put to rest last Christmas when she'd inadvertently come upon Sebastian and Grace kissing in the stables.

The sight had hit her like a hard slap with an icy rag, snuffing out the tiny flame she'd foolishly nursed in the most secret recesses of her heart that maybe, just maybe, Grace would fall in love with someone other than Sebastian. *That he'd fall in love with me.*

A humorless sound escaped her. How ironic that the two most memorable moments of her life both involved kisses from Sebastian. Unfortunately, only one of those kisses had involved Addie.

With a sigh, she tucked the charm back beneath her gown. She glanced at her bed, and knowing sleep would not come, she exited her bedchamber and headed toward the kitchens, as a mug of warm cider often rendered her sleepy. Anything to fall into the forgetfulness of sleep, to stop the images of what she could not have from flashing through her mind.

She made her way down the corridor to the wide, curved staircase. The scent of cinnamon lingered in the air mixed with the fragrant Christmas greenery that abounded in the house, creating the heady bouquet experienced only at this time of year. As she drew near the billiards room, the distinctive clack of balls hitting together reached her ears and a knowing smile tugged at her lips. James was clearly practicing for their traditional Christmas Day match—as well he should. Her younger brother had yet to best her, an outcome he was determined to reverse, for at age fifteen, he now considered it his manly duty to do so.

The door was ajar and she approached on silent feet, reveling in the delicious thought of catching her devilish brother unawares as he so often did her. *Heh, heh, heh.* Wouldn't he be surprised when she came up behind him and tapped him on the shoulder? Hopefully he'd jump a yard in the air and let out a yelp of fright as she had the last time he'd sneaked up on her in such a manner.

Cautiously she peered around the door. Then froze. At the sight of Sebastian leaning over the baize-covered table, his brow furrowed with concentration as he lined up his next shot. He potted the red ball, then slowly rose, and her breath caught. He'd removed his formal jacket and waistcoat and rolled back the sleeves of his snowy-white shirt, revealing strong forearms dusted with dark hair. His shirt was unfastened at the throat and her gaze riveted on the fascinating bit of skin showing in the shallow opening—far too much for propriety's sake, but not nearly enough for her hungry eyes. His hair looked rumpled, as if he'd run his fingers through it, and the slight shadow of whiskers that would be shaved away in the morning shaded his jaw. She'd often seen him casually dressed, but not lately, and certainly not so very casually. Or so deliciously…er…scandalously undone.

Her inner voice commanded her to retreat and, with a great deal of reluctance, she decided to obey. After one last ogle…er…glance she was about to step back when Sebastian's deep voice asked, "Are you planning to skulk in the doorway all night, Addie—or would you rather play a match?"

Botheration! The man had eyes like telescopes. "I wasn't skulking," she said, her voice full of pride, as she moved around the partially open door to stand on the threshold. "I was merely…standing."

"Yes, but before you were merely *standing*, I heard you walking down the corridor."

Apparently he also possessed ears the size of dinner plates. "How did you know it was *me* who was walking?"

He shrugged. "I know the sound, the rhythm of your gait. Plus, you've never known the meaning of the word *stealth*."

She lifted her chin a notch. "There was no reason for me to be stealthy as I wasn't aware anyone was about. Which begs the question—why *are* you about?"

"Couldn't sleep." His gaze flicked over her white cotton-and-lace robe, and although the garment covered her from chin to toes, as did the nightgown beneath it, she suddenly felt very exposed. "You?"

"I wanted some cider."

"Cider?" With his gaze never leaving hers, he set down his cue stick then moved around the table, walking toward her with a slow gait that somehow made her feel as if he were a very large cat and she a very small mouse. He halted when a mere arm's length separated them—a distance that was simultaneously much too close, and not nearly close enough. "There's no cider here, Addie," he said in a deep, husky voice. "Only me."

Yes. Only him. Looking so devastatingly handsome she couldn't tear her gaze from him. And her. Wearing her nightclothes. With her heart pounding so hard she feared he would hear it.

She cleared her throat to locate her suddenly missing

voice. "I was on my way to the kitchens when I heard someone playing. I thought it was James."

"I'm guessing you wish it was." A teasing glint sparkled in his eyes. "Him you can beat."

Addie raised her brows. "You don't think I can beat you?"

"No. I don't."

"You realize you've thrown down a gauntlet."

"That's me—Lord Throw Down a Gauntlet."

"I suppose you like that better than Lord Lovely."

"Absolutely. Now, the question remains—are you going to pick it up?"

"Obviously you've forgotten that I'm the undefeated champion billiards player in this household."

Sebastian made a dismissive gesture. "That isn't saying much as your father detests the game, Grace fears striking the balls too hard and James has no aim whatsoever."

Humph. Very vexing that she couldn't argue with any of that. "I can beat Evan."

"*Grace* can best Evan."

"And I can best you. I've done so in the past."

"True, but not recently. I've learned a few tricks since we last played." A wicked grin curved his lips. "Care to see them?"

Dear God, she wanted to see anything—everything— he cared to show her. So much so that she knew she should leave. Now. Before she said or did something she'd regret. But the temptation to spend these few unexpected moments alone with him was too strong to deny. As was the desire to prove him wrong.

She imitated his dismissive gesture. "It is skill, not tricks, that win matches."

"I am very skillful with the tricks."

"And arrogant in the extreme. Indeed, I think I shall dub you Lord Thinks Very Highly of Himself."

"I'm merely confident."

She shook her head and made a tsking sound. "I fear your confidence will suffer greatly from the taste of crow in your mouth after losing to me."

"There's only one way to find out. Unless..."

"Unless what?"

He took a step closer and planted a hand on the doorjamb next to her head, and Addie utterly forgot how to breathe. He leaned toward her and the scent of freshly laundered linen mixed with something else she couldn't define—something that smelled warm and musky and tempting beyond belief—inundated her senses. "Unless you're afraid," he murmured.

God help her, she was afraid. Not of him, but of herself. Of what she wanted to do. Of what she wanted him to do.

She shot him her haughtiest look. "I'm not afraid. It's merely that—" she glanced down at her attire "—this is hardly proper."

"I won't tell if you won't."

Addie couldn't help but smile at his softly spoken statement—one they'd frequently made to each other while growing up when engaging in some mischief or another, most often at her instigation. He grinned in return and she suddenly felt as if they were once again adolescents, plotting a tree-climbing or frog-hunting expedition they knew their parents wouldn't approve of.

"I'm going to win," they said simultaneously. Then they both laughed softly.

"Only one of us can be correct," said Sebastian.

Addie looked toward the ceiling. "Well, that's obvious—" Her words cut off and she froze. And stared. At the object hanging in the doorway directly above her head. "Wh-what's that?"

Sebastian looked up and she sensed him go still. "It appears to be a kissing ball."

It was indeed. The globe made of mistletoe, rosemary, sage and lavender dangled from a bright red satin ribbon.

"But…but how did it get there?" she asked.

"I imagine one of the servants must have hung it there."

She shook her head. "No. I personally supervised the placement of the kissing balls, and one was not put there."

"Obviously there was an extra and someone hung it here."

"What is that floating about around the ball?" asked Addie, craning her neck. "It looks like—"

"Pink sparkles," they said in unison.

She lowered her head and discovered Sebastian regarding her with an unreadable expression. "'If a young lady standing under a kissing ball isn't kissed, she will not be married that year,'" Sebastian softly quoted the legend of the traditional decoration.

A nervous laugh escaped Addie. "As the year is nearly over, I'm not overly concerned." Indeed, she wasn't concerned with ever marrying, as the man she loved would soon be married to her sister. The man she loved…who stood a mere two feet away, who she wanted to kiss more than she wanted to draw her next breath.

"Legend also says that a young lady found standing beneath the kissing ball cannot refuse a kiss if offered."

Yes, that is what legend said, and because of the kissing ball that had appeared above her head as if by magic, she had the perfect excuse to accept a kiss from the man she loved.

Except to know that she couldn't. For while a quick peck under the mistletoe might appear chaste and proper, in her heart she'd know it wasn't—at least not to her. What for Sebastian would amount to nothing more than a meaningless bit of holiday tradition would to her mean far too much.

And she knew, just *knew* that if he kissed her, no matter how innocently, she wouldn't be able to hide her emotions. Dear God, her feelings for him trembled so close to the surface right now, she stood in true danger of inadvertently revealing them to him. If they kissed, he'd surely see her hopeless, helpless love, and then she'd never be able to face either him or Grace again.

Panic welled in her chest. "I must go," she said, inwardly wincing at the strain so evident in her voice, then turning to leave.

"Addie, wait—"

But she didn't wait. Instead she strode as quickly down the corridor as she could without actually breaking into a run and didn't slow until she reached her bedchamber and closed the door behind her. Breathing heavily, she leaned her back against the oak panel, closed her eyes and swallowed the sob that rose in her throat. Guilt stabbed her and a pair of tears leaked down her cheeks. God help her, she'd barely summoned the strength to walk away from him—from the man her sister loved and would marry. What sort of person did that make her?

Clearly the sort of person who could not be trusted to be alone with Sebastian. Only a few more days...then this hellacious holiday would be over and she'd be on her way to Paris, far away from Sebastian. That should have made her feel better, but she couldn't ignore the brutal truth that it broke her heart.

CHAPTER FOUR

ROSE FLOATED AROUND the ceiling of Addie's bedchamber and twisted her hands, sending a shower of pink sparkles skittering down toward her fitfully sleeping charge. Oh dear, things were not going well. Not going well *at all*. She'd thought for certain if she could get Addie and Sebastian to kiss, True Love would take its course and everything would work out as it should. And she'd come so close! Placing the kissing ball above Addie's head had been a stroke of genius, if she said so herself, but unfortunately Addie had possessed enough fortitude to resist and return to her chamber, where she now tossed and turned.

"I didn't want to have to do this, Addie," Rose muttered, rolling up the sleeves of her robe, "but you leave me no choice." She floated down and plopped herself on the mattress, then firmly tapped Addie on the shoulder.

ADDIE WAS HAVING THE strangest dream. She was outdoors, floating swiftly through the night air next to a tiny creature that looked like a cherubic pink angel wearing spectacles.

"Don't worry, dear. You're perfectly safe," said the diminutive being with a beatific smile.

"Who...what are you?"

"My name is Rose, and I am the Angel—or rather, the *Ghost* of Christmas Present."

Addie's eyes widened. "Like in Mr. Dickens's tale?"

"Precisely."

Fear and confusion suffused Addie. "But what do you want with me? I'm no Scrooge. I've committed no grievous acts of unkindness for which I must repent."

"No—but there is something I wish for you to see. Look."

Addie realized they'd stopped outside the window of a modest house in a village she did not recognize. "Where are we?"

Rose nodded toward the window and repeated, "Look."

Addie peered through the glass. A young dark-haired man and a blond woman stood in a small foyer. The muted hum of conversation, laughter and piano music indicated a party elsewhere in the house.

"It was lovely seeing you, Martin," the young lady said, handing him his top hat and gloves. "I'm glad you were able to come to the party." She looked up at him and Addie's breath caught at the naked longing shining in her eyes. Never had she seen such restrained love and desire.

"Thank you for the invitation, Lily."

"I…I hope you have a safe trip."

"Thank you." He stood, holding his hat and gloves, looking at her through serious dark eyes. Addie could practically see the tension shimmering in the air, feel Lily's palpable anticipation. Hope shined like a beacon on her lovely face. Finally, Martin cleared his throat. "Lily, I wanted to say…"

"Yes, Martin?"

"I wanted to say…Merry Christmas. And…goodbye."

All the hope and anticipation leaked from her expression. "Merry Christmas," she whispered. But he'd already closed the door behind him. Addie watched Lily bury her face in her hands then dash out of the foyer and up the stairs.

Addie turned to Rose and asked, "Who are they?"

"Just two young people."

"She loves him very much."

"You saw that?"

Addie nodded. "It was painfully obvious."

"Perhaps to you. But not to Martin. If he knew she loved him, he wouldn't be sailing to America tomorrow."

"How could he not know it?" Addie asked in an incredulous tone. "'Twas as plain as the sun in the sky."

Rose shrugged. "She's never told him. He loves her, as well, even attempted to court her several years ago, but at that time she was infatuated with someone else and rebuffed Martin. I'm certain you've heard of the proverb, once bitten, twice shy? I'm afraid it applies to poor Martin. He fears risking his heart to her again."

"I suppose that is understandable, but clearly her feelings have changed."

"Clear to you, but not to him." Rose made a tsking sound. "It's really quite sad. Two people who love each other not being together… Such a shame."

"Why doesn't she simply tell him how she feels?" asked Addie, feeling an inexplicable sense of urgency for a couple she didn't even know.

"She can't see that his feelings for her never changed. She's afraid that after hurting him, he'd reject her."

"But if she told him she loved him, surely he wouldn't go to America."

"No, I'm certain he wouldn't."

"Is she going to tell him?"

"I'm afraid not."

Something that felt like panic bloomed in Addie's chest. "Can we tell him?"

Rose shook her head. "He can't see or hear us." Rose heaved a sigh then quoted, "'When love once pleads admission to our hearts, in spite of all the virtue we can boast, the woman that deliberates is lost.'"

Addie blinked. "That's from Addison's *Cato*."

Rose's smile beamed. "Indeed it is. How fortunate that you are so well-read. 'Tis a pity that Lily didn't read those words—and act upon them."

Feeling sick with loss and regret and something else she couldn't name, Addie watched the lone figure of Martin walk slowly away from the house until he disappeared into the shadows. "What happens to them?" she whispered.

"Neither of them ever falls in love with anyone else."

A tear slipped down Addie's cheek. "That is so sad."

"Tragic," agreed Rose. "If only she'd seized the moment. If only she hadn't deliberated. If only she'd let him know how she felt. If only she'd let him know…"

ADDIE AWOKE WITH A GASP. Heart pounding, breathing labored, she sat straight up in bed, her gaze darting about the room. A full minute passed before her breathing calmed. She pressed her hands to her cheeks and felt wetness against her palms. Had she been crying? She'd cried in her dream—

Her dream. She wrapped her arms around her upraised knees and shivered. Never in her life had she experienced such a vivid dream. Clearly, her reading of *A Christmas Carol* had adversely affected her imagination. She'd make certain the next book she read was a comedy. She glanced toward the window and saw the first streaks of mauve indicating dawn staining the sky. Christmas Day had arrived.

She lay back down and stared at the ceiling, still unnerved by the memory of her dream. She tried to push it from mind, but the words quoted by the tiny pink Ghost of Christmas Present kept echoing through her mind: *The woman that deliberates is lost.*

CHAPTER FIVE

THANKS TO THE ABILITY to mask his true feelings—
which he'd been forced to perfect over the years—Sebastian knew he appeared to be enjoying the sumptuous
Christmas Day feast and conversation. He smiled and
chatted as he partook of roasted goose, standing rib of
beef with Yorkshire pudding, potatoes, dressing, freshly
baked breads and tender green beans, but inwardly the
tension and sick sensation that had gripped him since
last night's encounter with Addie in the billiard's room
had grown to nearly unbearable proportions.

All morning long, during the opening of the gifts,
then during the Christmas Day services at St. Peter's
he'd wanted to speak with her—other than the pleasantries they'd exchanged—but really, what could he
say? *I want you so much I can barely think? I love you
so much it actually hurts? If I'd kissed you last night,
I don't think I'd have been able to stop?*

Bloody hell. He'd wanted to kiss her more than he
would have believed it possible to want anything. He
should have ignored her when he realized she was
watching him from behind the door, but as he'd often
done while they were growing up, he'd baited her into
joining him for a game, telling himself that they were
friends, would soon be related through her marriage to
Evan—as soon as his brother got around to proposing

to her—and there was nothing untoward about them engaging in an innocent game of billiards.

But he'd been lying to himself, rationalizing a situation that he knew, in his heart, was far from proper, especially given his desire for her. Yet the sight of her in her nightclothes, regardless of the fact that they were virginally modest in the extreme, had practically brought him to his knees. And rendered him unable to listen to his conscience which screamed warnings at him that being alone with her was wrong. Inappropriate. And far, far too tempting.

And then they'd seen the kissing ball. He would have sworn it wasn't hanging there when he entered the billiards room, but obviously he was mistaken, and he didn't care to question something that he decided in an instant of selfish madness was an omen. He'd wanted nothing more than to kiss her, and suddenly the perfect excuse to do so was hanging right above their heads. Again he'd lied to himself—a nasty habit to be sure— that a kiss under the mistletoe was naught more than a meaningless holiday tradition. Certainly it would be for Addie, and since he'd grown so adept at hiding his feelings, she'd never know that it meant more to him.

His gut twisted as he recalled her expression just before she'd fled—a combination of panic and distress and something else he couldn't decipher. Damn it, in spite of his best efforts to keep his expression blank, had she read something in his eyes, somehow sensed his desire? Logic would indicate yes, yet she'd been perfectly pleasant to him all day, giving no indication in her manner or conversation that she was upset with him or unsettled in any way. He wanted very much to conclude that her distress and abrupt departure merely stemmed from the fact that she was improperly attired, yet, his gut told him it was something more. Something he apparently wasn't destined to know.

What he did know, however, was that he'd nearly given away the show and revealed the feelings he struggled so hard to hide. For while he could lie to himself all he wanted, there was no running away from one brutal truth: if he'd taken advantage of the opportunity to kiss her, he would have been incapable of concealing his desire.

The double doors opened and a liveried footman entered, bearing the Christmas Plum Pudding on a silver platter. Everyone gasped and applauded as the flaming dessert was set before Lord Gresham. After the flame burned out, the earl asked for a blessing on all who had prepared the pudding. Then he sliced and served the creation with great ceremony while anticipation ran high as to who would find in their portion the ring, coin and thimble that were traditionally tossed into the batter.

Not even a minute had passed before James proclaimed, "I have the coin!"

"That means wealth is coming your way," said the earl.

"Excellent," chimed in Addie, "as he owes me three pounds from his losses at the billiard table this morning."

"By God, Addie, you have the devil's own luck," James grumbled. "Never seen anything like it."

"It's not luck, brother dear," Addie informed him with a smug, sisterly grin. "It's called skill."

"The fact that James couldn't hit water if he fell out of

a boat helps your cause considerably, Addie," Sebastian added in a dust-dry tone.

Everyone laughed, even James—after he'd leveled a look on Sebastian that could have curdled milk. Seconds later Evan exclaimed, "I found something... It's the thimble. 'A happy but single life' for me," he quoted.

Sebastian thought he saw something that looked like pain flicker in Evan's eyes, but before he could decide, his brother twisted his face into an exaggerated pout and said in a woebegone tone, "Surely *some* poor woman, *somewhere* will take pity on me and have me."

Sebastian glanced at Addie and his jaw tightened at the bright blush blooming on her cheeks. He knew damn well who that woman would be. Evan wouldn't have to worry about living his life as a single man. Which had Sebastian once again wondering when Evan planned to propose to Addie. Bloody hell, waiting for the announcement to be made was like having a pistol held to his head and waiting for the shot to be fired.

"Any woman would be lucky to have you, Evan," Grace said softly. She looked down at her lap. "Very lucky indeed."

Murmurs of concurrence circled the table, then Sebastian's father asked, "What about the ring? Who has it?"

Eating resumed and half a minute later Sebastian heard Addie say in a tone that sounded both surprised and confused, "I...the ring. I got the ring. That means—"

"Marriage," Evan said. Smiling, he reached out and patted her hand. "What a lucky man he'll be."

Addie's face resembled a setting sun and Sebastian

forced himself to look away. He finished his pudding, eating by rote, anxious for the meal to end. When it finally did, the group retired to the drawing room, where the gaily decorated Christmas tree scented the air with pine, the crystal Nuremberg angel topping the tree reflecting the light from the gas globe lamps.

"What game shall we play?" asked Grace.

"Not billiards," said James, shooting Addie a mock glare.

"Charades?" suggested Evan.

Addie bent down and picked up something from the rug in front of the Christmas tree. "What is this?" she asked, holding aloft a length of black silk.

Grace joined her. "It's the scarf we use for Blindman's Bluff. How did it come to be on the floor?"

"I've no idea," said Addie. She gave the scarf a shake and what looked like pink dust fluttered from the material.

"Seems like a clear message," Evan said with a laugh. "Blindman's Bluff?"

Everyone agreed, and although he truly wanted nothing more than to retire, Sebastian felt churlish doing so. Besides, what harm could come of a simple parlor game?

"Who will wear the blindfold?" asked Grace.

"I vote for Sebastian," said Evan, taking the scarf from Addie.

"Why not you?" asked Sebastian.

Evan pushed up his spectacles, then grinned. "Age before beauty."

Sebastian snatched the scarf from him and grinned in return. "Pearls before swine."

After securing the scarf around his eyes, Sebastian turned in five circles while the others scattered, seeking hiding spots within the room. At the conclusion of his fifth turn, Sebastian called out, "Stop!" Upon his command, everyone had to freeze in place, and it was his objective to locate and identify them.

He stood still for several seconds to orient himself and listen for any telltale sounds that would offer clues. He heard the slight clearing of a throat and inwardly smiled, wondering if Lord Gresham even realized that he possessed such a habit. With his hands out in front of him to maintain his balance, he started forward. He'd taken only a few steps when his shin connected sharply with a piece of furniture.

"Ouch," he muttered. He heard a muffled laugh coming from his right. James. He'd get him right after the earl. He took several more steps and his knee found a table.

"There is far too much furniture in this room," he announced. Two steps later he bumped into a body. Although he knew it was Lord Gresham, Sebastian pursed his lips and proceeded to pat his hands over the earl's jacket. "Hmm. Definitely not Grace or Addie..." He lifted his hands and patted the top of the earl's bald head, then smiled. "Ah. Lord Gresham."

The earl conceded, and the game continued. He next located James and took great pleasure in yanking on the young man's ear lobes and mussing his hair in the name of identifying him. That brought several guffaws, which helped him determine the locations of the other players. In spite of bumping into furniture, walls, nearly causing the demise of a porcelain shepherdess, and being jabbed in the buttocks by a Christmas tree branch, he next found and identified his father—who good-naturedly accepted Sebastian tugging on his facial hair.

With his father out of the game, Sebastian paused and listened. And heard the faint rustling of material just to his left. A lady's gown. He turned in that direction and drew a slow, deep breath. And detected a faint whiff of jasmine. His pulse jumped.

Addie.

He extended his hands at shoulder height and carefully moved forward. On his third step his fingers encountered what he realized was the intricate beaded fringe dangling from the short sleeves of Addie's emerald-green velvet gown. He knew it was her. Hell, he'd known it was her before he'd even touched her. He should identify her, step away and continue on with the game.

But he simply couldn't. Couldn't not take this unexpected opportunity to touch her. He wouldn't do anything untoward or improper and no one would know he already knew damn well it was her. Only he would know. And what was one more layer of guilt at this point? He'd play the game—and play to his audience.

Heart pounding, he moved his hands down several inches, until his fingers curved around the velvety smooth skin of her upper arms. He heard her quick intake of breath. "Unless Evan has removed his jacket and shirt, I've been fortunate enough to locate one of the ladies," Sebastian said.

"You have a fifty percent chance of being correct on your first guess," James called out from the direction of the sofa where those who had been found remained until the game was finished.

"And a one hundred percent chance of being correct on his second guess," Lord Gresham said.

While the bystanders joked and egged him on, as was the duty of those out of the game, Sebastian glided his palms up and down Addie's upper arms. Bloody hell, he'd never felt anything so soft. He slowly skimmed his hands upward, brushing his fingertips over her collarbone and the delicate hollow of her throat. Up her neck, then he gently traced her features, memorizing the curve of her satiny smooth cheekbones. He cupped her face in his hands and slowly brushed the pad of his thumb over her plush mouth. Her full, soft lips parted slightly and her breath warmed his fingers.

"Best beware, Sebastian—she looks like she's going to bite you," James said with a laugh.

With great reluctance, Sebastian shifted his hands from her face and smoothed his fingers over the artfully arranged silky curls brushing her shoulders. How many times had he imagined plucking out all the pins and other feminine contraptions that confined her hair and watching it unfurl down her back? And then plunging his fingers into that glossy mass of curls? Too many times to count.

"I believe I've aged a decade over here," Evan said.

"Yes, Sebastian, get on with it," said his father. "What's your guess?"

Sebastian slowly lowered his hands, imprinting the feel of her in his brain. "Addie."

The group on the sofa applauded, and the game continued. Several minutes later he found Grace who, as the last person discovered, was declared the winner.

At the end of the game the party broke up. As much as Sebastian wanted to speak to Evan to find out when he planned to propose to Addie, he had to put off doing so until tomorrow. Right now he felt too...raw. Too unsettled. He couldn't talk to Evan when Addie's scent still filled his head, when the feel of her soft skin, the texture of her hair and the plump softness of her mouth lingered on his hands and fingertips. Tomorrow. He'd talk to Evan tomorrow. Then afterward, after the Boxing Day festivities were finished, he'd tell his father he couldn't marry Grace—a blow that would hopefully be softened by news of Evan's plans regarding Addie. And the day after tomorrow he would return to Hartley House. And try to forget her.

The instant he entered his bedchamber, Sebastian leaned against the door, tipped his head back and closed his eyes. He covered his face with his hands—and breathed in the scent of jasmine on his fingers. This was torture. Had he actually thought that game would provide nothing more than an evening's harmless entertainment? What a fool. Instead it would result in but yet another sleepless night, wanting the one woman he could never have.

CHAPTER SIX

THE DAY AFTER CHRISTMAS, in keeping with the Boxing Day tradition, Addie and Grace spent the morning helping the servants box up the leftover food from the Christmas Eve ball and Christmas Day feast to be donated to the less fortunate people of Buntingford and the nearby parishes of Little Hormead, Throcking and Wakeley.

Addie normally enjoyed the task, but after another night spent tossing and turning, reliving the exquisite torture of Sebastian's strong hands gently touching her during Blindman's Bluff, she possessed little energy. Dear God, she'd barely been able to breathe as his fingers had glided over her skin. Touched her hair. Brushed over her lips. Thank goodness for the protective layers of her gown and petticoats that hid her shaking knees, and for her restrictive corset which would have provided a handy excuse had she succumbed to swooning—a true threat when with each passing second she'd failed to breathe as he continued to touch her.

Also detracting from the usual gaiety was the fact that Grace was clearly troubled. Her normally clear blue eyes looked as tired as Addie's felt, her complexion was wan and drawn and she lacked her usual sparkle. Although Grace insisted she was fine in reply to Addie's inquiry, Addie knew her sister was lying. And she knew exactly what had her normally sunny sister in the doldrums—the fact that Sebastian had failed to propose.

By God, she felt like boxing his ears. What on earth was the man waiting for? Clearly he was planning some grand surprise, which, given that the house party concluded tomorrow, must be planned for today. For which she could only give thanks as it would end the awful suspense and sick sense of dread that had all but suffocated her for so long. And relieve poor Grace, who looked as wilted as a flower that hadn't been watered in weeks.

Still, surely Grace had to know that while the delay was nerve-racking, Sebastian would certainly propose today, while everyone was together to celebrate the news. Therefore something else must be troubling her. Had they perhaps argued? Annoyance sizzled through Addie toward Sebastian for distressing Grace—an emotion she wholeheartedly embraced instead of the usual unwanted, hopeless love that haunted her—and she was determined to find out what was wrong, and how she could help fix the problem.

With the last box sealed and the footmen set on the task of loading the carriage for the goods to be delivered, Addie and Grace exited the kitchen.

"The snow has stopped and the sun is shining," Addie said. "Why don't we sneak off to the pond to skate—just the two of us?"

A slight smile touched Grace's lips. "Like when I was a child."

"Hmm…yes, but also like last winter, if I recall correctly," Addie said with a laugh.

Grace chuckled and relief filled Addie at the show of good humor. "Remember how Mother brought us skating at the pond every year?"

A lump caught in Addie's throat as it did every time she thought of their beautiful mother. "She was so graceful on her blades."

"Yes. But you're the one who really taught me to skate. One of my earliest memories is of you holding me up while I wobbled horribly." Grace rested her hand on Addie's arm, and they stopped in the corridor. "You held on to me and never let go," Grace said, her eyes serious and grave. "Not even when my feet would slide out from under me and I dragged you to the ice when I fell."

"Half those falls were my fault, Poppet."

Grace shook her head. "Not unless I tripped you." She reached out and grasped Addie's hands. "You've always taken care of me, Addie."

"You make it sound as if being your sister is a chore. I assure you, it's my greatest pleasure."

"But you've been more than a sister to me. You've always been my champion. My best friend. And like a mother to me after she died. You've given up so much—"

"Is that what's bothering you?" Addie broke in. Relief filled her, as this was a problem she could fix. "Grace..." she gently squeezed her sister's hands "...we all feel melancholy at this time of year over the loss of Mother, but you mustn't be sad, especially on my behalf. I gave up nothing."

"But you did." Tears glistened on Grace's lashes. "Mother died just days after your come-out. You lost that season for mourning, and while I didn't realize it at the time, I now know that you passed up all the subsequent seasons because you were so busy being a mother to me. And to James."

"I gave up nothing important, Grace. *You* were important. You and James. Always. Still." Which was completely true. Yet guilt slapped her because, while love for her siblings and determination that all their mother's hopes and dreams for them came true, Addie couldn't deny that she'd had no desire to attend all those soirees anyway. They were all merely designed to find a marriage partner, and there was only one man she wanted to marry. And that man was destined for Grace.

Twin tears tracked down Grace's cheeks, and Addie marveled that her sister could look stunning even when she cried. "It's not just that," Grace continued. "I recently shared some very enlightening conversations with Aunt Margaret. I never realized how much you shielded me from Father's disappointment that I was born a girl. Or how much you bore the brunt of that disappointment alone until James came along."

"It's only natural Father wanted an heir to inherit the title," Addie said, making light of the pain that had driven her as a young girl to behave as boyishly as possible, to climb trees and catch frogs and ride and run like the wind in the hopes of lessening her father's displeasure in her gender. Although Father had never *said* anything to her, Addie could see, could feel his disappointment, and she'd been determined that Grace would never feel that same sting. It wasn't until James was born, when Addie was ten and Grace five, that Addie recalled ever seeing their father truly happy, a happiness that had faded significantly when his wife died eight years later.

She pulled Grace into a hug. "You were never a disappointment, Poppet. Indeed, you were such an extraordinarily beautiful child, everyone who saw you—including Father—fell in love with you." She drew back and smiled. "They still do."

But Grace didn't smile in return. "But you'd still love me even if I were ugly. How many people would do the same?"

"Everyone. Because you're also beautiful inside. In your heart. Where it truly counts."

Instead of looking comforted, a fresh wash of tears glistened in Grace's eyes. "I...I'm not as good as you think I am, Addie. I wish I were more like you."

More guilt walloped Addie. Grace wouldn't think her older sister so admirable if she knew Addie's desire for Sebastian. So, as she had countless times before, Addie shoved aside her unrequited feelings and focused on her profound love for her sister. "You're wonderful, Grace. In every way."

Another tear dribbled down Grace's cheek. "So are you, Addie. You've always made me feel so loved, so special. So treasured. You are the most unselfish sister anyone could ever ask for. I would do anything for you."

"And I for you."

"And that's why I love you so." She leaned forward and kissed Addie's cheek. "I hope you know I only want your happiness."

Addie forced a smile through her guilt. "Of course,

Poppet. As I want yours." She gave a quick laugh. "Heavens, we've become maudlin. Let's go skating."

Grace nodded and they continued down the corridor. When they reached the stairs, Addie set one foot on the bottom tread, then issued the challenge that had echoed throughout their childhood. "Race you to the pond!"

They both dashed up the stairs, their seriousness replaced with the laughter that always flowed so easily between them. As soon as they hit the upper landing, they headed in opposite directions to their respective bedchambers. Addie rang for her maid to help her change into her skating costume, then ran to the massive wardrobe near the window. She yanked open the door and dropped to her knees to drag her skates from the corner.

It seemed as if an eternity passed before she was finally ready to leave, her departure delayed by the need to replace one of her skate's laces, which was badly frayed. With her skates slung across one shoulder, she practically skidded into the foyer.

"Has Grace left the house yet, Wilson?"

"About five minutes ago, Lady Adelaide," intoned the stately butler. He opened the door for her and a blast of cold air swirled inside. "Lord Channing and his brother left several minutes ago, as well. On their way to the stables, they said."

Addie nodded then ran outside. Her skates thumped against her back as she trudged along as quickly as the ankle-deep snow allowed. She noted the three sets of footprints marring the pristine layer of white—the small one obviously Grace's, heading toward the pond, then two larger sets leading toward the stables. Her mind instantly conjured an image of Sebastian standing before her, a blindfold covering his eyes, his fingertips tracing her face. With a growl of self-directed annoyance, she ruthlessly pushed aside the mental image and increased her pace. Sunshine poured down from a cloudless blue sky, warming her skin and forcing her to squint against the near-blinding whiteness reflecting off the glistening snow.

Several minutes later she spied Grace through the copse of trees, stepping onto the edge of the ice. How had she managed to don her skates so quickly? Addie quickened her pace, puffs of vaporous breath from her exertions fogging the air in front of her. By the time Addie reached the stone bench where she sat to put on her skates, Grace had reached the center of the huge pond. She turned in a graceful arc, then seeing Addie, she stopped and waved.

"I win!" Grace called.

Addie slipped her gloved hands from her ermine muff and waved. She opened her mouth to yell back a reply, but before she could make a sound, a blizzard of what looked like pink sparkles swirled around Grace, obscuring her view. "What on earth?" Addie muttered, cupping her hands around her eyes, trying to see through the flurry of pink. A few seconds later the sparkles cleared and she saw Grace.

Grace stood in the middle of the pond, wide-eyed, surrounded by a rapidly expanding web of cracks. The terrifying sound of ice breaking reached Addie's ears, but before she could scream out a warning, Grace cried out and fell through the ice.

CHAPTER SEVEN

SEBASTIAN AND EVAN had nearly reached the stables—where once they were astride and riding through the woods, Sebastian planned to finally get the answers he sought regarding his brother's wedding plans to Addie—when a high-pitched cry rent the air. They froze.

"That sounded like Grace—" Evan began, turning toward the trees behind them, where the sound had come from.

"Grace!" That single shouted word from Addie, filled with terror, turned Sebastian's blood to ice. "Help!"

Sebastian broke into a run. The pond. The cries had come from the direction of the pond, and he greatly feared the worst. Addie continued to shout for help. With his heart pounding hard enough to bruise his ribs, he sprinted as fast as he could toward the sound. He broke through the thick trees, with Evan close behind him. His heart stalled at the sight of Grace, struggling to hold her upper body out of the water by clinging to the ice where she'd fallen through near the center of the pond, and at Addie, crawling on her stomach on the ice, dragging a rope with her, to rescue her sister.

"Addie, stop!" Sebastian ordered, his voice tight with dread and fear. "You'll fall in, too."

She shook her head and continued to inch forward.

"The rescue rope isn't long enough. This is the only way."

Sebastian stepped onto the ice. "Then let me do it. You come back. Now."

"No!" yelled Addie. "Your weight will crack the ice."

In spite of the warning, Sebastian started forward, determined to get her to safety, but before he'd taken half a dozen steps, the surface beneath his boots began to crack. He quickly dropped to his stomach to more evenly distribute his weight. "Run to the stables and get more rope," he ordered his brother. "Hurry!"

Evan took off as if he were shot from a cannon and for the next few agonizing minutes Sebastian inched closer to Addie, but it quickly became clear from the groaning sounds emitting from the ice around him that he'd never be able to get as close as he needed to be without further risking her safety. It damn near killed him to retreat, but he did so knowing he'd be better able to pull them to safety if he was standing, yet also knowing that if Grace went under or Addie broke through the ice, he'd bloody well swim through ice or fire to get to them. He wasn't certain how long he stood there—waiting, praying, dying inside—but they were the longest, most agonizing moments of his life, watching Addie creep forward and a shaking Grace struggle to cling to the edge of the ice to keep her head and shoulders above the water.

"Hold on, Grace," came Addie's voice, calm and controlled. "I'm almost there. Just keep looking at me and holding on."

"I...can't," came Grace's terrified reply. "I can't hold on—"

"Yes, you can! Look at me. Look in my eyes. I'm almost there."

What appeared to be a circle of pink dust surrounded Grace. Sebastian squinted. What the devil was that? Obviously a trick of the sun reflecting off the ice, yet it almost seemed as if it were some sort of life ring holding her up. Seconds later he watched Addie slip the looped end of the rescue rope over Grace's head and shoulders. She helped Grace lift one arm then the other through the loop and wrap her fingers around the rope. "All done," came Addie's voice. She held on to Grace's forearms. "Now we're going to pull you out. All you have to do is stay still and hold on to the rope. Don't let go."

"Move back, Addie," Sebastian called. "Evan will be here any second now with more rope and you'll need to tie the ends together."

"All right," she called. Then he heard her say to Grace, "I'm going to back away so we can pull you out. I have the other end of the rope and I won't let go."

"P...promise?" asked Grace.

"I swear on my life, Poppet."

Sebastian held his breath as Addie slowly inched her way backward, talking to Grace the entire time in that same calm, soothing tone. The ice groaned, but didn't break through. When he finally heard Evan approaching, he ran to meet him, grabbed the rope from his winded brother and rushed to the edge of the pond.

Calling on every bit of expertise he'd honed in the Navy, he quickly coiled the rope, then holding one end, he took careful aim and threw the coil. The rope unfurled in the air, the end landing directly next to Addie, who quickly tied it to the end of the rope Grace clung to. The instant Addie yelled, "It's secure," he and Evan heaved on the rope and pulled Grace from the water. Addie, still on her stomach, pushed herself to the side to lessen the weight on the ice as Grace was pulled to solid ground. The instant she reached them, Sebastian pulled the rope off her shaking, dripping form. "Get her to the house," he said tersely to Evan as he re-coiled the rope. "I'll get Addie."

Without hesitation Evan scooped Grace, whose complexion resembled wax, except for her lips which were blue, into his arms and ran toward the house. Sebastian tossed the rope to Addie, and again his aim was true. With Addie clinging to the rope, he pulled her to safety. Then snatched her into his arms, holding her tight against his pounding heart.

"Grace?" she whispered, the word muffled against his heavy wool coat.

"She's fine. And you…?" His throat slammed shut and several seconds passed before he could speak again. "My God, Addie." His voice sounded as if he'd swallowed glass. He leaned back far enough to frame her face between his hands, which shook inside his gloves. His gaze scanned her features and his stomach sank at the sight of her ghostly pale complexion. Her dilated pupils swallowed her brown irises, making her eyes look like twin black pools. "Tell me you're all right," he demanded in that same harsh tone. "Bloody hell, tell me you're not hurt."

"Not hurt," she whispered. "Just frightened." Her

teeth began to chatter. "And cold. But not nearly as cold as Grace."

Not hurt. The two best words he'd ever heard. "We'll have you warm in no time. Hang on." He lifted her into his arms then swiftly headed toward the house, holding her as close to the warmth of his body as he could. She snuggled her icy face against his neck and the area surrounding his heart went hollow.

"Are *you* all right?" she asked against his skin.

"I'm fine," he lied. But it was a falsehood of gargantuan proportions as he was the exact opposite of all right. Never in his entire life had he been so frightened. Felt so helpless. "Except for the decade that was just shaved off my life."

"I think two were shaved off mine," she said in a trembling voice. "I saw her fall. One second she was smiling and waving to me, and the next there was this odd pink dust swirling around her and then in a blink she went down. When I saw the water close over her head…" A shudder shook her entire body and he clasped her tighter and increased his pace. "For several seconds I couldn't move, couldn't breathe. Then her head broke the surface and there was more of that odd pink dust all around her."

"I saw that same dust. It must have been a reflection of the sun against the ice."

"I suppose. Grace somehow managed to pull her upper body out of the water. It was almost…magical how she was able to do it, and so quickly. As if an invisible hand were helping her. I grabbed the rescue rope and immediately realized it wasn't long enough, so I yelled for help and went after her." She lifted her head and looked into his eyes. "And then you came."

"I—we—heard you."

"I knew you would. Knew you and Evan were headed toward the stables." Her bottom lip trembled and his heart seemed to tear in two. "You saved us. I never could have pulled her free by myself, especially not while lying on my stomach."

"You were the brave one. The one who got the rope to Grace. All I did was pull." He squeezed her tighter. "You're the bravest girl I've ever known."

She huffed out a breath. "I was utterly terrified."

"Bravery has nothing to do with lacking fear—it has to do with acting in spite of your fear. And you, my darling girl, did that most admirably."

To his alarm, two fat tears dribbled from her eyes. "I don't feel admirable. Or brave. I'm shaking inside and, oh...oh dear, I'm going to cry." Her face crumpled and she buried her face against his neck and sobbed as if she'd just lost everything that mattered to her.

He had no idea how to comfort her, so he just kept walking as fast as he could and spoke what he prayed were soothing words. After a minute, her sobs subsided, and unable to keep from doing so, Sebastian pressed his lips to her temple. And nearly smiled. "How is it possible that even after all you've been through, you still smell like jasmine?"

The fact that the noise that escaped her almost sounded like a laugh loosened a bit of the tension gripping him. She again raised her head and looked at him. The sight of those beautiful toffee-colored eyes dampened by tears nearly undid him. "I think you're just being gallant. Indeed I'm not certain whether to dub you Lord Gallant or Lord Big Fat Liar."

"In this case only Lord Truthful will do. You smell... lovely. Perfect. Just the way the bravest girl in the world should smell."

Several seconds of silence passed, then they said in unison, "I'm glad you didn't fall in the water." She smiled—a gentle tremulous smile that brought with it a wave of love that damn near drowned him. He had to physically bite his tongue to keep from telling her. Had to corral every bit of his willpower to refrain from setting her on her feet and dragging her into his arms and showing her how much she meant to him. From showing her that she meant *everything*.

Instead he dragged his gaze back to the path in front of him and teased, "You may smell like flowers, but your nose resembles a tomato."

She pulled one of her gloved hands from around his neck and covered her nose. "I'm certain my skin is all blotchy, and my eyes red-rimmed, as well. I'm a fright when I cry."

"You're stunning," he said, meaning it from the bottom of his heart. The most beautiful woman he'd ever seen—tomato nose, red-rimmed eyes, blotchy skin and all.

"Clearly, you smacked your head on the ice. But thank you anyway."

"You're welcome."

"You *could* have offered me your handkerchief, you know." The mock glare she sent him let him know more than anything else could have that she was settling herself.

"I suppose I could have," he agreed, nodding solemnly, "except my hands have been rather occupied carrying you. Of course, if you'd prefer I dump you in the snow…" He raised his brows and waited for her answer.

"Not today, thank you," she said primly, tightening her hold around his neck.

He heaved a put-upon sigh. "Very well. Tomorrow."

"I'm leaving tomorrow."

And with those three words the bit of levity that had sprung up between them instantly evaporated. Yes, she was leaving tomorrow. As was he. Both of them off to different places, to separate lives. The next time he saw her would probably be at her wedding. To his brother.

Silence descended and Sebastian quickened his pace to a near run. They arrived at the house less than a minute later where they were greeted by a group of worried servants, James and Sebastian's father, who also looked very concerned, and Lord Gresham, who practically wilted in relief at the sight of his daughter.

"She's unhurt," Sebastian said. A collective sigh of relief filled the air.

"I'm fine," Addie confirmed. "Just cold."

"A hot bath's being drawn," the earl said, leading the way up the stairs while Sebastian followed with Addie in his arms. "And Dr. Everly has been summoned."

"How is Grace?" Addie asked.

"Very cold, as you can imagine," said the earl, "but thank God she was able to pull herself partially out of the water. She's in a hot bath now."

When they reached the water closet, he gently set Addie on her feet. Steam rose from the taps where hot water spilled into the large wood-encased porcelain tub. Addie's maid, Henrietta, immediately clucked over her like a mother hen. "I'll take good care of her, my lords," the rotund woman pronounced. "We'll have her warmed up in no time, then the doctor can check her."

Sebastian and the earl exited into the corridor, and the door was closed behind them with a click. He pulled in a shaky breath and dragged his hands down his face.

"You look as if you could use a brandy," the earl said.

A humorless sound escaped Sebastian. "I feel as if I could use several."

The earl clasped Sebastian's shoulder. "You and Evan saved my girls. I don't know how to thank you."

"It's actually Addie you have to thank for saving Grace. She got the rope out to her. The ice wouldn't have held mine or Evan's weight."

A look of pain crossed the earl's face. "I can only give thanks you were both about. I cannot believe a rescue rope that was too short to reach the middle of the pond was in place. I can assure you it's an error that won't be repeated."

"Good. Although, this incident has put me off skating for the foreseeable future."

"Me, as well," agreed the earl. "Now, how about that brandy? We'll ask your father to join us. He could use one, too."

Sebastian knew he should take this opportunity to talk to both his father and Lord Gresham, to tell them an engagement between Grace and himself would not be forthcoming, but that conversation—as well as the one he still needed to have with Evan—would have to wait until after he'd had an opportunity to pull himself together. He felt like he'd been hit with an ax.

"Thank you, but perhaps later? I'm afraid I'm a bit... unsettled."

"Of course. Completely understandable. Why don't you take a rest in your bedchamber? You're looking rather pale."

Relieved, Sebastian agreed and he headed for his bedchamber. The instant he entered the room, he jerked off his coat then headed directly for the decanters and poured himself a generous brandy. The potent liquor burned a fiery path down his throat, but it did little to melt the ice that seemed to surround him like a frozen blanket, or relieve the pounding that had commenced in his head.

He finished the drink, poured another, then sat heavily on the edge of the bed. Setting his elbows on this thighs, he leaned forward and stared into the snifter of brandy dangling from his fingers. And allowed himself to feel all the emotions, the sick sense of panic and dread he'd ruthlessly tamped down since the moment he'd come upon the scene at the pond.

His eyes squeezed shut and an image of Addie on her stomach, surrounded by cracked ice, inching her way to Grace, rose in his mind. Bloody hell, he'd never be able to erase that horrifying image. It was branded into his brain.

How, *how* could he have stood it if Addie had fallen through the ice? Had died? The mere thought eviscerated him. Left his heart bleeding. What had his expression, his eyes given away when he'd looked at her? Had she seen all the feelings that he wasn't certain he'd been able to hide? He didn't know. Indeed, the only thing he did know was that he couldn't bear this any longer. Couldn't bear being near her yet not having her. Couldn't bear the thought of her belonging to someone else. Couldn't bear the reality that she loved his brother. Something had to be done.

But what?

CHAPTER EIGHT

SEBASTIAN OPENED HIS eyes and blinked several times, trying to get his bearings. And realized he was lying down. On top of the royal blue velvet counterpane in his bedchamber.

With a groan, he sat up. He must have fallen asleep, not a complete surprise he supposed, given he'd barely slept the past two nights. He glanced at the ormolu clock on the mantel, then blinked and looked again. Surely it couldn't be nearly midnight. He gaze flew to the window. When he'd entered the room, bright sunshine had flooded through the windows where the silvery glow of the moon now seeped.

He raked a hand through his hair and noted the dinner tray on the bedside table—right next to his empty brandy snifter. He was normally a light sleeper, but clearly the combination of alcohol, exhaustion and the fright he'd experienced had all but rendered him unconscious.

He stood and noticed a note on the dinner tray. He snatched up the missive, broke the seal he recognized as his father's and scanned the few lines.

Didn't want you disturbed as you were obviously exhausted. Both Addie and Grace are well and, except for being as tired as you, are none the worse for the accident.

Sebastian briefly closed his eyes at the news. Thank God. He then resumed reading:

Looking forward to you feeling well rested in the morning as there is much to discuss, namely a certain announcement...

A frown pulled down his brows. Was his father referring to the announcement he expected Sebastian to make regarding a betrothal to Grace? Or had Evan finally proposed to Addie and that was the "certain announcement" to which he referred? Surely it was the latter as Addie was leaving tomorrow.

Sebastian's jaw tightened. If Evan hadn't proposed this evening, then damn it, he needed to do so in the morning. And Sebastian had to be prepared to depart immediately afterward. Because he wasn't certain he could hide his feelings. Didn't trust himself to keep in place the mask of indifference he'd worn for so long. At least not now, when he felt so battered, so raw.

He shoved his hands through his hair. Were they engaged? Damn it, he had to know. Now. Had to talk to Evan. Now. Have the conversation with him that he'd planned to have this afternoon, before everything had gone awry. His better judgment told him to wait until morning, but his feet moved toward the door. He was halfway across the room when a knock sounded. Frowning, he crossed the Turkish rug and pulled open the door.

Evan stood in the corridor, looking more troubled than Sebastian had ever seen him. "We need to talk," Evan said in a tight voice. "May I come in?"

"Of course." Sebastian stood back to allow his brother

to enter, then closed the door. "Oddly enough, I was just on my way to see you."

Sebastian expected Evan to ask him regarding what, but instead it appeared as if his brother hadn't heard him. He moved to the fireplace and paced in front of the hearth several times, then turned to face Sebastian. His face was drawn and pale, and his eyes behind his spectacles utterly somber.

"There's something I must tell you, Sebastian." He tunneled his hands through his hair, wreaking havoc with the already disarrayed strands. "It concerns Grace."

Concern filled Sebastian. "Is she unwell?"

"No, no, she's fine. It's just that... Damn it all, there's no way to say this other than to simply say it." He pulled in a deep breath then squared his shoulders. "I love her."

Sebastian huffed out a laugh. "Well, of course you do. Everyone loves Grace."

Evan shook his head so vigorously his spectacles slid down his nose. "No, I mean, I am *in love* with her."

The pronouncement seemed to vibrate in the air between them. It took Sebastian several seconds to locate his voice. And even then, certain he'd misheard, all he could manage was, "I beg your pardon?"

"I'm in love. With Grace." Evan drew another bracing breath then said in a rush, "I've hidden my feelings for her for years, but after today's accident something inside me just snapped and I...I kissed her. I couldn't stop myself. And I kissed her." His torrent of words ended and a look of utter misery filled his eyes. "I'm sorry, Sebastian. I didn't mean to do it, and I've felt horribly guilty, but I couldn't not confess. I can only hope, pray, that you do not hate me."

Sebastian slowly walked toward Evan, his mind in a whirl. When a mere arm's length separated them, Sebastian reached out and clasped Evan's shoulders. "Allow me to make certain I understand this. You are in love with Grace."

"Yes."

"You are not in love with Addie."

Bright red suffused Evan's pale cheeks. "I love her—but only as I would a sister."

A crack formed in the wall Sebastian had built around his heart, allowing a ray of hope to shine where only darkness had previously dwelled. "You have no desire to marry Addie."

"None."

"This kiss you gave Grace—what was her reaction?"

Evan's face flamed even brighter. "She, um, well... kissed me back."

Sebastian blinked. "Well, I'll be damned."

"I'm truly sorry, Sebastian. We both are—"

"She loves you as well?"

Evan nodded, his expression a combination of elation and misery Sebastian would have thought impossible to achieve.

"Well, I'll be damned," he repeated. Relief and joy hit him so hard he felt a sudden need to sit down. Evan didn't love Addie! He loved Grace—and Grace loved Evan! By God, it was nothing short of a Christmas miracle. Except—

Addie was in love with Evan.

Reality returned with a thump, taking the wind out of his sails. Bloody hell, this development was going to devastate her.

"You know that Father—everyone—expected you to propose to Addie this holiday."

Evan nodded. "Yes. Just as they expected you to propose to Grace. Waiting for you to do so has felt like walking on hot coals. I want you to know that, if not for Grace's accident, I never would have kissed her or confessed my feelings to her. Everyone knows, as I've always known, that she's yours."

"Apparently not," Sebastian murmured.

Some of the color drained from Evan's face. "I have no excuse for my actions except that I was just so… undone. So sick at the realization that she could have died. Seeing her in that pond…" He briefly closed his eyes and swallowed hard. "I believe I went a bit insane."

Yes, that perfectly described Sebastian's state of mind when he'd seen Addie out on that cracked ice.

"I have another confession, Sebastian. As much as I wish I could swear to you that if you and Grace had already announced your betrothal I wouldn't have kissed her, I…I'm not sure, given the circumstances of her accident, that I would have been able to refrain from doing so. I can however swear it was only the accident that precipitated my unguarded behavior. But regardless of the reason, the outcome remains the same." Anguish filled his gaze. "I'm sorry. I'm a horrible brother. I—"

"Does Grace know you're here?"

"No. I told her I would speak to you in the morning, but I couldn't wait."

"I'm glad you didn't. Evan—you're not a horrible brother. And there is nothing to forgive."

Evan frowned. "That is far too generous of you."

"It is nothing of the sort. I have a confession of my own to make. I'm not in love with Grace."

Evan stared at him as if he'd spoken a foreign language. He cleared his throat, then said, "Huh?"

Sebastian nearly laughed at his dumbfounded expression. "I'm not in love with Grace. Never have been. I intended to tell Father in the morning that I have no intention of marrying her. I'd put off breaking the news to him, hoping you'd propose to Addie and fulfill his dream of joining the two families." A half-smile pulled at his lips. "Seems that they'll be joined after all."

"You…you're not angry?"

"Not a bit. Greatly relieved, actually. I didn't have any wish to crush Father's dreams, but I was prepared to do so, rather than marry a woman I don't love."

"I can't believe you don't love her," Evan murmured in a bemused tone. "How can that be? She's the sweetest, most ravishing woman on the planet."

This time Sebastian couldn't hold back a laugh. "Spoken like a man truly in love. I feel about Grace the way you feel about Addie—I love her, but only as I would a sister."

Hope flared in Evan's eyes, replacing the anguish of moments ago. "Then you're not heartbroken?"

"Not in the least."

"And you're not going to toss me into the Thames?"

Sebastian pretended to consider, then said, "I might perhaps do that someday as you can be a colossal pain in the arse, but today is not that day."

Relief bloomed on Evan's face. "Do we have your blessing?"

"Absolutely."

Sebastian pulled him into a hug that turned into a back-thumping bone crusher that left them both laughing. When they broke apart, Evan said, "How will I wait until morning to tell Grace?"

"By knowing she needs her rest after today's ordeal."

"Yes, yes, of course. The doctor prescribed a tisane to help her sleep. Besides, I'll need to be rested to face tomorrow, too. There's Father and Lord Gresham to talk to, and Addie, as well." Some of the happiness leeched from his expression. "Neither Grace nor I want to hurt her."

As Sebastian couldn't offer any reassurances that Addie wouldn't be heartbroken, he simply said, "I wish you luck."

"Thank you, Sebastian. For everything. And most of all, for not loving Grace."

Sebastian huffed out a laugh. "My pleasure."

They bid each other good-night, then Evan quit the room. As soon as the door closed behind him, Sebastian scrubbed his hands down his face. A cyclone of thoughts and emotions battered him from all sides, vying for his attention, but he could only focus on one thing.

Addie.

He blew out a long slow breath, and tried to fight the elation careening through him. Tried to remember that just because the problem of Evan's feelings were solved, didn't mean the problem of Addie's were. There was no reason to go to her, yet the need to see her, to assure himself she was all right, overwhelmed him. Seeking her out now was madness. His common sense reminded him of his father's note that stated she was fine. He knew it—yet he couldn't stop himself.

He exited his bedchamber and headed toward Addie's.

CHAPTER NINE

ADDIE PACED IN HER BEDCHAMBER, her night rail and robe flowing out behind her. Dear God, she simply couldn't stand the strain any longer. Why on earth hadn't Sebastian declared himself to Grace today—especially after such a frightening episode? Good heavens, you'd think the man would want to immediately propose to the love of his life after almost losing her. The waiting for their betrothal to be official was torture, and if it was so for Addie, surely it had to be as well for Grace. Unfortunately, Addie hadn't had the opportunity to have the conversation she'd intended to have with Grace to find out what the delay was regarding Sebastian proposing.

Well, Addie was leaving tomorrow, and if the betrothal hadn't been announced by the time her train departed, then so be it. She couldn't stay here another day, wanting Sebastian so badly yet not having him. She'd been terrified he'd be able to see her feelings while he'd carried her back to the house. Would sense how much she'd wanted to press her lips to the warmth of his neck. Then kiss her way up to his mouth. It had taken every bit of her strength not to lean forward and kiss him. Or even worse, beg *him* to kiss *her*.

Which was why she couldn't wait to get away from here.

She paced across the hearth rug once again, and was about to repeat the action when a knock sounded on her bedchamber door. She glanced at the clock and concern filled her. Nearly midnight. No one knocked at this hour because they were the bearer of good news.

She hurried across the room and pulled open the door. "Grace! What are you doing here?" Her concern doubled when she saw how pale and drawn her sister looked. "Why aren't you in bed?"

"I couldn't sleep." She brushed past Addie and walked to the fireplace, then turned. Her beautiful blue eyes resembled huge pools of distress. "I must speak with you on a matter of the utmost importance and urgency."

"Of course." Addie joined her and gently took her hands. "Whatever is wrong, Poppet? Are you feeling unwell?"

"No, I'm fine. That is to say, I'm most decidedly not fine, but not due to anything regarding today's incident—although, my anguish is directly the result of today's incident."

"I'm afraid I don't understand."

"Addie...I have a confession to make." Tears swam into Grace's eyes. "And I'm so afraid you're going to hate me."

Addie would have laughed at such a ridiculous notion, except it was obvious Grace truly believed such an outcome was possible. She raised their joined hands and kissed the backs of Grace's slim fingers. "I could never hate you, Poppet."

"I hope you'll recall you said that." Grace drew a deep breath, then said in a barrage of words that shot from her like cannon fire, "Evan kissed me and I'm so sorry I never meant to hurt you and I just feel so horribly, horribly *bad!*"

Addie wasn't certain what she'd been expecting, but it certainly hadn't been this—although, she wasn't exactly sure precisely what she'd just been told. "Evan kissed you and you're..." Addie searched Grace's distraught features. "Upset?"

"No, I'm happy," she said, then promptly burst into tears.

"I must say, you don't *look* particularly happy. But why would a kiss from Evan have you in such a state? He's kissed you many times over the years."

Her cheeks turned scarlet. "Not in the way he kissed me tonight."

Understanding dawned and Addie nodded slowly. "I see."

"Oh, Addie, I'm so sorry. I know you love him, and I've tried so hard to keep my feelings for him hidden, but when he kissed me, I...I lost my senses and kissed him back. It was all due to the accident, you see. My falling through the ice scared him so much, it prompted him to kiss me, and me to return his kiss. And then he told me that he loved me, and the fact that I love him just spilled out of me and—"

"Wait," Addie broke in. "You love him? You love *Evan?*"

"Yes. I'm so sorr—"

"But what about Sebastian?" Dear God, Addie felt as if the floor beneath her feet shifted. "I thought you loved Sebastian."

"I do love him—but not in the same way I love Evan. I love Sebastian like a brother. I'm *in love* with Evan."

"I…I need to sit down." Addie staggered the three feet to the settee and sat down with a thud. Grace, her beautiful face tight with distress, sat beside Addie and held her hand. Addie cleared her throat then said, "But you and Sebastian are supposed to marry. Everyone is expecting your betrothal to be announced this holiday."

Shame filled Grace's eyes. "I know what everyone expects, but I simply cannot marry him. Not when I'm in love with someone else."

"Not just 'someone else,' Grace—his brother! I cannot even begin to imagine how he's going to feel about this. He loves you. He wants to marry you."

"I cannot defend what I've done, Addie, but I must point out that Sebastian has never told me he loves me, nor has he asked me to marry him."

"How long have you felt this way about Evan?"

"When *haven't* I felt this way about him? It feels as though I've been in love with him my entire life."

"But I saw you and Sebastian kiss just last Christmas! In the stables."

Another layer of crimson stained Grace's cheeks. "That was at my initiation. I knew everyone expected us to marry, and I was hoping, praying, that if I kissed him it would ignite the sort of feelings I had for Evan. Unfortunately, it didn't. As for Sebastian—while I am of course concerned about how he will take the news, it is *you* that I am most troubled about. I don't want you hurt."

"Why would *I* be hurt?"

"Because you love Evan."

"Well, of course I do—" Addie's words broke off

as realization dawned. "You think you've broken my heart. By kissing Evan. By being in love with him. Is he in love with you?"

Grace nodded. "Yes. He told me so tonight. I'm so sorry, Addie. I feel absolutely horrible. I don't know what to say or do—"

Addie touched her finger to Grace's lips to stop her words. "Poppet, please don't distress yourself any further on my behalf. I am not now, nor have I ever been, in love with Evan."

Grace's jaw dropped. "I beg your pardon?"

"I'm not in love with Evan," she repeated slowly and distinctly. "If you two love each other, I'm delighted for you and you have my full blessing."

Grace blinked, then a dazzling smile lit her face. "I...I cannot believe this. It's a true Christmas miracle! I've been so miserable, waiting for you and Evan to announce an engagement. Now, not only are you not in love with him, but he's in love with me and me with him and... Oh my, everything is simply perfect!"

"Not quite everything," Addie said quietly, trying to ignore the rapid thump of her heart that seemed to scream with every beat *Grace loves Evan! Grace loves Evan!* Because really what difference did that make, other than to result in Sebastian suffering from a broken heart? "Just because you're not in love with Sebastian, doesn't mean he's not in love with you, Grace. He is sure to be devastated to lose you, especially to his own brother."

"Neither Evan nor I want him hurt." Grace chewed on her lower lip, then asked, "Would you speak to Sebastian, Addie? Before Evan does so tomorrow?"

"Oh, Grace, I don't think—"

"Sebastian respects your opinion," Grace hurried on, "and he'd listen to you. You could talk to him and soften the blow so that when Evan speaks to him, he'll be prepared to listen." She squeezed Addie's hands. "Please, Addie. Will you intervene with Sebastian on my behalf?"

Addie drew a deep breath and desperately searched for the words to refuse Grace's request. Dear God, she wanted to say no. She had no desire to deliver the news that would shatter Sebastian's dreams. How could she bear to watch him suffer? Watch his heart break over losing the woman he loved?

Yet one look at the hopeful plea in Grace's eyes and Addie knew she couldn't refuse. Finally she nodded. "I'll do whatever it takes to make you happy and to make things right for you, Poppet."

Gratitude glowed in Grace's eyes. "Thank you, Addie. I love you so very much."

"And I love you. Now you need to return to your room and rest. Tomorrow is going to be an eventful day."

She walked Grace to the door, gave her a last quick hug, then leaned in the doorway and watched her walk down the corridor. After she turned the corner, Addie re-entered her room and closed the door. She leaned her forehead against the oak panel and squeezed her eyes shut and tried to think of something, anything, other than the mantra reverberating through her mind. *Grace doesn't love him. Grace doesn't love him.*

She knew she should wait until morning to talk to him—going to him now was nothing short of insanity and completely lacking in propriety. Yet the need to impart the news she'd promised to deliver, to say it and get it over with, gripped her in a vise from which she couldn't escape. Her inner voice informed her that what she really wanted to do was to see him. Be near him.

She told her inner voice to be quiet.

And headed toward Sebastian's bedchamber.

SEBASTIAN STARED OUT THE window of his bedchamber with unseeing eyes, the conversation he'd overheard just moments ago outside Addie's room echoing through his mind.

Please, Addie. Will you intervene with Sebastian on my behalf?

I'll do whatever it takes to make you happy and to make things right for you, Poppet.

He hadn't meant to eavesdrop, but Addie's door stood ajar, so it was impossible not to hear the conversation taking place between her and Grace inside her bedchamber as he'd approached. As he had no wish to be discovered by either sister, he'd swiftly returned to his own room. And couldn't erase what he'd heard from his mind.

What precisely would Addie do?

A quiet knock interrupted his thoughts. Clearly this was his night for visitors. He quickly crossed the room and opened the door. His heart stuttered at the sight of Addie, her beautiful eyes reminding him of smooth toffee. His gaze took in her white, lace-trimmed robe—a virginal-looking garment that covered every inch of her skin from the neck down, but his imagination instantly conjured up a vision of generous womanly curves beneath the voluminous material.

She moistened her lips, drawing his gaze to her mouth and sizzling heat through him. He barely stifled the groan that rose in his throat. Bloody hell, Addie being anywhere near his bedchamber in the middle of the night was unwise in the extreme.

"You're awake," she whispered.

He cocked a brow. "I could say the same to you."

She glanced up and down the corridor, then said, "I know this is very untoward, but may I have a moment of your time? I wouldn't ask if it weren't important."

His common sense coughed to life and demanded he refuse her request. Send her back to her own room. Immediately. Admonish her of the impropriety of coming to his bedchamber. Insist that whatever she wanted could wait until morning. And be said in the drawing room. Instead he stepped back and indicated she should enter.

"Thank you." She walked past him, and he drew in a sharp breath when she brushed against him in the doorway—a breath that filled his head with the delicate scent of jasmine. He gritted his teeth against his body's swift reaction and prayed for strength. He closed the door slowly, taking an extra few seconds to get himself under control. When he turned, he was startled to find her standing less than an arm's length away.

Silence swelled between them and he fisted his hands to keep from snatching her into his arms, a nearly impossible urge to resist now that he knew she and Evan wouldn't be getting married.

"What do you want, Addie?"

"I want...I want..." Her gaze dropped to his mouth, and he felt as if she'd lit him on fire. Unable to stop himself, he took a step closer to her.

"What do you want? Tell me."

Her gaze settled on his and he saw exactly what she wanted. Before he could move or react, she threw herself into his arms and kissed him. And sanity fled. The instant their lips met, his every thought, his every good intention, simply evaporated. With a low groan, he deepened the kiss, exploring the velvety sweet warmth of her mouth with his tongue. She rose up on her toes, pressing herself against him, obliterating in a single second the years of restraint he'd practiced.

Without breaking their kiss, he stepped back until his shoulders hit the door. He spread his legs and pulled her into the vee of his thighs. Then simply drowned in her. In the incredible feel of her body straining against his. The scent of jasmine rising from her soft skin. The feel of her hair sifting through his impatient fingers. He tried to be gentle, wanted to go slow and savor each second, but he simply couldn't. Any miniscule chance he might have had of keeping his desires in check was obliterated by Addie's fervent response. Her fingers combing through his hair. Her breasts crushed against his chest. Her palms gliding over his shoulders.

He slanted his mouth over hers again and again, his kisses fueled by more than a decade's worth of longing and love and frustration and desire that rushed from the dam that had burst inside him the instant she'd touched him.

More. Wanted more. Needed more. He tugged on the sash of her robe, then slid his hands beneath the

cotton. While one hand slowly stroked up and down
her back, he flicked open the tiny pearl buttons running
down the front of her nightgown. He kissed his way
down her neck, touching his tongue to the base of her
throat where her pulse beat hard and fast. He dragged
his mouth lower, into the opening he'd created in her
gown and brushed his lips over the hard peaks of her
nipples, visible through the light cotton.

She gasped, then moaned. Plunged her fingers into
his hair and arched her back, offering more of herself.
"Sebastian..."

Her voice penetrated the fog surrounding him, allowing a modicum of sanity to seep through. And suddenly
her earlier words drifted through his glazed mind. *I'll
do whatever it takes to make you happy and to make
things right for you, Poppet.*

Bloody hell! In the space of single heartbeat common
sense returned and he froze. Clearly she *would* do anything to make things right for her sister—including
coming to his bedchamber and initiating this kiss, this
kiss that had quickly burned out of control, and sharing intimacies with him. Anything to deflect his attention from the fact that the woman he supposedly loved
wanted his brother instead.

A wave of anger and disgust washed through him. At
her, for allowing him to kiss her so passionately when
she was in love with his brother, even if doing so was
out of love for Grace. And at himself for falling on her
like a starving beast, completely losing the control he
prided himself on.

He drew an unsteady breath and set her firmly away
from him. And swallowed a groan. By God, she looked

beautiful. Aroused and ripe, flushed and tousled. In spite of his anger, he was barely able to stifle the urge to drag her right back into his arms and take whatever she'd give him, for however long, whatever her reasons. And damn it, that weakness infuriated him. He quickly walked to the center of the room to put some distance between them.

Addie pressed a hand to the wall as her knees had gone missing and she sucked in a series of ragged breaths. Good heavens, she felt as if she'd melted. Still breathing heavily, she turned to face Sebastian. And stilled at his expression. She'd never seen his eyes look so cold. So bleak. So angry or filled with disgust. Mortification all but choked her.

Dear God, what had she done? She'd only meant to talk to him on Grace's behalf, but the instant she saw him, all the feelings she'd suppressed all these years had rushed to the surface. And she'd suddenly recalled her dream and seen in her mind's eye the pink Angel of Christmas Present. The words she'd quoted had echoed through Addie's brain—*the woman that deliberates is lost.*

Addie decided in that instant to deliberate no longer and threw herself at the man she'd loved her entire life.

Her skin prickled with humiliation at the brutal truth, at the wanton way she'd behaved. Their kiss had left her breathless. Aching. Desperate for more. Good heavens, she'd practically *begged* for more. Her stomach cramped with shame, not only for her own actions, but from the profound embarrassment of his rejection. While he'd initially responded, the way he'd pushed her away—as if she'd stung him—and the way he was looking at her now made it abundantly clear the desire she'd experienced was one-sided. And killed all hope that she'd ever find herself in his arms again.

She hadn't deliberated, yet she'd still lost.

Wishing the floor would open up and swallow her, she tried to refasten her gaping nightgown, but her hands shook so badly she fumbled the task. Her gold chain was tangled on one of the buttons, and she carelessly shoved the necklace into the opening at her neck.

"I'm sorry," she said in a shaky whisper. Unable to meet his gaze, she mumbled, "I must go." Then she bolted from the room. And managed, just barely, to contain her tears until she reached the safety of her own bedchamber.

CHAPTER TEN

ADDIE SAT IN THE Buntingford train station, staring at the giant clock hanging on the wall, willing the minutes to pass quickly. She hadn't planned to leave Kendall Manor until late afternoon, but she'd done so directly after breakfast, claiming a need for extra time in London to settle her affairs before traveling to Paris. Her departure barely caused a ripple as everyone was so excited about the announcement of Evan and Grace's engagement.

Everyone except Sebastian. Because he wasn't there.

According to Wilson, Sebastian had left the house before dawn, telling the butler he wasn't certain when he'd return. When Addie heard the news of his departure, another knot tightened in her stomach. Evan had told her that he'd confessed his love for Grace to Sebastian last night, a fact that only made Addie's already crushing humiliation and devastation more complete. Clearly she'd caught Sebastian at a very vulnerable moment, thus his initial heated response to her kiss. She'd merely been a stand-in for the woman he really wanted. The woman who had just broken his heart. Obviously he'd left because he couldn't bear to hear the engagement announcement. And no doubt he wished to avoid Addie. Probably believed she'd throw herself at him again and he'd be forced to hide in alcoves to evade her.

A half laugh, half sob rose in her throat at the mental image of Sebastian peeking out from behind velvet curtains. Dear God, she was going to miss him—not only Sebastian the man she loved, but Sebastian, her very dear friend—as her actions of last night had clearly caused a rift between them. How would she ever be able to look him in the eye again? At the very least, she owed him an apology for pouncing on him as if she were a hound and he a pork chop—a more substantial apology than the *I'm sorry* she'd croaked last night before dashing from his bedchamber. She'd resolved to write him once she and Aunt Margaret were settled in Paris, and beg his forgiveness. And then she'd strive to put the entire incident from her mind.

Good luck, her annoying inner voice chirped. Good luck indeed, for how could she ever hope to forget the feel of his lips, his tongue, on hers? The heat of his body melting into her. His clean scent surrounding her. His hands in her hair. Smoothing down her back. Unbuttoning her nightgown. His mouth on her breast.

Unable to stop herself, she closed her eyes and allowed herself to relive those magical, perfect few moments in his arms, and knew that no matter how hard she tried, she'd never, ever be able to erase them from her mind.

She heaved a sigh and opened her eyes. And stared. At Sebastian, who stood directly in front of her, looking down at her with an inscrutable expression. She blinked, certain he was a figment of her imagination but then he spoke. Surely figments of one's imagination didn't speak. Did they?

"Are you all right, Addie?" he asked. "You look flushed."

Good lord, no doubt because she'd just been thinking of his hands roaming her back and his warm breath caressing her breast. And now here he stood, looking more beautiful than any man had the right to—although there was no missing the fact that his hair was mussed and... were those pink sparkles clinging to the dark strands? She stood and tried to ignore the shaking in her knees and the heat creeping up her neck.

"Yes, I'm fine. Merely surprised to see you. What are you doing here?"

"I wished to speak to you."

Panic fluttered through her. She had no desire to discuss the humiliating events of last night at all, let alone in a public place. She looked around. Only one other passenger waited, an ancient-looking man who sat on a bench at the opposite end of the building and appeared to be dozing.

"When I returned to the house," Sebastian continued, recalling her attention, "I was told you'd already departed for the station."

"I decided to take an earlier train."

"Which is why I didn't delay getting here. Indeed, I arrived in absolute record time. I don't believe Pericles has ever galloped so fast. Blew my hat right off my head. He actually left a trail of dust behind him. Pink dust. It encircled his head—and mine—as well." He shook his head, looking bemused, and several pink sparkles floated from his hair to land on his shoulder. "Oddest thing I've ever experienced. Must be something new in his oats."

"Since you've been back to the house, I gather you heard the announcement?"

"I did."

Neither his tone nor his expression gave any hint to his feelings. As she'd failed in her promise to Grace to discuss the matter with Sebastian last night, she said, "About the engagement—I hope you're…happy for them."

"I wish them only the best. But that isn't what I want to talk to you about. I want to talk about last night. About when you came to my bedchamber."

Addie's stomach dropped to her toes. No point in praying for the floor to swallow her—she'd already tried that and it hadn't worked worth a jot. Clearly, she'd have to face her disgrace here and now. Drawing herself to her full height, she forced herself to look him in the eye. "I'm sorry, Sebastian. My behavior was inexcusable. I hope you'll accept my sincerest apology."

He regarded her through unreadable eyes for several long seconds then shook his head. "I'm afraid I can't do that, Addie."

To Addie's dismay, hot tears pushed behind her eyes. She looked at the ground and blinked furiously, willing the moisture away. "I see. Well, in that case—"

"Why did you kiss me?"

Addie's head snapped up. "I beg your pardon?"

"Why did you kiss me?"

"Why did *you* kiss *me?*" she countered.

"Well, for one reason, because *you* kissed *me.*"

Botheration. She wracked her brain for a believable

lie and failed. And surely if she mentioned an all-too-real dream involving a pink, literature-quoting Angel of Christmas Present, he'd question her sanity. "I simply… forgot myself. It was not my intention to anger you, and I'm truly sorry that I did."

He nodded slowly. "Yes, I was angry."

"Obviously."

"Before you came to my room last night, I went to yours. Your door was ajar and I overheard you talking to Grace."

Addie's heart stumbled. She frantically tried to recall what they'd said to each other. "What exactly did you hear?"

"I heard Grace ask you to intervene with me on her and Evan's behalf. And I heard you promise to do whatever it took to make her happy and to make things right for her."

He watched her while the implications of his words sunk in. When they did, she drew in a horrified breath and heat raced into her face. "Good heavens. You believe I came to your bedchamber and…and…"

"Ruthlessly kissed me," he supplied helpfully when words failed her.

"Yes. And ruthlessly kissed you in order to…" Again words failed her.

"Distract me from the heartbreak of learning that the woman I was supposed to marry was instead enamored of another man, namely my own brother."

"Precisely," Addie said, in an outraged tone. "That's what you thought?"

"It is indeed."

"You believed me capable of such duplicity?"

"I was a complete and utter ass. Indeed, I shall save you the trouble of dubbing me Lord Utter Ass and do it myself."

She gave an elegant sniff and made a huge show of looking about. "Utter ass—you'll notice that no one is arguing with you."

"In my own defense, I'd like to point out that, first, my better judgment was seriously compromised at that moment due to my being ruthlessly kissed. And second, I quickly realized my grievous error."

"Oh? Why didn't you share that realization with me? Oh, I know why! You were too busy pushing me away and glaring daggers at me."

"I couldn't tell you last night for two reasons. One, because you'd already left my bedchamber."

"I'd suffered quite enough humiliation for one night."

"And two, because if I'd gone after you to tell you what a complete and utter ass I was, we would have ended up doing this." He took her in his arms and kissed her. A slow, soft, deep, tongue-dancing kiss that left her knowing precisely what melted butter felt like. When he lifted his head, she stared at him, dazed and grateful he hadn't released her, lest she become a puddle on the floor.

"We would have done that?" she said.

"Definitely. And this, as well." He leaned forward and slowly brushed his tongue down the length of her neck.

"Oh, my…" A train whistle sounded in the distance, and reality returned. "I mean, good heavens, have you lost your mind?"

He straightened and looked at her with such heat flaming in his eyes, she felt as if she stood in a ring of fire. "Yes. My mind, and my heart." He cupped her face between his palms. "Addie, my darling Addie. Can you forgive me for doubting you for even one minute last night? As I said, my only excuse is that you'd badly addled my wits. I wanted you so much it's no wonder I couldn't think properly. But then I saw it and realized that the reason you kissed me was the same reason I kissed you back."

"Saw it? What are you talking about?"

Without taking his gaze from her, he slowly pulled the slim gold chain she wore, until the gold apple charm slipped from beneath her clothing and dangled between them. "You were wearing this. There's only one reason why you would still wear the gift I gave you twelve years ago. Only one reason you would kiss me so passionately. Allow me to touch you so intimately. It's the same reason the painting you gave me all those years ago still hangs in my bedchamber at Hartley House and is my most-cherished possession."

Addie gazed into his beautiful eyes and went perfectly still. Incredibly, miraculously, everything she'd ever wanted was shining in those deep blue depths. Passion. Desire. And all the love in the world.

"I love you," they said in unison. Then they both smiled.

"I...I can't believe this," she whispered. "Is this a dream?"

"Best dream I've ever had." He lifted her up and spun her around until she was breathless with laughter. "All these years I thought you loved Evan," he said setting her back on her feet. "You have no idea the torture I've suffered."

"I most certainly do, because all these years I thought you loved Grace." She shook her head, bemused. "How is it that you don't?"

"My darling Addie. I've loved you since the day you taught me to climb my first tree. There's never been anyone else. You're the other half of my heart. You're just…everything. You always have been. The only reason I didn't tell you how I felt was because I thought you and Evan loved each other." He leaned forward and touched his forehead to hers. "I had no intention of marrying Grace. I planned to tell both our fathers this holiday."

She leaned back in the circle of his arms. "I never revealed my feelings because I thought you and Grace loved each other."

"And all this time Grace and Evan were in love."

She shook her head. "What a tangle."

"But we're all straightened out now."

"Yes—but why did you leave the house so early this morning? I thought it was because you couldn't bear to hear Evan and Grace announce their engagement. And also because I thought you were avoiding me."

His eyes seemed to darken and he leaned in to nuzzle her neck with his lips. "Avoid you? Hardly. Much more likely that I'd drag you into the nearest alcove and—"

"Ruthlessly kiss me?"

"Every chance I get," he promised.

She laughed, then squirmed until he lifted his head. "I may have to name you Lord Ruthless Kisser."

"You'll *definitely* have to name me that. For starters."

Oh, my. "You still haven't told me why you left so early."

He shot her a mock glare. "Because you keep distracting me. I wanted to go to you last night, but I knew if I did…well, I knew I wouldn't be able to leave you and I wanted to do this the right way. So, at dawn, I rode to Hartley House to fetch this." He reached into his pocket and pulled out a small velvet box. Addie's heart lurched and, feeling as if she were once again dreaming, she watched him lower himself to one knee and open the box. An oval topaz surrounded by diamonds glittered in a nest of white satin.

"It was my mother's," he said softly. "I recall seeing this ring for the first time when I was ten and thinking that it was the same color as your eyes." He took the ring from its satin nest and extended it to her. "Addie, will you marry me?"

A half sob, half laugh erupted from Addie. "God, yes. Please, yes. Yes, yes, *yes!*"

Sebastian rose to his feet, removed the glove from her left hand and slipped the ring on her finger. Then right there, in the Buntingford train station, with one ancient man dozing in the corner, Lady Adelaide Kendall once again threw herself at the man she'd loved her entire life and kissed him for all she was worth. After several moments, Sebastian raised his head. Addie dragged open her eyes and saw the deep love she felt for him reflected right back at her.

"I hope you don't want a long engagement," they said in unison, then they smiled. What appeared to be a shower of pink sparkles rained down on them. If either had looked up, they might have seen the fluttering of shiny new pink wings, but Sebastian was far too busy kissing his future wife, and Addie was far too busy being kissed by her One True Love to notice.

* * * * *

TOMORROW'S DESTINY

Hope Tarr

* * *

"Ghost of the Future!" he exclaimed, "I fear you
more than any specter I have seen. But as I know
your purpose is to do me good, and as I hope to
live to be another man from what I was, I am
prepared to bear you company, and do it with a
thankful heart. Will you not speak to me?"

It gave him no reply.
The hand was pointed straight before them.

"Lead on!" said Scrooge,—"lead on!"

—*A Christmas Carol:
Being a Ghost Story of Christmas*
by Charles Dickens

For Raj

PROLOGUE

MacPherson and Daughter Booksellers
Covent Garden, London
December 23, 1890, 4:00 p.m.

"YOU WILL BE HAUNTED," resumed the Ghost, "by Three Spirits."

Bookshop proprietress Fiona MacPherson intoned her favorite Dickens quote a final time, savoring the delicious, shivery feel of saying the words aloud. She closed *A Christmas Carol* and set the slender volume upon the tea table. She, Lady Adelaide Kendall and Miss Claire Halliday had been gathering about that very table to discuss their beloved books for two years. What had begun as a pleasant pastime between bookseller and book buyers had solidified into firm friendships.

Their monthly book club was the mainstay of Fiona's social life. It *was* her social life. Though their spheres rarely intersected in the larger world of London, snuggled within her bookshop's four walls the trio had forged a bond that sustained each woman in the wake of life's tragedies and trials.

First there was Claire. Her fiancé, Stephen. suffered an untimely death four years ago—at Christmastime, no less—and his family, the Mayhews, were still smothering poor Claire. If not to death, then straight to spinsterhood.

Then there was Addie. Fiona privately believed her ennui had to do with a certain dashing young man, her sister's beau. Sebastian Hartley, Viscount Channing, entered Addie's conversation with astonishing frequency for all that she professed him to be "only a friend." Fiona would wager her final farthing the viscount had a great deal to do with Addie's sudden decision to study art in Paris for the next several months. Once she went, Fiona feared their little literati would disband altogether. It was a bleak thought.

Last, but not least, was Fiona. Her accident five years before—a foolish fall on an icy patch of train platform—had left her with a limp and a fear of crowds, both of which had ended her dancing days. Still, she'd had her dear Da, her cat and her book club friends as recompense. Her Da's death last month, though not unexpected, was a buffeting blow all the same. And now the very future of her beloved bookshop stood in peril. The latter she kept to herself for fear of spoiling her friends' holidays.

Beyond frustrated, she blurted out, "I far fancy Mr. Scrooge before his reformation."

Her friends turned to her with predictably appalled faces. "Fiona, truly, how can you say such a thing?" Addie protested, nearly choking on her morsel of lemon-poppy-seed cake. "He was such a miserable, mean-spirited old miser."

"Fi, dearest," Claire suggested more gently, setting her teacup upon its saucer. "We know Christmas is especially sad for you this year, but do you not go too far in your humbugging? It pains me to see you stand so resolute, so…Scrooge-like against a season devoted to peace on earth, goodwill and, above all, love."

Fiona felt her gaze falter and a lump lodge in her throat. Looking down to her lap, she smoothed a hand over her black bombazine skirts, the solely acceptable fabric for full mourning. Underlying her gloom was yet another thing she'd kept carefully concealed from her two friends. Christmas Day, December twenty-fifth was her birthday. Not just any birthday but her thirtieth. By the time the clock tolled midnight, tomorrow, she would be well and truly on the shelf. On a chirpier chime, at least it would be a bookshelf—if she found a way to hold on to her shop.

Composing herself, she looked up. "No, I do not believe I do." Reluctant though she was to send her friends off to celebrate the season on a sour note, she prided herself on her honesty even if, admittedly, that honesty frequently ran to a fault. "Certainly Scrooge was overly harsh with all his blathering of workhouses and treadmills and decreasing the surplus population, but at least he was no hypocrite. Why *should* we feign a gaiety we cannot feel simply because the calendar decrees it to be Christmas? It's all so horribly false and I, for one, want no part of it." Impatient, she swept back a copper-colored curl from where it had fallen over her blue eye. "What reasons have any of us for making merry at Christmastime or any other?" she demanded, capturing their gazes in turn.

The two thought a moment. "We have our health," Claire offered.

Addie swallowed deeply, her golden-brown eyes

dimming. "And surely we…or certainly you two have some…romantic prospects." Color swept into her cheeks and she looked quickly away.

Regal in her simply styled navy woolen skirt and jacket, Claire shook her head. "Addie, for all you know, you may meet your One True Love while sketching in a park in Paris." She looked to Fiona. "And you, Fi, may well meet yours as you met Addie and I—in this very shop."

Holding back tears, Fiona divided her gaze between them. Little did they know it, but the shop, the books and indeed the very table at which they'd passed so many pleasant hours might at any moment be snatched away.

For their sakes, she summoned a smile and reached for the teapot to refill their cups. "Whatever this holiday season and new year may bring, with wonderful friends such as you, what do I need with a man?"

"WHAT, INDEED!" GRIMACING, Fern, Fiona's guardian angel-in-training, turned to her fellows, Periwinkle and Rose, floating above the bookcases beside her. "Poor Fiona hasn't only given up on Christmas, she's given up on True Love, too—and 'tis all my fault!" She punctuated the pronouncement with a sob, sending turquoise sparkles joining the dust motes milling about in the still air.

She hadn't forgiven herself for the accident five years ago. Fiona had been set to accompany her father to an estate auction in Hungerford near Oxford, a lord's library of rare and collectible books where she was to have met her One True Love. Only, at the train station where Fiona and her father waited to board, Fern had fallen down on her guardianship duties. Distracted by another passenger's pretty shawl, turquoise, of course, she'd turned her attention away from Fiona for a blink of time—but it was enough. Caught up in the crowd, Fiona had slipped upon a patch of ice and fallen. The resulting wrenched ankle had forced her to stay behind—and made Fiona miss meeting her One True Love, the single soul who could be counted upon to make her truly, blissfully happy. The accident also left her with a very slight limp and a very great fear of crowds, both which she'd turned into reasons for putting herself on the shelf well before her time.

"Don't be so hard on yourself," said Rose, Adelaide's angel, patting Fern on the shoulder with her plump hand and sending pinkish-red sparkles scattering.

"We all make mistakes," added Claire's angel, Periwinkle. Waiving her hand, she added her blue sparkles to the mix.

Brushing off the flecks, Fern shook her head. "Easy for you two to say. Rose, admittedly you've missed some opportunities with Lady Adelaide, but you've yet to allow anything truly harmful to befall her." She whipped about to Periwinkle, spearing the newcomer with a look that sent the timid angel shrinking. "And you've been assigned to Claire for only three weeks now. Three weeks! You're coming at this assignment fresh as a daisy."

The Powers That Be had given each apprentice angel until the final stroke of midnight on New Year's Eve to unite Claire, Adelaide and Fiona with their respective One True Loves. If the angels failed, they wouldn't have another chance to earn their wings for a century, an eternity in earth years and no pittance in astral time, either. And their three ladies would live out their lives as spinsters. Such was The Rule.

Wringing her hands, Periwinkle echoed Fern's worries. "I only hope The Powers That Be have given us sufficient time. One earth week isn't a great deal of time to work what amounts to a miracle—*three* miracles! Looking dejected, she propped her cheek in her palm.

"Do stop dithering and calm yourself, Periwinkle," Fern ordered, her customary confidence returning. "Our plan to adapt Mr. Dickens's book to our purpose is sheer brilliance."

Rose shook her silvered head so fiercely her spectacles slid down her nose. "A book on Christmas and yet there isn't a single angel in it, only ghosts. Ghosts! I can't fathom what Mr. Dickens could have been thinking—or drinking—when he sat down to write such rubbish."

Determined to stick to their plan, Fern said, "I quite agree. Still, the book has implanted in the fertile soil of our ladies' imaginations, and so casting ourselves as the *Angels* of Past, Present and Future should work quite nicely."

Mindful of the ticking time, she shot her gaze down to the shop floor where Fiona hugged each of her friends in turn, Claire and Addie duly bundled for the fast-falling snow and Fiona doing her brave best to send them off with a smile. Smile or not, Fern could feel her lady's heart all but breaking, but then, she had been with Fiona since birth. Fern had fond memories of playing peek-a-boo with Baby Fiona in her crib and of guiding the toddler on her first shaky steps. Her charge had been able to see her back then. Now that she was grown up, Fiona no longer acknowledged her angel's existence and yet their spiritual bond was unusually strong all the same.

Adelaide and Claire left, the shop door closing behind them, the blasted bell reporting that somewhere yet another angel had earned her wings. Shoulders slumping, Fiona turned back inside and limped over to clear away the tea things. Looking on, Fern blinked away what felt suspiciously like mortal tears.

Rose tapped Fern on the shoulder. "I don't think Fiona's little limp bothers her half so much as her eyes do. She's self-conscious on account of their being…well, mismatched."

Distracted, it took Fern a moment to make sense of the remark. "Why, that's positively absurd! Having one blue eye and one green eye is a rare gift from The Powers That Be." She spread her arms to indicate her splendid heavenly raiment, one half in hues of deepest leaf green and the other in celestial blue. "Fiona's eyes are the portal to her free-spirited soul, as well as the trait by which her One True Love shall know her."

Fern only hoped Fiona would cooperate and recognize him in return. Even an angel in the service of The Powers That Be could but do her best. Free will was every human being's birthright. That's where casting herself as the Angel of the Future came into play. Giving her charge a grim glimpse into how her future would unfurl should she continue her humbugging might seem heavy-handed, but it was also a necessary evil. She couldn't afford to be faint-hearted. Fiona needed a sound push if she was to move beyond her grief and get on with her life. Little did she know it, but her One True Love was due to arrive at the bookshop that very evening. There wasn't a moment to waste.

Fern looked back to Rose and Periwinkle. "Our ladies have gone their separate ways for the holiday. Time to roll up our robe sleeves and get to work."

"Are we not...f-forgetting something?" Periwinkle asked in her tremulous voice.

"We are angels even if we are still in training," added Rose.

Secretly ashamed to have forgotten protocol, Fern nodded. "Quite, I was...er...testing you."

Without further words, the three formed a circle. Each angel made a steeple of her hands and concentrated on pooling her energy with that of the others. In unison they sang, "On a wing and a prayer let us deliver three Christmas miracles to our three most deserving young ladies and let this Noel be remembered fondly, merrily and *lovingly* for many an earth year to come."

CHAPTER ONE

FIONA FINISHED CLEARING the table. Brushing the cake crumbs into the dust bin, she tried not to think of how lonely she felt. Now that Addie and Claire had gone, the shop felt depressingly empty, the ticking of the cuckoo clock and the snoring of her cat in the bow window the only stirrings to dent the stillness.

She set down the stack of dirty plates with a heavy sigh and walked over to the window. Curled up on the cushion with eyes closed, the Grey Ghost didn't budge. Reaching over him, she scoured a fist over the frosted pane and looked out. The streetlamp illuminated the fast-falling snow, and the snow-covered sidewalk was without a single footprint. Home to the Royal Opera House, as well as myriad music halls, public houses, Turkish baths and brothels, ordinarily Covent Garden teemed with life, both the seedy and sophisticated sides of it. But tonight the flower sellers and fruit peddlers, the tavern owners and even the streetwalkers seemed to have closed up shop for the holiday. Fiona wouldn't have thought it possible, but she missed the customary carousing. Mr. Dickens's Scrooge indeed had the right of it.

Christmas was a great lot of humbug!

And yet there had been a time when she'd seen both the holiday and her birthday as a gateway to a new year of bright beginnings and marvelous miracles poised to unfold. That time, only five years ago, seemed as far away as the moon and as much a fairy tale as Father Christmas himself. Oh, to believe again!

Thinking over her recent book club gathering, she wondered if she hadn't been overly harsh. Admittedly, she'd never been particularly adept at diplomacy. As the cherished only child of her widowed father, a big bluff Scotsman, she'd grown up encouraged to speak her mind and read her fill.

"I want to be a witch when I grow up," she'd announced one day after reading The Grimm Brothers' fairy tale "Hansel and Gretel." It wasn't the sweets-thieving children but the poor, put-upon witch whose home they'd invaded who'd won her sympathy.

Her Da had laughed, ruffled her copper curls and proclaimed her to be precocious. "She'll grow out of it in time," he'd assured subsequent horrified adult listeners.

Fiona hadn't.

Only, the tall, red-haired, freckled reflection she met in her wardrobe mirror each morning was as un-witchy as visages could be. Even her mismatched eyes weren't scary as much as freakish. Nor was her cat particularly spectral. Weighing nearly two stone, he waddled when he walked, his thumping paws and sluggish gait rendering birds and mice perfectly safe.

Stepping back from the window, Fiona felt her problems, which she'd set aside for her book club friends, descend upon her shoulders like bricks. Chief among those burdens was The Honorable Tobias Templeton, a gentleman scholar and collector of antiquities, and for the past five years her father's chief rival in the acquisition of rare books. Like a vulture descending upon carrion, Mr. Templeton had scarcely waited for her Da to grow cold in his grave before descending upon Fiona with his demands. According to him, he'd purchased the bookshop and the entirety of its contents from her father the month before his death. He meant to take possession of his property on the first of the new year!

The shock had hit Fiona like a second death. If Mr. Templeton's claim was true, and the letter from his solicitor seemed to support its veracity, in another week she would be required to vacate the premises. On balance, she would receive a bank draft for five thousand pounds. Five thousand pounds. It was a modest fortune. Still, the bookshop was the only home she'd ever known, her sanctuary since her accident and the seat of cherished memories. Though she'd yet to set eyes upon its new owner, she hated Tobias Templeton with all her heart.

Mr. Templeton seemed to particularly care for a rare and little known translated text by Aristotle. Five years earlier, her father had snapped up the volume at auction apparently all but under Mr. Templeton's nose. Fiona would give a great deal to turn back the clock so that she might attend the auction and witness the blackguard's face when he realized the coveted book was as good as lost to him. Indeed, she'd been en route there with her Da when a tumble on the crowded, iced-over railway platform had forced her to stay behind.

For the past five years, no matter of pressure Mr. Templeton brought to bear could persuade her Da to part with his treasure. His failing health must have caused him to relinquish his position at the last. "I mean to see my girl settled," he'd said more than once in his final few months, and it wasn't until Mr. Templeton's communiqué that Fiona had realized just how sincerely he'd meant it. Thinking of her dear father using his final breaths to assure her security simply hurt too much. So far she'd dealt with Mr. Templeton's prodigious pile of letters and telegrams by simply ignoring them. If he wanted her shop and his blasted book so bloody badly, then let him come to London and claim them!

She turned the shop sign over to Closed and gave Grey a gentle nudge. "Come along. We might as well go to bed. With any luck, I'll sleep through Christmas Eve and Christmas Day and perhaps New Year's Day entirely."

I shouldn't count on it, dear.

Fiona stalled in midstep. The chuckling voice, female, had seemed to come from just above her, which was both silly and impossible. Other than Grey, she was quite alone in the shop. Still, she could have sworn…

To be sure, she searched both front and back rooms, and then checked the bolt on the door not once but twice. Mounting the creaking stairs, she caught herself looking back over her shoulder, but only Grey followed. Inside her room, she turned up the lamp, yanked back the moth-eaten bed curtains and knelt to look beneath the bed. No bogey man or bogey woman peered back, let alone a ghost. Feeling foolish, she rose and limped over to the wardrobe, her chilly fingers starting down her gown's queue of jet buttons. It was a relief to relinquish her heavy mourning gown and petticoats, corset and pantaloons, step out of her shoes and unroll her mended stockings. Shivering, she pulled on her night rail and robe, and then hung the gown on a peg alongside the brightly colored ones she wouldn't wear for another year at least.

She came back to the bed, turned down the lamp and crawled beneath the chilly covers. Pulling them up to her chin, she vowed to banish Christmas, birthdays and, most of all, Tobias Templeton from her mind.

TOBIAS TEMPLETON hunkered down between the raised collar points of his mackintosh and steeled himself to ignore the nettle-like stinging of the snow striking his cheeks. He hadn't been an hour in the saddle when the first misting of rain had solidified to sterner stuff. A normal person would have turned back. A normal person would have, at the very least, sought shelter for the night.

Tobias wasn't remotely normal and never had been.

Born pearlescent pale with white-blond hair and opaque eyes painfully sensitive to sunlight, he looked more a ghost than a man. So far none of the physicians who'd examined him over the years could do more than document his strange condition.

As an only child among a family known for its dark beauty, Tobias wasn't only a freak in the greater world but an outcast in his own home. It was no coincidence his parents had declined to try for a second child. They were afraid the mistake, the curse, might be repeated. Even now his widowed mother acted as though she could scarcely stand the sight of him.

Fortunately for them both, she didn't have to, certainly not very often. Tobias kept to his own suite of rooms, his library especially, and let her have free rein over the rest of the big, rambling manor house. Goggles outfitted with dark-colored lenses, a contraption he'd contrived, allowed him to venture forth in daylight when he absolutely must. For the most part, though, it was simpler to wait out the day indoors with the curtains drawn.

And so instead of setting out from his manor house in Hungerford at sunrise as a normal person would, he'd waited until twilight when the waning light would be kinder to his skin and eyes. By the time he'd reached the train station, the last train to London was poised to pull out, the private compartments booked for the holiday. Tobias declined to purchase a seat in second-class, but not because he was a snob. Traveling in the close confines of the communal carriages would mean weathering the stares of his fellow passengers. If he wasn't inclined to celebrate Christmas, at the very least he meant to spend it without being made to feel a carnival freak.

But more unsettling than his physical defects was what he feared might be some flaw in his mind. From his first recall, he'd been beset by the sense he was but half of a whole and that an integral part of him was simply...*missing.* The obsession had haunted him since boyhood. Equally persistent was the recurrent dream of a tall, flame-haired woman swathed in ghostly white, her one green and one blue eye fixed in horror upon his face, her full mouth hanging open on a scream sufficient to wake the dead and undead alike. His Ghost Girl, or so Tobias thought of her.

Tobias had dealt with his strange affliction as he would any yet-to-be explained phenomena. He'd made a study of it. He'd read books, a great lot of them. Metaphysics, he'd become convinced, was his only avenue of hope. After years of dead ends, he still believed that some explanation might yet be found and from it a cure contrived.

It seemed only fitting that the answer to his quest should reside between the covers of a book. Not any book, but a rare volume, a recently unearthed treatise on metaphysics by the very father of the field, Aristotle. The book was reputed to contain the recipe for the legendary *lapis philosophorum,* or philosopher's stone. Tobias had become convinced the stone wasn't legend at all. Unlike those who'd chased after it in the past, he wasn't especially interested in turning base metals into gold or even seeking eternal life. Indeed, the three-and-thirty years of earthly existence he'd so far experienced had been quite a trial. Through his reading and research, Tobias had developed a theorem for adapting the classical elements of hotness, coldness, dryness and moistness to correct, or even reverse, the imbalances in his body's own obviously imbalanced system. But before he could proceed further with his research, he needed to know the composition of the stone so he might replicate it in his laboratory.

Tobias had hunted down the sole surviving volume with the vigor most Englishmen reserved for riding to hounds. Its location had been a lord's estate mere leagues from Oxford and Tobias's own manor house. The contents of the library were to be auctioned. Unfortunately, by the time he arrived to the sale, a Scotsborn bookseller by the name of MacPherson had already acquired the volume. Despite Tobias's repeated attempts to purchase it for thrice its worth, MacPherson insisted it "wasna" for sale. He'd left for London directly thereafter, ostensibly to nurse his ailing daughter. That was five years ago. Biding his time, Tobias had kept up a correspondence with the fellow. Through their letters, he confirmed that the Aristotle remained unsold and kept under lock-and-key in the proprietor's private collection. The month before, his patience was at last rewarded. MacPherson contacted him to say that failing health rendered him willing to entertain an honest offer.

MacPherson's body might have been failing but his will was ironclad. If Tobias wanted the Aristotle, he would have to purchase the London bookshop. Tobias had agreed to the terms without haggling or regret, not because he wished to go into the bookselling trade—he didn't—but for the sake of securing his book.

But before he could take possession of his property or make arrangements to view it, the bookseller died. In the month since, Tobias had made every effort to contact MacPherson's daughter, Miss Fiona MacPherson, so far without result.

The prospect of greeting yet another new year no closer to a cure was intolerable and unthinkable. Christmas holiday or no, his every instinct screamed he dare not wait any longer. The time was here, the time was now! Fueled by that surety, Tobias rode on, not pausing for food or lodging or even to stand before a public-house fire long enough to dry his drenched clothes. Despite the foul weather, he reached Covent Garden at what must be have been a record-setting rate.

The theater district was eerily quiet, the columned portico of Saint Paul's deserted save for a few homeless taking refuge there, the fruit and vegetable market shuttered against the snow. MacPherson's bookshop was situated on a side street south of the main market square. His steel trap of a brain had memorized the direction, but Tobias was too meticulous to trust something so crucial to memory. Drawing up beneath a streetlamp, he dipped numbed fingers inside his coat and pulled out the damp deed of sale. His heartbeats quickened. He was closer than he'd thought. After five years of agonizing waiting, he was minutes from taking possession of his prize.

Christmas holiday or no, he meant to have that book!

CHAPTER TWO

"PSST, WAKE UP. FIONA, dear girl, wake up!"

Fiona started. "What...who, where?" Cracking open an eye, she peered into the pool of turquoise light leaking through her parted bed curtains, curtains she was certain she'd drawn.

"It's me, Fern."

Pushing herself upright, Fiona saw the turquoise sparkles gradually take the shape of a very handsome albeit very green-and-blue woman. At least she assumed her visitor was female. So far only the figure's haloed head had taken firm form.

Halo!

Fiona shrieked. Recovering her composure, she snapped the sheet up to her chin. "I don't know who you are or how you managed to get in, but you are to leave at once."

Her visitor chuckled. "Mind you don't take that tone with me, young lady. I was there when your mother put on your first nappies."

"That's impossible."

The specter sniffed. "On the contrary, it's entirely possible. It *is*. I'm your guardian angel, Fiona. I used to visit you in your bedroom every night when you were wee, and we'd play peek-a-boo and a great many other jolly games. I was there with you the night your dear mother passed. I held your hand as you sat at her bed-side with your father, the poor man too beside himself to comfort you. Don't you remember me?"

Fiona took stock of her situation, willing herself to stay calm. The insane asylum, Bethlehem Royal Hospi-tal, lay on Lambeth Road, a rather long walk especially in the snow and yet possible, she supposed. She remem-bered reading somewhere that some lunatics exhibited extraordinary craftiness. Did the intruder truly know of her mother or was she hazarding a lucky guess based on the portrait in the hallway below? Fiona hugged herself. Undoubtedly the voice was the very same she'd heard downstairs before retiring. Who knew how long she'd been hiding in the house.

"How can I remember someone I've only just met?" she asked, mentally calculating her odds of bolting up and making it to the chamber door.

The woman sighed. Like warm breath striking frigid air, the sigh produced a cloud of blue-and-green crystals. Lunatic or not, the magician's trick was impressive.

"Just as well, I suppose. For tonight, you may con-sider me the Angel of Christmas Future."

"The Angel of Christmas Future," Fiona repeated, suddenly suspicious.

Had Addie or Claire enlisted a family friend or ser-vant to play a practical joke upon her? But no, surely neither of her two friends would go so far as to hire a housebreaker to prove their point.

"Quite," the "angel," Fern, answered with a brisk bob of her green-and-blue braided head. "But we haven't time for further chitchat. We must be off."

Fiona left off hugging herself and hiked the covers

higher. "I'm not budging from this bed unless it's to call for a constable, so I strongly suggest you leave—now!"

"Tsk, tsk, stubborn as you ever were," the lunatic, Fern, chided. She stretched out an arm, the glittering blue-and-green sleeve falling back to reveal a slender wrist, and clasped Fiona's hand. "Hold on."

Fiona tried to pull free. Only, she couldn't. Gentle as Fern's touch felt, it was ironclad.

"Up, up and away!" Fern called out. Her voice, though soft, seemed to ricochet from the very walls, ushering a great gusting wind.

The window must have come loose from its casement, or so Fiona tried telling herself, her curls lashing her cheeks. Her kerchief flew off. Reaching for it, she felt her body levitate from the mattress.

Hovering above the bed, she whipped about to Fern floating beside her. "I must be dreaming. I must!"

Fern shook her head. "Hold on, Fiona," she called out, her soft voice rising above the wind.

Fiona held on for dear life. Together they swept across the chamber and then out the window. The night was snowy and yet the air felt oddly mild, almost balmy. Once outside, Fern picked up pace, towing Fiona along. Looking down upon gabled rooftops, London Bridge, Westminster Palace and Big Ben, Fiona assured herself she would awaken at any minute.

They flew higher, skirting the fog and finally the very clouds. At last, they alighted. Fern released her. Fiona let out a relieved breath as her bare feet met earth once more. It was night still and snowing and yet, despite being barefoot and in her nightclothes, she felt toasty warm. The neighborhood where they'd landed resembled her current one, but the street was wider and several of the constructions taller and more modern. Only one structure stood out as an eyesore, its roof on the brink of caving, its entrance denuded of all but a few chips of peeling paint. Feeling an odd sense of connection, Fiona looked up. A broken sign hung from its rusted chain above the door. *MacPherson and Daughter Booksellers.*

She whipped about to her guide, too caught up in relief to care if Fern was a lunatic, a magician or an actual angel. "Da's bookshop. It's still here! I must have found a way to save it from that blackguard Templeton after all!" Her spirits dipped as she took in the sagging front steps. "Only, whatever happened?"

Fern's face clouded. "Enter and see for yourself."

Fiona hesitated, a tremor of foreboding dragging down her high spirits. "I'm not sure I should. I mean, it is rather late."

"Enter," Fern commanded, her tone leaving no room for disobedience.

Taking hold of the weathered wooden rail, Fiona climbed the three short steps to the door. Despite the late hour, the front door stood open. She hesitated and then stepped inside, Fern floating behind her.

Fiona caught her breath. Cobwebs congregated in corners and piles of dusty books littered the unswept floor. More books were crammed haphazardly onto the sagging shelves. Rotund silver-coated felines, not the Grey Ghost but his progeny perhaps, roamed the room, occasionally stopping to feed from the numerous bowls scattered about. There was such a general atmosphere of chaos, neglect and despair that Fiona almost missed seeing the room's one human occupant.

A grizzled woman wearing a rusty black gown perched on a stool by the settle, the gnarled fingers of both bony hands clasped about a crockery cup from which a gray, unappetizing steam arose. Her corkscrew curls bore a few cinnamon-colored streaks but were for the most part snowy-white.

Turning away from the sad-eyed creature, Fiona faced Fern. "Spirit, I don't understand. What is this place? Who is that poor, derelict woman?"

Fern shook her head. "I'm not a spirit, dear. I'm your Angel of Christmas Future. We haven't all night, so do try to keep up."

"Sorry," Fiona said to placate her. Whatever else she was, Fern was Fiona's ticket home.

Fern's angelic features eased. "The scene before you is Christmas Eve 1915, twenty-five years hence. But don't take my word for it. I know these days you only credit the proof of your eyes." She patted Fiona's shoulder as if she were a puppy. "Enter and have a closer look."

Fiona hesitated. "I'm afraid."

"Poppycock, there's nothing to fear. She is but a shadow of events that may come to pass. She can neither see nor hear you and even if she could, you'd find her bark far worse than her bite."

A gentle push propelled Fiona forward. She braced for her weak ankle to fold but it didn't. In fact, it felt every whit as sturdy as her other—proof indeed she must be dreaming. Still, determined to discover all she could, she crept closer.

The ringing of the shop's bell sent both Fiona and the crone starting. The latter lifted her face from the bowl and Fiona gasped. The sour-faced crone was her!

Trembling, she spun about to Fern. "That can't be me! It simply can't."

Fern's voice was gentle yet firm. "It can be. Indeed it is you. Or rather, you twenty-five years hence, this bookstore your only home, a cup of gruel your only Christmas Eve repast, your cats your only family."

Fiona wished with all her heart to walk away and yet she couldn't. Repelled though she was, she was also morbidly fascinated. How could she possibly have come to such a pass?

She shook her head to clear it. "I must be dreaming. I must!"

The angel shook her haloed head. "I'm afraid not, dear. You're having a vision of your possible future, and that is quite different from a mere dream."

Two females stepped inside the shop. Beribboned baskets looped over their wrists, they swept past Fiona and Fern. Staring, it struck Fiona that their straight-skirted carriage gowns must be in the first stare of some strange new fashion. The above-ankle hemlines seemed, to her, shockingly short. Peering beneath the brims of their fashionable hats, she found herself looking at Addie and Claire. Both women had aged with the utmost grace. Their lightly lined faces radiated happiness and health, and their figures remained straight-backed and slender.

Beyond relieved, she rushed to her friends. "Addie, Claire, it's me, the *real* me." Circumventing her future self, she threw open her arms but neither woman seemed to so much as register her presence.

Deflated, Fiona dropped her arms and took a backward step. "They don't know me."

Fern floated up beside her. "They, too, are but shadows of the future. They cannot see or hear you." She settled a consoling hand upon Fiona's shoulder.

Tears in her eyes, Fiona shrugged it off. "Then what is the point?"

"The point? There you go again with all that overthinking." Tsking, Fern shook her head. "Listen, watch and, beyond all, look to your heart. The point, or rather, the answer resides there."

"But—"

"Hush!"

For a supposed angel, Fern was bloody bossy. Fiona opened her mouth to say so but before she got out the first word, the triad began speaking.

Fiona's future self rose on creaking knees. "You're late." Scowling, she dragged her thin, bent body toward her two visitors. Fiona winced to see that her limp was bad beyond what she'd ever feared it might become.

Addie spoke up. "It is my fault entirely, Fi. I got so caught up in helping Jemma choose the trim for her wedding gown that I quite lost track of the time."

"Jemma is Adelaide's eldest daughter," Fern whispered, answering Fiona's unspoken question. "Unlike you, Addie married her soul mate. She and Sebastian have so far shared twenty-five years of wedded bliss during which they've been blessed with five beautiful children."

Certain she must have misheard, Fiona repeated,

"Addie married Sebastian Hartley? But everyone was sure he would wed her sister, Grace."

Fern cut her off with a nod. "Addie and Sebastian followed their hearts. They have two girls and three boys, grown now. Inspired by her parents' happy example, Jemma will wed her young man on New Year's Day. With the wedding but a week away, Addie is a busy mother of the bride."

Claire's voice drew Fiona back to the scene unfolding. "I am to blame, as well. Simon brought the twins over and, this being their first Christmas, I couldn't tear myself away from the little darlings."

Fiona suspected she knew the answer and yet she couldn't keep from asking, "The twins?"

Fern bobbed a nod. "Yes, Claire's grandchildren, the first of many to come. Like Addie, Claire followed her heart and wed her soul mate. They had a boy, Simon, and now Simon and his wife have twins. This holiday season promises to be a happy hubbub for both Addie and Claire."

"And yet they still find time to visit an old friend," Fiona whispered, tears welling.

"Nice of you to find time to visit an old friend," Future Fiona croaked, sarcasm dripping.

Shocked, Fiona swung about to Fern. "Surely I would never be so rude."

Fern shrugged. "The seeds of bitterness sewn in the present have had twenty-five years to grow into a twisted tree."

Fiona turned away from the angel, too ashamed to meet her gaze.

Ahead, Claire blinked, registering surprise and,

Fiona fancied, hurt as well. "Of course we would. Our book club meetings may be long ended, but still you're our oldest friend, Fiona." Claire set her basket atop the counter and came around to take Future Fiona's hand.

Addie came up to the crone's other side. "Won't you come with us now? Sebastian and I would dearly love to have you as our guest for Christmas Eve dinner."

"And I should be honored if you'd join us on the morrow for Christmas supper," Claire added with a hopeful smile.

Fern leaned in and whispered, "As you see, your friends have stuck by you all these years."

A lump lodging in her throat, Fiona observed her future self's craggy face softening ever so slightly. "I thank you both for remembering me, but I've made my feelings plain for these past twenty-five Christmases and it seems I must waste yet more breath to do so again. Christmas is a great deal of rot and rubbish, a great deal of humbug. What reason do I have for gratitude or for making merry on Christmas Day or any other?"

Addie and Claire exchanged sad-eyed looks. "I suppose we should be going," Claire said.

Solemn-faced, Addie nodded.

Setting down their baskets, they turned to go.

Fiona ran toward them. "No, don't go. Addie, Claire. I'm sorry. Come back. Come back!"

They couldn't hear her, of course. Watching her two best friends disappear out the shop door and into the mist, Fiona choked back a sob. "In the future, I feel as though I have nothing for which to be grateful, nothing at all? This is beyond dreadful. It's…tragic."

"It *is* tragic," Fern agreed. "And yet did you not say much the same earlier this very day?"

Fiona didn't bother to deny it. "Is there nothing that can be done to alter the outcome?"

Fern hesitated. "The scene before you is one possible outcome. There is one more for you to see." She held out her hand. "Come with me."

Fiona hesitated but the angel took hold, and once again she felt herself towed along as if carried by the tide. All at once the motion stopped. Fiona opened her eyes. They were in the bookshop still but in the back room used for storage. At least she thought so. Waltz music filled the air. A champagne bucket brimming with ice stood beside a cozy cloth-covered table set for two. A lone man stood at the window, contemplating the snowy streetscape. His pale hands were clasped behind his broad back, and his white-blonde head bent as if in deep thought. Abruptly, he turned about, and Fiona found herself staring into handsome features sculpted as if from marble—and crystal clear eyes. Opaque irises widening, he started toward her—and froze.

Her breath catching, Fiona drew back. "Who is he?" Unlike the future versions of Addie and Claire, he alone seemed to see her.

For the first time, Fern smiled. "He is your One True Love, and he has been waiting for you for some time— five years now. The only question remaining is, are you ready to receive him? Are you, Fiona? For both our sakes, I hope so."

Gaze trained on the man, still frozen in midstep, Fiona swallowed hard. "For both our sakes? What do you mean?"

For the first time, Fern looked less than self-assured. "It is nothing. I'm not allowed. Oh, do forget I—"

Fiona folded her arms. "I want to know."

The angel sighed. "Oh, very well, if you must know, The Powers That Be have given me until the final stroke of midnight on New Year's to unite you with your One True Love. If we—I—fail, you will live out your days as a spinster, and I will have to wait a full century for another chance to earn my wings."

Striving not to be obvious, Fiona glanced around the angel. Indeed, no wings were in evidence. "You mean to say you would be penalized for my failing to find true love?" At Fern's sad-eyed nod, Fiona felt a stab of sympathy. "That hardly seems fair."

Fern sighed. "Fair or not, those are The Rules."

"I'm not sure I'd recognize true love if it knocked on my door," Fiona admitted. Considering she was still dreaming, there was no point in dissembling.

Fern hesitated. "Let us hope and *pray* that is not the case. Still, I've done all I can for one night. I must take you back to the present now. It's coming on midnight."

"What happens at midnight?" Fiona asked, wondering if she really wanted to know.

Fern opened her mouth as if to answer, and then pressed her lips tightly together. "From here on, my dear, that depends entirely on you."

CHAPTER THREE

FIONA AWOKE TO A loud drubbing. Disoriented, she kicked free of the tangled covers, pushed herself upright and tore back the bed curtains. The window, so far as she could see, remained firmly closed. Feeling through the darkness, she found the bedside lamp and turned it up. The dream of her Angel of Christmas Future had been so very real she half-expected to find Fern's robed form standing at her bedside.

No one was there, of course. Except for Grey, tail twitching at the foot of her bed, she was alone. She straightened her kerchief and willed her palpitating heart to settle. She was a woman of logic and letters. Angels, like ghosts and fairies, simply did not exist. The culprit was that damnable Dickens tale. Small wonder she loathed Christmas. Everything about the holiday seemed to wreak havoc upon her peace.

More banging from below assured her that her late-night caller was no imaginary figment but flesh-and-blood real. She got up. Padding barefoot across the chamber, she peered outside. A horse stood hitched to the post, a trail of human footsteps leading toward her shop. Her caller, whoever he or she might be, must be standing on her stoop. Her thoughts flashed to her two friends. Addie, she knew, had a day of travel ahead.

Fearful that some ill might have befallen one or both of them, she pulled on her robe and hurried out into the hallway.

STANDING FROZEN ON THE bookshop stoop, one shoulder raised against the snow avalanching from the roof gutters, Tobias struck the door knocker against the weatherworn wood, lightly at first and then with increased vigor. A dozen or so strikes in, he took stock of the deserted street and considered that the hour must not be merely late but unseemly so. If the tolling of the nearby church chimes could be credited, it was midnight. Still, he'd come this far and the light showing in an upstairs window suggested that someone, no doubt the disagreeable Miss MacPherson, was both at home and awake.

A key's scraping from the other side of the door snapped Tobias to attention. He watched, breath bated, as the brass knob slowly swiveled. The door swung back. A tall sylph shrouded in white stood on the threshold. Framed by corkscrew curls, her oval face was pale and freckled, her wide mouth full-lipped. But it was her eyes that froze his blood and sent him searching for his next breath. One green and one blue, they stared up at him in abject horror as though he was the one of them performing the haunting. Whether she was a ghost or not remained to be seen. Regardless, Tobias knew to a certainty he'd come face-to-face with his destiny. Before he could absorb that stunning epiphany, she opened her mouth and screamed.

For the first time in his life, Tobias didn't pause to ponder. He didn't pause to think or, indeed, to breath.

For the first time in his life, Tobias followed his instincts and simply acted. He seized the beautiful specter by the slopes of her slender shoulders, pulled her to him and claimed her mouth in a searing, silencing kiss.

CAUGHT UP AGAINST A hard male chest, her mouth possessed by lips that felt soft, supple yet firm, Fiona felt like snow subjected to the suddenly blazing sun of a January thaw—helpless to do other than melt.

He is your One True Love, and he has been waiting for you for some time—five years now. Or so Fern, her guardian angel, had said in her dream.

Another dream, she thought, *a delicious one this time.* She sank against her Dream Man with the complete confidence that this encounter, like her recent foray into the future, must be pure fantasy. But such a lovely fantasy and so very vivid! The scents of wet wool and bay rum and old books engulfed her. Strong male arms banded her, holding her firmly yet gently, as she'd secretly yearned to be held but never before had.

Fiona kissed the fantasy figment back with more than a decade of shored-up fervor. She reached up and stroked the back of her hand down one lean jowl. Despite the cold and his unnatural pallor, he felt surprisingly warm. He hadn't shaved. Stubble, as pale as snowflakes, scored her skin, a delicious diversion from his lips, which felt entirely too soft and good moving over hers. For the second time that night Fiona felt as if her feet had left the earth, as if she and her spectral suitor were spiraling up toward the snow-banked sky.

A tongue's velvet sweep snapped her back to her

senses. She planted both palms upon his chest and pushed—hard.

Flustered, Fiona stepped back. "You, sir, are not only a rake but a trespasser. I must ask—no, *insist*—you go on your way at once or…" Fiona paused to think. Really, what could she do? "Or I shall scream again, bloody murder, and this time I shan't stop until the bobbies arrive to cart you away."

If the intruder was cowed, he didn't show it. He fixed his unblinking, opaque gaze upon her face. "I am Tobias Templeton and the deed in my pocket makes this bookshop my property. Only one of us is the trespasser here and that person, Miss MacPherson, is you."

"MISS MACPHERSON," TOBIAS SAID, dripping melting snow onto the woven hearth rug in the bookshop's back parlor, "please forgive my earlier…lapse. I assure you, I do not go about…embracing strange women out of turn."

By now he ought to be accustomed to streetlamps flickering out as he passed, to black cats streaking across his path and to beautiful women such as the bookseller's bluestocking daughter loathing the very look of him. Fiona MacPherson was hardly the first female to recoil at the sight of him, though admittedly she was more vocal than most. Considering not only his freakish looks but his unannounced appearance on her doorstep at such an ungodly hour, her screaming seemed a perfectly logical response. Still, it had cut him to the quick. Then again, she was the woman of his dreams, his Ghost Girl, the ethereal female he'd always thought of as the harbinger of his destiny. Only,

Miss MacPherson wasn't ethereal nor was she a girl. From the way she'd kissed him back, she was entirely a woman.

"You think me strange?" Perched on the edge of a worn settee, Miss MacPherson tilted her head and regarded him with keen, mismatched eyes.

Tobias peeled off his gloves and held out his hands to the fire. "Of course not… I did not mean to imply… Dash it, Miss MacPherson, I cannot say what came over me out there. But when I heard you scream, I was overtaken with this…strange compulsion to kiss you."

That she'd recovered so swiftly, and with such equanimity, spoke to her apparent sound sense. He only hoped she would employ that most admirable trait to honor the terms of his agreement with her late father.

"Pray let us speak of it no more, sir." Miss MacPherson pressed four fingertips to her temple. "I am not usually of such a nervous nature, but it has been a most trying evening."

"I am sorry to hear it."

And he was. At the same time he felt queerly comforted that his unannounced appearance was apparently not the only happening to have rattled her.

Butting against his boots had him looking down. A silver-colored cat, the biggest and broadest he'd ever before seen, stropped his legs.

"Hullo, there." Tobias stooped to scratch between the silver ears. "You're a fine, fat fellow, aren't you? And what might your name be?" he inquired, mindful of Miss MacPherson watching.

The cat replied with purring but no real information.

Miss MacPherson, however, supplied, "I call him the Grey Ghost."

"That's a substantial name for a cat."

She smiled stiffly as though she wasn't much used to it. "He's rather a substantial cat."

"He seems as though he must be fond of his food," Tobias ventured.

She nodded. "He is. Other than climbing and descending the stairs once a day, he takes no exercise. I suppose I should let him outside to prowl, but I couldn't bear the thought of any mischief befalling him."

She looked vulnerable suddenly and achingly young for all that he guessed her to be nearing thirty. To his best knowledge, she had no remaining immediate family. All alone in the world, Tobias well knew how that felt.

Filled with the compulsion to comfort her, he found himself saying, "He strikes me as more of a homebody than an explorer. I'll wager he's perfectly content lounging about the shop."

A frown found its way back to her face. "If you are seeking to soften me up by pandering to my pet, you can spare yourself the trouble."

He stepped away from the fire, wondering when or rather if she intended to invite him to sit. Eying a comfortably worn wing chair with particular envy, he answered, "I wasn't pandering as you put it. I rather fancy cats and dogs, too, although not when it's raining them as it was when I set out today." He tried for a smile.

She didn't smile back, but her gaze traveled over him. "You are wet through," she said as if seeing him for the first time. He almost fancied her voice carried a note of sympathy. "Fancy a drink?"

Tobias hesitated. He wasn't much of an imbiber, and he'd already lost control of himself once. There would be no repeat of that mad and altogether magical kiss, he assured himself, vaguely wondering why the vow had him feeling more wistful than relieved.

He shook his head. "I shouldn't wish to impose."

"It's rather late to worry about that, don't you think?" Rising, she lifted a slender hand to waive away any further objections, and Tobias found himself recalling how those long light fingers had felt on his flesh.

He inclined his head. "I'll take a spot of sherry if you have it."

A less than ladylike snort was her response. "My father was a Scot, Mr. Templeton, and my late mother Irish. Whiskey is the sole spirit we keep, Scotch whiskey from the stills of Dinwiddie Diddle."

"Dinwiddie Diddle?" he echoed, wondering if she might be toying with him.

She answered with a reverent nod as though the silly-sounding place was some sort of Elysian Field. "It is a little hamlet in the Scottish Lowlands known for its stills and the quality of Scotch whiskey produced. My father was born there, and supposedly, I have cousins there still."

Her hitching stride brought her to the mahogany side-board, and suddenly he understood why she'd insisted he precede her through the bookshop to the back of the house. Miss MacPherson was crippled, though until now she'd done a bloody fine job of hiding it. Seeking to save her both steps and embarrassment, he met her at the sideboard.

"You've not been?" he asked, mindful of the accident her father had mentioned five years ago.

Back to him, she poured out the whiskey. "No."

"Perhaps you'll visit someday soon?" Once he signed over the five thousand pounds sitting in a certain London bank account, she could well afford to travel the earth's four corners.

Avoiding his gaze, she turned and handed him a glass. "I shouldn't think so."

Their fingertips brushed, and Tobias felt as if an electrical current shot up his arm, the soft humming settling in his fingertips. Admittedly, his skin was more sensitive to temperature and touch than a normal person's and yet her wide-eyed gaze told him she'd felt it, too.

She raised her glass, which was every bit as full as his. *"Sláinte,"* she said, somewhat shakily, or so it seemed to him.

He lifted his drink in salute, feeling less than steady himself. "Bottoms up."

They settled into two chairs by the fire. Like everything else in the shop, the needlepoint cushions showed signs of wear, but Tobias found the effect more homey than shabby. Installed in her snug little back parlor—his parlor now, he supposed—Tobias could almost believe they were conducting a social call. Almost.

Miss MacPherson apparently wasn't only a tippler but a connoisseur of the spirit. Warming the glass between her palms, she expertly swirled the Scotch, then lifted it and took a whiff. The aroma apparently pleased her, for her features relaxed and her full mouth widened into what looked to be a smile, the satisfied smile of a woman thoroughly sated. Watching her, Tobias couldn't help wondering if she would wear a similar expression after making love. He dealt himself a brisk mental shake. He could ill afford to entertain such lascivious thoughts, not when the Aristotle was as good as within arm's reach.

To distract himself, he regarded his glass. Following her lead, he swished the amber liquid about and then lifted the glass to his nose. The fumes singed his nostrils, but he forced a smile. "Indeed, Miss MacPherson, I am looking forward to this."

Miss MacPherson set the rim of her glass against her lips, her luscious lips, and tilted it ever so slightly back. Lowering it, she ran her tongue along her bottom lip, and Tobias felt a telltale and most inconvenient tightening in his groin.

"Small wonder the Scots call it the water of life, aye, Mr. Templeton?"

"Quite." He tipped back his glass and swallowed. Lowering it, he felt as if someone held a lit match to the back of his throat. He regarded Miss MacPherson through streaming eyes. "I appreciate your hospitality, Miss MacPherson, but as we are both quite awake despite the ungodly hour, I propose we settle our business so that I may be on my way."

Cinnamon brows winged upward. "I fail to see what business we have."

Tobias stiffened. "There is nothing to be gained by playing coy. You have received my numerous correspondences, including the letter from my solicitor—received, but not answered them. You are aware I purchased this shop and its contents from your father shortly before his demise for a handsome sum."

Miss MacPherson pulled back her shoulders and shot up her chin. "My father did not consult me. Had he, I would have told him that I had no wish for him to sell. At any price."

Regarding her fierce face, Tobias regretfully conceded that the social aspect of their visit was officially ended. The gloves were off, the die cast. Under other circumstances, he might have found himself admiring her foolhardy if stout spirit. Dash it, he did admire her. But as much as he might wish for more time to sip his Scotch—and indeed, it was tasting better by the moment—and admire the fetching picture she made in her nightclothes, he hadn't the luxury of it.

His gaze settled on her slipper-shod feet, one pinkish toe peeking out from the hole atop the badly frayed footwear. "Whether you wish it or not is immaterial. Your father wanted it for you. Our arrangement will allow you to live anywhere you wish, travel anywhere you wish." Feeling overly warm suddenly, he slipped a finger beneath his shirt stock.

She drew back and shuddered, putting him in mind of a child confronted with a spoonful of medicine. "But I do not wish to go anywhere. This is my home. I am quite content to remain as I am."

Tobias prided himself on understanding people, as well as phenomena, but Fiona MacPherson baffled him. Owing to his condition, his "traveling" was confined to the books he read from his armchair. Greece and Pompeii, Italy and India—what he wouldn't give to experience even one of those fascinating places first-hand, to stand out on the deck of a steamer ship and let a dazzling Mediterranean sun wash over him. Quite obviously Miss MacPherson did not share his passion. The little fool was looking a fortune and freedom in the face and choosing to turn her back on them.

He swallowed more of the Scotch and considered his options. Threaten her with legal action, he supposed. He would be entirely within his rights to do so. Indeed, if she forced his hand he would do so, and yet he detested the thought of bringing her greater grief.

Tobias blinked. His eyes felt so heavy he could scarcely keep them open. Finding a bed for the night suddenly seemed a most pressing concern. Let her keep her bloody shop. It was the Aristotle he was after.

He gave his head a shake to clear the cloudiness. "Very well, you may stay on as my tenant if you wish. Hang tenancy, I shall sign the shop back over to you provided you…hand over my book. The Aristotle," he clarified, wondering why his tongue suddenly felt so exceedingly thick.

She set her jowl and scowled. "I am sorry to say, sir, you have come a long way for naught. That particular volume is not for sale."

His vision, ordinarily so keen at night, was becoming more bleary by the moment. He leaned closer and matched his blurred gaze to hers as best he might. "Fortunately, I have no need to buy it. I already own it."

"You are mistaken, sir." She sniffed, the delicate tip of her nose flaring, putting him in mind of a thoroughbred filly. A filly that, despite his fatigue, he badly wanted to mount and, yes, tame. "That particular volume resides in my father's private collection, not the shop's inventory, and hence you have no claim upon it." She set her glass down on the settle and stood. "Now I must ask you to leave."

Tobias rose as well, the room seesawing. "Hand over the Aristotle and I will gladly go."

Gladly indeed, for by now it was abundantly obvious what was wrong with him. Miss MacPherson had got him drunk! He advanced a step toward her, aware that he was weaving. Only, the foot he'd picked up seemed to be fashioned of lead. Dropping it back to the floor, he crashed backward into the chair.

Her extraordinary eyes widened. "Mr. Templeton!"

Tobias fitted a hand to his head, willing the world to cease spinning. "Just a bit…woozy is all. Only need… to…h-have…a lie-down."

"Mr. Templeton," she intoned, her doubled faces looking dire indeed, "you cannot possibly stay the night. We are without a chaperone."

Tobias opened his mouth to reply but even that small effort sent him tipping.

Slight as she was, she caught him against her. "Mr. Templeton!"

"Call me Tobias." Sliding down the length of her, the silken, supple length of her, he landed them both on their knees. "Not a ghost…not a ghost after all." He peered into her extraordinary eyes for a long, soul-searching moment, then the lights dimmed and the world went black.

HELPLESS, FIONA LOOKED down at the white-blond head pillowed upon her breast. "Mr. Templeton. Mr. Templeton!"

Snoring was his only response. The man was out like a lamp turned low.

What the bloody hell had just happened? She'd known some lightweights in her time—Addie became beset by the giggles after only a few sips of sherry—but never before had she known anyone, a man, to become drunk so quickly. Mr. Templeton had had only the one glass. Aside from his impulsive and quite…stirring kiss on her stoop, he'd seemed perfectly sober upon his arrival— sober and entirely determined to get *his* bloody book.

Unbidden, the myth of the Norse god of thunder, Thor, popped into her mind. She recalled one tale in particular wherein Thor had accepted a challenge to drain a drinking horn dry. Only, it was a sucker's bet. The horn was bottomless, for it contained the very sea. The god drank and drank and yet the level in the vessel remained steady.

Holding up Mr. Templeton, his large body pinned against her, she glanced over her shoulder to the sideboard. Unlike Tobias's drink, the decanter of Scotch stood at three-quarters empty. Three-quarters empty! The drams she'd poured them, while generous, should barely have dented the contents.

Soft tinkling, a cross between wind chimes and a woman's light laughter, echoed throughout the room.

"This is not funny, Fern. Not funny at all." Fiona firmed her lips. "If you are listening, if indeed you even exist, note I am not amused."

Bracing up her burden, she considered her options. Assuming she could get him up and herself, as well, she might struggle him to the front door and set him out on her stoop. Doing so would only serve him right.

But it was beastly cold and snowing heavily. He might well freeze to death or, barring that, catch his death of cold. Enemies though they were, she didn't care to live with a death on her hands.

Beyond that, if the angel in her dreams might be believed, Tobias Templeton was her One True Love.

She turned back to him. His hair had fallen forward over his brow from whence it grew in the most splendid widow's peak. Resisting the impulse to brush it back, she shifted his weight against her. His strangely colorless, strangely beautiful eyes were closed but by now she knew them to also be both large and luminous, and generously fringed in feathery white lashes. And his lips, scarcely darker than the marbled white of his face, had felt not cold at all but most warm as he'd taken possession of her mouth.

But she could ill afford to think about that now. Wrapping an arm about his waist, she somehow maneuvered them from their knees to their feet. Panting, she paused for breath. Her cheek pressed against his pale one—they were almost of a height—she steeled herself to ignore how very good he smelled.

"Let us get you to bed, sir. One True Love or not, it seems *someone* is *hell-bent* on seeing that you spend the night."

CHAPTER FOUR

December 24th, Christmas Eve Day

CONTRARY TO HIS CUSTOM, Tobias awoke before noon the next day. He would have expected a splitting head and a cotton wool–lined mouth—indeed, it seemed he richly deserved them—but instead he felt uncommonly rested and refreshed. Thankfully, the window curtains were still drawn though he sensed the sunlight peaking in along the edges. Lifting the blanket that Miss MacPherson had thoughtfully pulled over him, he was equally thankful to find that other than his cravat he wore his full complement of clothing.

He sat up in bed and surveyed his surroundings. The chamber was Spartan by modern standards and yet unmistakably feminine, the chintz curtains and needlepoint carpet and frilly white robe hanging upon the back of the door proclaiming it to be a woman's room. Not any woman's room. Miss MacPherson's room!

Tobias leapt onto his knees, scanning the chamber for her possible whereabouts. His gaze struck the floor at the foot of the bed. A mussed blanket and pillow were left out. She must have spent the night there. Her cat occupied that spot now. Stretching, the beast yawned and looked at him but did not bother getting up.

Tobias considered the previous evening. What had

happened? Might Miss MacPherson have drugged his drink? He didn't like to think so. The last thing he recalled was feeling woozy and asking to lie down. Quite obviously he'd passed out completely. What must she think of him? Tobias scarcely knew what to think himself. How a sylph like Fiona MacPherson had managed to haul him upstairs and into bed, with her limp, no less, was a mystery he had no time to ponder.

Feeling like a churl, he rose and walked over to the washstand. Staring into the moisture-spotted mirror, he confirmed he looked a fright. White-blond hair stood out from his head at odd angles and a day's growth of bristle blanketed his jaw. Impatient as he was to take possession of his book, still he was a civilized man. He could hardly seek out Miss MacPherson in his present disreputable state.

His leather satchel sat out atop the scarred mahogany dresser. After depositing him in her bed, Miss MacPherson must have hauled the heavy satchel upstairs herself. He'd had the forethought to pack his shaving kit if not much else. Tamping down his impatience, he lathered his face and carefully set about scraping away the stubble.

Dousing the razor in the chipped china urn, it struck him that the previous night had not been an utter disaster. He might not have the Aristotle in his possession, not just yet, but a part of the mystery surrounding his "curse" was solved. His Ghost Girl was no ghost at all, but a flesh-and-blood woman. Recalling their kiss, and the enthusiasm with which she'd kissed him back, he would be hard-pressed to name anyone more fully, passionately alive than Miss Fiona MacPherson.

Admittedly, he might not have much—indeed *any*—experience in these matters. As with traveling, he'd had to rely on what he'd gleaned from books. And yet he knew unequivocally that he and Miss MacPherson had most definitely "connected" in a very physical way. How warm she'd felt tucked up against him, and how infinitely right it had felt to hold her thus. For the span of several heartbeats, he'd almost found himself forgetting the book—almost.

He rinsed the razor and dried it along with his face. Guilty though he felt and rightly so, he couldn't allow himself to be diverted from his purpose. The previous night, he had permitted a surfeit of spirits and a pair of pretty ankles to interfere with his judgment and his mission. There would be no more lapses.

His ablutions completed, he took out his silver-backed pocket comb and ran it through his hair. His clothes looked as though he'd slept in them, which of course he had. There was no help for that. Restored to something approaching respectability, he stepped out into the hallway and made his way downstairs to face Miss MacPherson and the proverbial music.

He found her in her office at the front of the shop. Seated at the small secretary desk, she didn't bother looking up, though she must have heard his approach on the uncovered floorboards. Tobias hung back, taking his opponent's measure. Her abundant hair, so gloriously wild the night before, was pulled into a low bun at her nape. Her slender, straight-backed figure was covered from neck-to-toe in black bombazine, the queue of jet buttons reaching just below her chin. A pair of wire-framed spectacles perched on the bridge of her nose, which he noticed was delectably turned up at the tip and, he felt sure, infinitely kissable. Still, pouring over an open ledger, a fountain pen in one long-fingered hand, she looked to be all business. Then again, so was he.

Standing out on the threshold, Tobias cleared his throat. "Expecting brisk custom on Christmas Eve?" he asked from the doorway.

She didn't as much as glance up. "One never knows. There were a few customers yesterday, browsers mostly but there was one sale during my book club meeting."

"You're in a book club?" Intrigued, he edged closer. "What do you read?"

She shrugged. "A good many things—biographies, histories and, on occasion, novels. We read Mr. Dickens's *A Christmas Carol* this month but then that's tradition." She still hadn't looked at him, but at least they were talking.

Tobias had read the book, too. He hadn't much cared for the story, not because he found it all that farfetched but because the sense of being haunted struck too close to home. "What did you think of it?" He entered the room without being asked.

She reached up to keep the spectacles from sliding. "It's a rather silly story, I suppose, but Claire and Addie fancy it." She made a notation on the margin of one ledger page, a few angry slashes that Tobias felt certain must mean grim news.

"Claire and Addie are your book club mates, I gather?"

"They are." She put down the pen with a huff and glared up at him. "But I'm quite certain you're not here to query me on my reading interests or my friendships, are you, Mr. Templeton?"

"No, I am not," he admitted. "Actually, I'm here to make you an apology, a *second* apology. It wasn't my intention to…er…put you out of your bed."

Her beautiful mismatched eyes bored into him. "Putting me out of my house is perfectly acceptable but evicting me from my bed merits an apology? You have a curious concept of chivalry, Mr. Templeton."

"You might have put me in your father's room," he suggested.

That she looked daggers at him told him he'd uttered sacrilege indeed. "No one sleeps there."

"Sorry." Tobias grimaced. "I see I am in your black book still."

Her silence sealed it. Leaving him in limbo, she went back to her ciphering.

Tobias was accustomed to being stared and laughed at, to being screamed at and occasionally fled from, but being ignored was altogether new to him. He found he did not like it, not one whit.

He walked up to the desk. "I regret having to disappoint you, Miss MacPherson, but I am not going to disappear simply because you wish it."

"Hmm, that *is* disappointing."

"If you wish to see the back of me, then you know what you must do."

"So you've said." She smothered a yawn behind her hand.

But Tobias was undeterred. Two could play at this game, but there could only be one winner.

Tobias was determined the winner would be him.

Bypassing the desk, he strolled over to the fireplace. A glass-framed photograph of a woman with dark hair and eyes took pride of place on the plaster wall above the mantel. Her gown's leg-o'-mutton sleeves and bell-shaped skirt proclaimed the picture to be several decades old.

"Your mother perchance?" Her sudden stiffening confirmed he'd made a lucky guess. "She is lovely."

Tobias didn't think the petite, dark-haired woman could hold a candle to her daughter's vibrant, if unconventional, looks, but "lovely" seemed a safe enough remark to make.

Miss MacPherson closed the ledger, pushed back from the desk and stood. "She is." The rustle of stiff skirts announced she was making her way over to him. She joined him by the portrait. "I always wanted to look like her."

He turned away from the photograph to study her bright eyes and freckled face. His gaze strayed to her mouth, her bee-stung bottom lip especially, and he felt his own mouth water and his sex harden.

Stepping back from the portrait, she shuttered her gaze. "I follow after my father, I'm afraid."

"You sound sorry for that."

She didn't deny it. "When I was little, I was fascinated with anything to do with the supernatural. Ghosts, goblins and witches were my heroes, not the pansy princes and princesses they supposedly harassed. In point, I wanted to *be* a witch. While other little girls were playing with dolls and putting on pretend tea parties, I was gathering talismans and casting spells, or trying to. I even went so far as to dye my hair black, or at least that was my intention. My father found me out and intervened before I might do so. That was the only time he ever sent me to my room without supper." Her face took on a wistful expression.

Curious, he asked, "What do you imagine to be amiss with your looks?" Even swathed in mourning black, she was a stunner.

She frowned. "They're so blasted...*sunny*."

Tobias was astonished. He rather fancied "sunny" in no small part because sunshine had always been forbidden him. Fortunately, looking at Miss MacPherson didn't hurt his eyes. Not in the least. In point, he found her piquant freckle-cheeked face, brilliant green-and-blue gaze and abundance of radiant red hair quite easy on the eyes. Under other circumstances, he might find himself content to stare at her for the better part of a day.

But he had business to conduct.

He blew out a heavy breath. "I realize this bookshop is your childhood home and must hold many such fond memories. I have no desire to 'put you out' of it, as you say. Nor do I have any particular need or desire to possess it. Indeed, when I contracted with your father to purchase it, at his insistence, I'd assumed I'd likely let the building to another shopkeeper or raze it altogether so that something more modern might be built."

A gasp greeted that pronouncement. "This shop may not look like much to you, sir, but indeed you are correct on one score. It is the only home I have ever known and the only one I shall ever desire. My father built this business when he was little more than a boy. He brought my mother here as a bride. I was *born* here."

Tobias felt himself on the cusp of losing patience yet again. Hadn't he just gone to great lengths to assure her he didn't want the bloody shop? If all women were as swine-headed as Miss MacPherson, his bachelorhood might well be for the best.

"And I am perfectly willing to sign the deed back over to you as soon as you hand over the Aristotle." Gentling his tone, he added, "You really have no choice, my dear."

She bit her bottom lip and Tobias found himself recalling in vivid detail how very good her mouth and tongue had tasted. "I will think on it," she finally said.

Tobias shook his head, which had commenced hammering and not because of any Scotch. "You have what remains of the day to cease your sulking—"

"Sulking!"

"And to deliver my book, so I advise you not to think overlong. I mean to leave for Hungerford by the moon's first light and when I do, I will take the Aristotle with me—or else."

LUNCHEON WAS A COLD COLLATION of sliced cheeses, salted meats and stale bread Fiona cobbled together from her pantry. Neither she nor her unwanted houseguest had exchanged so much as a word since sitting down to it. Still, she was finding that ignoring Mr. Templeton, or at least *pretending* to ignore him, was not the simple matter she might have supposed. Looking up at him through the veil of her lashes, she caught herself licking her lips much like the Grey Ghost did when eyeing a plump bird outside the window. Now that she'd grown accustomed to his strange, striking looks, she found him to be quite simply beautiful.

Nor could she rid herself of the previous night's madcap dream. Dream though it was, it had felt so frightfully real. In it, she had seen Mr. Templeton quite clearly. If her Angel of Christmas Future was to be believed, Tobias—Mr. Templeton—was her One True Love, her soul's mate. There was no denying Fiona had recognized him on the stoop—not only recognized him but permitted him to kiss her. And not only a peck but a true kiss. A kiss that was deep and searing and, yes, soul-searching. It seemed she was in peril of losing her mind or her morals or, perhaps, both. And yet neither prospect troubled her half so much as the grim dream image of her future self sitting sour-faced and alone in the ramshackle shop. Though Fern had admitted it was but a *possible* future outcome, the tragic scene had haunted Fiona for the rest of the long, sleepless night.

Across the table, Mr. Templeton cleared his throat. "You really ought to rethink your position, Miss MacPherson, for your own good. If I leave here without the Aristotle, the next person you deal with will be my solicitor and, I assure you, he is far less accommodating than I."

She picked up the cheese knife and sank the blade into the wedge of Stilton. "I suppose that is meant to frighten me." First Fern and now Mr. Templeton. It seemed scaring her witless was the order of the day.

"Perhaps it should." His clear-eyed gaze brushed over her face, oddly gentle.

Fiona shivered. Fighting the feeling he was seeing straight through her, she replied, "It doesn't."

That was a lie, of course. These days she found herself afraid of so very many things—being caught up
in a crowd, losing her shop and the legacy of beloved
books, including the Aristotle, that were her last link
to her father.

He picked up the napkin from his lap and used it to
wipe the corners of his mouth. Enemy or soul mate,
whichever he was, he had the most perfectly beautiful
manners. "Has it occurred to you that once you wed,
your husband may not wish to sell books? He might not
wish to live here at all."

She forced a shrug, the bite of cheese sticking in her
throat. "You are a bachelor, are you not?" Last night
she'd found his left hand to be without a ring, but then
some married men declined the custom. "Do *you* make
your every decision based upon how your future wife
might or might not feel about it?"

His opaque gaze flattened. "As I do not anticipate
entering into marriage, no, I do not."

Fiona was torn between relief that he was indeed
unmarried and a sinking sense of disappointment that
he was apparently a confirmed bachelor—so much for
her One True Love. "You do not desire a family?"

His pained expression had her regretting the question.
"Look at me, Miss Templeton. Look at me and tell me,
do you truly require an answer or are you simply being
cruel?"

The accusation caught Fiona unawares. Well-versed
as she was in her many faults, she'd never been deliberately mean. "I assure you, sir, I did not mean to
imply…" Rather than risk doing further damage, she
let the defense die.

His world-weary look lanced her heart. "I make it a point to avoid mirrors, Miss MacPherson, and yet still I must peer into one every morning in order to shave. I know full well how freakish I appear. And if I did not, the reactions of…strangers would confirm it."

In strangers, he clearly included her. Then again, they'd met only last night and unlike the romantic scenario of her dream, they'd met as enemies, not friends and most certainly not soul mates. And yet that kiss, that mad, amazing kiss, had been undeniably real and strangely…*right*. A day later, she could still feel the imprint of his hands on her body, the taste of his lips upon her tongue.

"On the contrary, sir, you are quite…beautiful."

The declaration slipped out before she could call the words back. Mortified, she fought the urge to bang her head upon the tabletop.

A tight smile greeted that most improper declaration. His gaze shuttered but not before she glimpsed the hurt reflected in the pools of those moon-pale irises. "Flattery from the fairer sex is not without its charm. Still, if you think for a moment that contrived compliments will deter me, you are mistaken."

"It was not my intention to gull you, sir." Toying with her teaspoon, Fiona scoured her brain for a safer subject. "But what of you? You certainly are free to do as you fancy. Do you travel? Do you see the world?"

His smile slipped. "It is different for me."

"How so?"

"Well, for one thing, I am a man."

Ordinarily, Fiona would have bristled at the implicit inequity of that statement. She did bristle and yet, still

recalling her close acquaintanceship with all that mas-
culinity standing on her stoop, she shivered as well—not
with cold but with heat.

She cleared her throat, which suddenly felt as though
clogged with a goodly dollop of the despised Christmas
plum pudding. "I am aware of that."

"Are you also aware that I suffer from a heretofore
undiagnosed disease, the main symptom of which is
sun blindness?"

Fiona feared she did a poor job of concealing her
surprise. She'd supposed that his striking looks must
be a family trait. "Is there no cure, no tonic you might
take?"

He hesitated. "None that I nor any of the physicians I
have consulted over the years have found. I have goggles
outfitted with a special tinted glass for those occasions
when I am compelled to go out in daylight but for the
most part it is easier to remain indoors. My manor is
both my sanctuary and my prison."

Fiona swallowed hard. The kinship she felt with this
strangely beautiful man made it increasingly difficult to
remember that, dream or not, in the real, waking world,
he was her enemy.

He startled her by saying, "You have rather unusual
eyes yourself."

Fiona stiffened. "I am well aware of my oddity," she
answered, hating how vulnerable she felt. "You need not
point it out."

Tobias blinked. He shook his head as if to clear it.
"My dear Miss MacPherson, were you any other female,
I would swear you were fishing."

Embarrassed, she drew back. "Fishing! I assure you, I am not."

"Then you mistake my meaning. You mistake *me*. Your eyes are beautiful. *You* are beautiful."

Fiona ducked her head. "I believe you are the one of us paying false compliments."

"Indeed, I am not." He locked his gaze on her as though willing her to look up at him. Powerless to resist the pull of those crystalline orbs, Fiona complied. "Everything about you brims with color, with life, while I am as pale and passionless as a specter."

"Mind you, I rather fancy specters," she admitted.

There was a protracted pause during which they shared a smile.

Rather than risk saying something stupid again, she set her napkin aside, pushed back her chair and rose. For once, her wobbly stance had nothing to do with her injury. "I should return to my...bookkeeping."

Mr. Templeton got up, as well. "I see I have offended you yet again."

Fiona shook her head, which felt to be swimming. "No, you have not. It is only that I am not much used to compliments, not since..."

Fortunately Mr. Templeton was too much the gentleman to press her. "In that case, I shall see you...later."

"Yes, later," she agreed, halfway out the door.

Fiona hurried out of the chamber. Gaining the front hallway, she paused to peer out the window. Outside, the wind howled. The fog rolled in. And the snow continued falling. It seemed The Powers That Be conspired against her yet again.

Despite his determination to be on his way, and hers to see him go, Mr. Templeton would not be taking himself or the Aristotle anywhere that day.

CHAPTER FIVE

CURSED, THAT SINGLE word seemed to encapsulate the theme of Tobias's life. Standing at the shop window and watching the blizzard through goggle-sheathed eyes, he confronted his most pressing problem. That problem was not the Aristotle, presumably safely hidden somewhere in the shop, nor even the physical condition that had created his need for it. No, Tobias's problem had a distinctly human face and form.

Miss Fiona MacPherson.

She'd been holed up in her room since luncheon. Though that meal could scarcely be said to have gone well, still he'd enjoyed parts of it. Miss MacPherson might be the most exasperating female he'd ever encountered—she *was* the most exasperating—but she was also the most exciting, intelligent and delectable one. He marveled he'd ever mistaken her for a Ghost Girl, a phantom. With her abundant copper-colored curls, beautiful blue-and-green eyes and sun-kissed countenance, she radiated warmth and energy and sunshine. And yet Fiona's light didn't hurt his eyes, not one whit. Quite the contrary, her radiance, her life force, drew him like the brightest of beacons.

The more time he spent in her company, the more convinced he became that her frosty facade was just that—a facade she'd erected to prevent being hurt again.

Having barricaded himself from normal living for three decades and counting, Tobias was well-acquainted with the feeling. Walls. How easy they were to build—and how damnably difficult to tear down.

Blizzard or not, book or not, Tobias felt compelled to stay on long enough for them to become better acquainted. He wanted Fiona MacPherson to like him, not because he'd decided to let her keep her bookshop or because he was paying her five thousand pounds. He wanted her to like him for himself. He wanted it rather a lot.

The pity was she loathed his very shadow.

Deep mewling, more croak than purr, drew his attention downward. The Grey Ghost flopped atop Tobias's booted toes and then rolled over onto his back.

Tobias chuckled. "We should all have such confidence."

He reached down to rub the cream-colored belly. As he did, he spotted a folded paper tucked inside the cat's collar. For a handful of heartbeats, Tobias considered letting it be, but his scholar's mind was fueled by an innate and rather burning curiosity. Unlike his mistress, Grey at least liked him. Speaking to the animal in a low, soothing tone, Tobias managed to retrieve the note without any bloodletting.

He stood with the paper, catching a whiff of Fiona's verbena scent as he opened it and read:

My dear sir, I hope you will forgive my rapid and rather rude luncheon departure. Please allow me to make recompense by accepting my invitation to supper at seven o' clock. —FM

Tobias stared down at Miss MacPherson's—Fiona's—

note. Spare though it was, still he felt thunderstruck. An invitation to sup was the very last thing he would have expected from her. But then it was Christmas Eve. Who knew, but perhaps The Powers That Be listened to prayers after all. He struck out for Miss MacPherson's office to find pen and paper so that he might scribble a response.

FIONA HAD RETREATED NOT TO her office but to her room. More than an hour later, she'd not scraped together sufficient courage to come out. Instead she stood at her bedroom window, losing herself in the falling flakes. It was as if The Powers That Be had exploded an enormous feather pillow over the city. Still, eventually the snow would stop, the roads would clear and Tobias—Mr. Templeton—would be on his way. Bleakly she admitted that at some point over the past few hours she'd begun holding on to the Aristotle for an entirely different, entirely selfish reason.

Once she gave up the book, Tobias would be gone.

Ever since she'd received his first telegram informing her of his acquisition of the bookshop, Fiona had envisioned Tobias Templeton as an ogre who'd taken advantage of a desperate, dying man. The circumstances of the past not yet twenty-four hours had forced her to revise, albeit grudgingly, her initial opinion. Intelligent and witty, learned and kind, Tobias was a man that any woman with a grain of sense would be proud to have for a sweetheart. No, not only a sweetheart but a soul mate.

They hadn't known each other for a full day, and yet already she was accustomed to his luminous eyes and marble-chiseled features. His crystalline eyes tipped in lashes of snow seemed to return her stare from another place and time. Looking at him, she felt her limp lessen and her fears subside. And then there were his lips, pale yet inviting, the bottom one so full and soft-looking she could scarcely hold back from reaching out to trace its curve with her finger.

A woman approaching the milestone age of thirty would do well to think upon her future. A woman about to attain said milestone on Christmas Day might well be inclined to ponder her future with especially careful scrutiny.

A human life was but a blink of time. Whether or not it was a dream, the previous night's journey with Fern was a wake-up call. In another few hours, she would turn thirty. Fiona still found that difficult to fathom. At this rate, it would be 1915 before she knew it. Did she truly wish to spend the next twenty-five years brooding in her bookshop? Should that possible Future Christmas indeed come to pass, Fiona meant to greet it with a smile, not a scowl, with sweet memories and good friends to bear her company along with the books and the cats.

Footsteps approaching her closed door had her turning about. But instead of the door opening, a folded sheet of foolscap was slid beneath. The sight sent her heart hitching. It must be a farewell note from Tobias. He must have decided to let his solicitor deal with her after all. Even so, her fears were all for him. The foolish man would catch his death riding in this weather, assuming he managed to make it back to Hungerford at all.

Breath bated, Fiona walked over and bent to pick up the paper. Hands shaky, she unfolded the vellum and read:

My dear Miss MacPherson, I accept your kind invitation to dine and anticipate it with great pleasure. Until seven o'clock. —TT.

Fiona clasped the letter to her breast, the same breast against which Mr. Templeton's—Tobias's—head had rested so snugly the night before. She didn't remember asking him to supper. Had she? Her lunchtime blathering was already a bit of a blur. Regardless, she quite clearly recalled that he'd proclaimed her to be beautiful. Beautiful! Feeling like a girl again, she hurried over to her wardrobe, in her haste, forgetting the limp. She had more pressing concerns than ruminating over a five-year-old injury.

Chief among them was the age-old question: whatever would she wear?

FIONA DREW UP TO THE threshold of the dining parlor just as the clock in the front hall struck its seventh and final chime. Peering inside, it struck her that she was about to step into, if not a fairy tale, then certainly the happy ending to the previous evening's dream. Candles blazed from myriad silver candlesticks. The gasolier hanging overhead shone as bright as a star, the once smoke-stained glass globes as crystal clear as Tobias's eyes. The small round table was covered in shimmering blue-and-green cloth. It held an epergne festooned with Christmas greenery, two flutes bubbling with what looked to be freshly poured champagne and two place settings of silver-covered dishes. Judging from the aromatic smells wafting her way, the latter must contain their Christmas supper, though so far as Fiona knew, her pantry was down to the bare bones. A silver bucket with what must be the rest of the champagne stood tableside. How *had* Tobias managed it?

Her dinner guest stood at the window, staring out onto the still falling snow, his elegant hands folded behind his broad back. He must have heard either the clock or her approach, for he turned. Limned by moonlight, he stole her breath and set her heart to haplessly hammering.

Clear gaze widening as it had in her dream, he started toward her. Fiona couldn't say for certain, but she fancied he caught his breath.

Drawing up before her, he acknowledged her presence with a deep bow. "Miss MacPherson, you look… enchanting."

Fiona couldn't say whether or not she met the standard for "enchanting," but for the first time in five years she no longer felt broken or faded or plain. It was the dress, of course. With its bustled back, the Nile-green silk was hopelessly out of vogue, and yet the nipped-in waist and deep jewel tone flattered her. A double strand of emerald-and-sapphire colored glass beads festooned the low, square-cut neckline. More beads glittered from the butterfly sleeves, waist and trained skirt. A doubled rope of pearls, her mother's, looped about her bare throat.

Feeling at once pleased and shy, she entered the room. "I decided to leave off mourning for the evening in honor of the holiday. Considering how my father loved Christmas, I do not think he would mind."

Tobias smiled. "I did not know him well, but I believe he would approve."

Fiona more than suspected that was so. Her father had been a merry man with scant patience for moping. Happy to turn the topic to a more neutral one, she said, "You look very fine, as well."

Fine was an understatement. He was positively splendid. Turned out in an ebony tailcoat with satin-faced lapels, cream-colored waistcoat and tailored trousers that might have been painted on his leanly muscled hips and calves, he was eerily, ethereally, perfectly beautiful. A sapphire stud, the only color on his person, winked at her like a shining star from his shirt stock.

The beginnings of a blush brought color to his handsome face at last. "Thank you." His gaze slipped away from hers. "It was most kind of you to make me a loan of your late father's clothes."

Fiona stared at him. It had occurred to her to wonder how he had fit a suit of evening clothes into his small satchel. "I assure you my father never possessed anything so fine."

Her Da had been no fashion plate. Other than his clan tartan, taken out from its cedar chest on rare special occasions, he'd worn the same rusty black suit of clothes every day of the year.

For a moment Tobias appeared startled and then his chiseled features relaxed. "A gift from the gods, then?" he suggested, his supple lips sliding into an endearing sideways smile.

"Or the angels," she added gamely. Looking about at her dream of Christmas Future come to life, she couldn't help but wonder if a certain apprentice angel might be doing more than *watching* over them.

He startled her by asking, "Will you do me the honor of dancing with me before we dine, Miss MacPherson?"

Sudden panic seized her. With her limp, she would likely fall flat on her face, a humiliating end to an evening that promised to be most pleasant, even magical. "But we have no music," she protested, seizing on the ready excuse.

"I shouldn't be so certain of that, Miss MacPherson. The gods have been generous indeed. In this case, they led me to your office closet. I was searching for pen and paper and instead I found this. I hope you do not mind."

He stepped aside, and Fiona saw what she had missed before. Sitting atop a pedestal in the chamber's far corner was her gramophone, the metal amplifying horn polished to a high gloss. After her accident, she'd packed both the music player and her collection of discs away, presumably for good, as she had her pretty party dresses and her dancing slippers and her hopes for a Happily Ever After.

Might Tobias have been rooting through her things in search of the Aristotle? Her brain answered with a "yes," but her heart assured her he had not. Fiona banished the black thought from her mind. In her dream, Fern had counseled her to listen to her heart and, for once, she meant to do so.

Tobias walked over to the music player and turned the crank. He stepped back, and the scratchy strains of Fiona's favorite waltz filled the small room.

Returning to her, he held out his hand. "Shall we?"

Fiona hesitated, whetting dry lips, and then gave him her hand. Holding her gaze, he carried it to his mouth and brushed his lips atop her satin-sheathed knuckles. She shivered, feeling as though every fiber of her being had suddenly become enervated, awakened—alive.

He gave back her hand with a wry smile. "I will try not to tread upon your toes, though as I have never before danced, I make no promises."

Fiona glanced down at her feet. She wore her black satin slippers, the darling ones with the pointed toes trimmed in black beading. She'd once danced many a waltz, polka and quadrille in those very shoes. She had not put them on since her accident.

Caught up in her own uncertainties, it took her a full moment to register what he'd just revealed. "You've never danced?"

He shook his head. "I have not." He blushed, and Fiona regretted having spoken so rashly. "When I was younger, my mother tried to teach me but I soon lost patience and so did she. I suppose neither of us really saw the need for it." His smile dimmed as though reliving a less-than-pleasant memory. "I did, however, read a book on ballroom dancing. A manual, actually."

Tenderness rushed her. She took back his hand. They both wore evening gloves, his of wrist-length cream-colored kid leather. Still, their clasped hands brought her enormous comfort—and confidence. "The waltz is likely the simplest dance with which to begin." It was also the most romantic, though she refrained from saying so.

She guided his right hand to the center of her waist,

shivering as his warmth seeped through the silk. "Place your palm on the small of my back, like so, and take hold of my hand with the other." She rested her hand lightly on his elbow. Tobias shuddered.

She withdrew at once. "It isn't only your eyes that are sensitive, is it? It is your skin, too."

He hesitated and then admitted, "I feel the cold and heat more keenly than others do, but I had not considered I might be more attuned to...touch." Flushing deeply, he reclaimed her hand, setting it back in place. "Attunement and discomfort need not be synonymous. In point, I find your touch quite...pleasant."

Fiona cleared her throat, marveling that the room suddenly seemed very warm. "From here, it is but a matter of sliding our feet, a simple one-two-three, and step in, step close. Mind how we are making a small circle?"

Staring down at their toe-to-toe stance, he nodded. "I do."

Tobias proved a swift study. After a few circuits about the room, he left off staring down at their feet and instead looked into Fiona's eyes, his movements as fluid as if he'd been dancing all his days. Now that he'd gotten the steps down, they glided along the room as though belonging to one body. Their very breaths seemed to match. Fiona scarcely felt her weak ankle at all.

"I forgot how much I adored dancing," she confided. Indeed, for the first time in five years, she felt well and truly whole.

Tobias swallowed, the ripple traveling along the corded column of his white throat, a throat Fiona suddenly wanted very badly to press her lips to. "I find myself enjoying it, as well."

Lest he see the lust in her face, she looked over his shoulder. Her gaze snagged the window, the draperies safely drawn back now that the sun had set. Moonlight streamed inside the glass panes though it snowed still. The rooftops and streets sparkled as if dusted with confectioner's sugar. A snowman with two coal lumps for eyes and a carrot for a nose stood guard by her front gate. It was as if The Powers That Be had dumped a bottomless bag of sugar upon London City and were willing to be more generous still.

Then again, it was Christmas or, at least, it would be in another few hours—Christmas, as well as her birthday. Amazingly neither eventuality struck the terror in her heart they would have just a day ago. Closing her eyes, she settled her hand back upon Tobias's shoulder and fitted her body more closely to his. Happy in the present and hopeful for the future, Fiona didn't only dance again. She felt as if she could fly.

CHAPTER SIX

SHORTLY BEFORE MIDNIGHT they parted company by the stairs.

"I shall take the sofa for my bed," Tobias announced, feeling deflated by the thought.

Still, he could not rightly expect Fiona to share her room with him a second night. That she'd slept on the floor the night before still shamed him.

"You will do no such thing," she told him, her former firmness returning. "That old thing is hard as bloody bricks and the needlepoint covering is most chafing. You must…take my father's room."

His gaze flashed to her face. "Fiona, I cannot."

"Of course you can. It lies at the opposite end of the hall from mine and though it's become a bit dusty, the linens are fresh." He started to protest again, but she cut him off with a look. "Da would want me to open it up just as he would want me to leave off mourning and celebrate Christmas and…my birthday."

"It's your birthday?" Tobias asked.

She hesitated and then admitted, "I was born on Christmas, just after midnight."

As if on cue, the hallway clock tolled. They both turned to it and then back to one another.

Tobias waited for the twelfth and final knell before saying, "I wish you had told me earlier. I might have persuaded the gods to come up with a cake to go with the very fine champagne and ginny fowl," he teased.

How Fiona had managed such a feast was beyond his reckoning. Based on the cold luncheon she'd cobbled together, he'd gathered she barely cooked at all. Fine as the supper fare was, they'd been too caught up in each other to do more than pick at their plates. The champagne, however, they'd polished off quite nicely.

"Tonight was perfect exactly as it was. One might even say it was a dream come true," she added with a smile as though enjoying a private joke.

"Not quite perfect. Belated as it is, allow me to wish you a happy birthday…Fiona." He said her name slowly, deliberately, though she'd yet to grant him the liberty.

She was within her rights to reprimand him. Instead, her smile broadened. "Thank you for making it such a memorable one…Tobias." She turned away and stepped up to the landing.

Watching her float up the stairs, the limp all but erased, Tobias felt his heartstrings snapping. If only things might be different between them. If only that blasted book might not stand in their way.

But as the saying went, "if wishes were horses, then beggars would ride." The adage was well-taken. Simply wishing for things didn't make them so. Action was what counted. In daring to dance for the first time since her accident, Fiona had shown tremendous courage. Tobias was proud of her.

Restless, he roamed the shop, randomly pulling books from the shelves but finding nothing that could hold his interest beyond a scattering of minutes. Finally, he conceded that his best course was to retire. It couldn't snow forever. On the morrow he would reprise the subject of the Aristotle. The sooner he had the volume in his possession, the sooner he might be on his way. He was becoming far too fond of Fiona MacPherson for the good of either of them.

He climbed the creaking stairs with a heavy heart. Stepping off the landing, he came upon her closed door. He hesitated, wavering. A sliver of light showed at the crack beneath. She must be up still. The temptation to enter was strong, too strong. As if pulled by an invisible puppet string, his arm lifted and he knocked.

"Come in," she called from within.

At the sound of her voice, Tobias began to shake. He wrapped a trembling hand about the worn metal knob and turned it. The door opened.

Fiona stood by the fireplace. Barring the double rope of pearls she still wore, she'd undressed for the night. With her copper curls streaming over her bare shoulders, and her lithe body sheathed in a low wrapper of some shiny, creamy fabric, she looked like a bride on her wedding night.

His bride.

"Mr. Templeton."

She smiled. Not a tentative smile or a tight-lipped smile but a full, generous smile, as warm and welcoming as the look in her eyes. Tobias felt the warmth of that smile wrap about his heart like an embrace.

"I came to wish you a happy birthday—again," he ended lamely.

He glanced to the bed, turned down but yet to be lain in, and then back at her. Reminding himself that he was a gentleman, as well as a scholar, he began backing out into the hallway.

Fiona called him back. "In that case, do come in." Her expression, it seemed to Tobias, was exceedingly tender.

He cleared his throat, which suddenly felt too thick for talking. "Were I to do so, Miss MacPherson, I could not swear to behave as a gentleman ought."

The light touches they'd exchanged during dancing had attuned him not only to her body but also her being. Though he'd always prided himself on his honor, Tobias doubted he could trust himself to do no more than hold her.

The twinkle in her eyes had him hardening. "What if I were to say that I do not wish for you to behave as a gentleman? The bald truth, Tobias, is that I do not wish for you to behave at all."

"Fiona!" This time the familiarity slipped out unbidden.

Barefoot, she crossed the creaking floorboards toward him. "Stay with me, Tobias, not because you want the Aristotle or the shop, but because you want me."

Tobias closed the remaining distance between them, meeting her in the room's center. "Of course I want you. *How* I want you. This pull between us...we cannot allow ourselves to give in."

"Can we not?" She caught his hand, her slender fingers enfolding his wrist. "We are both sufficiently mature to know our own minds and wants. I, for one, very much want...this."

Before now, Tobias had been more than a little

disdainful of those who gave in to their carnality. But gazing at Fiona, seeing the desire in her beautiful green and blue eyes, he finally fully understood what it meant to be human and fallible and weak.

She ran the back of his hand alongside her satiny cheek. "Tonight isn't any birthday for me. It is my thirtieth," she admitted, biting at her bottom lip.

Tobias wasn't surprised. When they'd first met, he'd judged her to be in her late twenties or thereabouts. The gravity with which she made the admission suggested she considered thirty to be a great age.

"Should I stay the night with you, Miss MacPherson, you have my word I shall never reveal it to another living soul. Still, I would despise myself if I thought I'd taken advantage of you."

Fiona let go of his hand. She leveled him a wary look. "Because I am as yet an innocent or because I am past my prime, or perhaps, both?"

"You are most certainly not past your prime. You are as fresh and lovely as any man might wish."

Fiona let out a long breath. "Well, then."

Holding his gaze, she took a step back and untied her robe's sash. The garment parted, revealing the peak of one pink-tipped breast and skin as creamy smooth as the pearls she still wore. She shifted her shoulders and the garment slid slowly off. Naked, she stood before him, all shy smiles and satiny peaches-and-cream skin. The sprinkling of sun-kissed flesh along her collarbone begged for kisses, but before they went any further, Tobias had an admission of his own to make.

"I've never before been with a woman." He swallowed hard. "I have, however, read a fair number of books on the subject." The fierce heat shooting into his face stalled further explanation.

She pressed the back of her cool hand to one of his burning cheeks. "Then once again we shall be perfectly partnered, like dancing."

"Like dancing," he echoed, and felt his lips relax into a smile.

They hadn't yet kissed, let alone coupled. Still, looking into Fiona's uniquely beautiful eyes, feeling the warmth of her spirit touching his, Tobias suddenly knew what it meant to be one with another person.

Sated.

Completed.

Whole.

FIONA SHIVERED AS TOBIAS laid his hands atop her shoulders. Closing the small space between them, he drew her against him. He bent his head and kissed her. Fiona's breath stalled. This time when his tongue slid along the seam of her lips, she neither screamed nor shoved him away. Instead, she opened for him like a flower. Tobias entwined his tongue with hers, his hands skimming her shoulders and breasts, hips and buttocks. Everywhere he touched, her skin skittered. A hot tingling overtook her. An urge so primal she could scarcely credit it as belonging to her pounded through her veins.

She dragged her mouth from Tobias's and pressed her lips to the blood-warmed pulse point at the side of his neck. She'd fantasized about that spot for the past several hours. Ravenous, she grazed him with her teeth. The slightly salty taste of Tobias's skin did not disappoint. He might look as though made of marble, but instead of chilly stone he was warm-blooded and alive.

Fiona dragged her mouth away and drew back. "Take your clothes off...please."

Tobias hesitated, but only for the span of a single heartbeat. He took a step back and began undressing. Watching buttons drop and clothing fall away, Fiona found herself licking dry lips.

Naked, he stepped out of the pool of clothing and Fiona caught her breath. As good as he'd looked in his evening clothes, he looked even better out of them. Pearlescent skin stretched tautly over lean muscles and elegant long bones, a Renaissance nude come to life. His shoulders were broad, his torso rippling with muscle. A narrow waist and hips descended into powerful thighs and calves that must owe their muscle to long hours spent in the saddle. Silver hair glittered from his pectorals and fine strong limbs, putting her in mind of the first dusting of Christmas snow.

That this oddly beautiful man desired her as she did him struck her as nothing short of a miracle, a Christmas miracle. No present left inside a hung stocking or beneath the bows of a festooned tree could have brought her nearly so much pure joy. Far from frightened, she couldn't wait to take in his magnificence.

Holding her hand, he led her over to the bed. Fiona lay down in the center of the turned-down sheets. Tobias joined her. Settling in beside her, he drew her into his arms. "Lest I become so caught up that I forget to wish you so later, happy birthday again, Fiona."

Smiling, Fiona lay a hand alongside his handsome face. "Merry Christmas, Tobias."

It was a merry Christmas and a happy birthday both. Tobias proved to be a thorough and attentive lover. Taking his time, he learned the landscape of her body, sprinkling soft kisses over her forehead and closed eyelids, the corners of her mouth and cheeks, her throat and shoulders and finally her breasts. Her freckles, of which she'd always been slightly ashamed, seemed to hold for him a particular fascination. Throughout, he frequently paused to look into her eyes, to smooth a stray curl back from her forehead or simply to repeat how beautiful he found her to be, how perfectly pleasing in every way.

His warm white hand cupped her. "Open for me, Fiona."

Fiona did. She drew a quaking breath. A steady, humming ache struck at her core and began to slowly build.

Tobias slid his big body down the length of her. His head disappeared between her parted thighs. His tongue swept over her, suckling and teasing at turns. As amazing as she felt, for her first time she did not want to climb Mount Olympus alone. She wanted to do so with Tobias.

As if reading her wish, Tobias lifted his head and looked up at her. Kneeling, he sat back on his heels and looked down at her, gaze raw. "I won't hurt you, Fi."

Fiona shook her head. "I'm not afraid anymore."

And the bald beauty was that she truly wasn't. Not of dancing or of standing among crowds or of ceding the whole of her heart to the possibility of true love, Christmastime miracles, and a New Year's filled with fairy-tale beginnings.

He shifted to straddle her. His sex pressed against

her lower belly. Bracing one palm beside her pillow, he reached down with the other and fitted himself to her.

Despite her brave declaration, Fiona tensed. From what she'd read, a first penetration usually involved some discomfort. Eager to get this part over, she lifted her hips to meet him. But Tobias refused to be rushed. He entered her slowly and carefully, his gaze never leaving her face.

The books hadn't lied. Fiona felt herself stretched and filled beyond any imagining. A sharp sting announced she was a virgin no more. Tobias stilled. Fiona kissed the side of his damp neck, laving the small bruise she'd made earlier.

"More," she whispered, nipping him again. Feeling the lovely tingling returning, she lightly raked her nails down his sweat-slick back.

Tobias groaned. He gave her more. He gave her all. Cupping her buttocks, he lifted her against him, stroking back and forth, faster and faster. The blunt pressure built, deepened and then bloomed into something that was more pleasure than pain. Though the chamber was chill, perspiration pearled on Tobias's brow. His strokes became longer and sharper and surer. Locking her legs about his torso, she met him thrust for thrust.

Tobias pulled out and then entered her fully. Suddenly, the peaking pleasure could peak no more. Something within Fiona, a golden thread, snapped, gave way, buoying her beyond her body. Only, she didn't wish to go anywhere, not without Tobias. She anchored her arms about him, feeling his fast-beating heart as though it was her own. Holding on to him, Fiona felt the last lock on her heart fall away. She still wasn't certain she believed in angels, but she believed in Tobias. He was indeed her One True Love, her soul's perfect mate. With Tobias in her heart and her life, all her future Christmases promised to be wonderful indeed.

SOMETIME LATER, FIONA turned to Tobias and asked, "Talk to me, Tobias. What about the Aristotle makes it so important to you?"

His gaze shuttered. "I'm afraid it's a rather long and complicated history. At the end, you may think me mad. I shouldn't blame you if you did."

"Try me." She propped up on one elbow and looked down upon him. "I love long, complicated histories." *I love you* she wanted to say but stopped herself. Surely it was too soon.

She'd already decided to give him the book, not in barter for the bookshop but as a Christmas gift. It wasn't fair to use it as a carrot to keep him here. So long as she withheld it, she would never know whether he stayed because of it or her.

He heaved a sigh. "I met your father for the first and final time five years ago. The contents of the Earl of Langsford's library were being auctioned off, the Aristotle among them. I believe it may contain the recipe for the legendary philosopher's stone and that stone might be put to use in transmuting not only metals but human tissue into a finer, more harmonious form."

"You seek a cure for your sensitive eyes and flesh?" Fiona asked, ashamed of what her stubbornness had put him through.

Tobias hesitated, and then admitted, "Yes. Only, a mishap made me late to the sale. The lens fell out of one side of my goggles, and the repair required longer than I'd supposed. By the time I'd arrived, the bidding for the Aristotle was completed and your father named its new owner. I tried any number of tactics to persuade him to sell it to me, but he wouldn't be bent."

Throat thickening, Fiona nodded. "That sounds like Da."

Tobias caught her gaze and smiled. "As well as someone else I know a good deal more intimately." Below the covers, his stroking hand settled over her hip.

The bed was warm, Tobias even more so. And his hands on her felt like heaven. It would be easy enough to become distracted.

Determined to hear the rest of the story, she prompted, "Go on."

"Over the following years I kept in regular touch in the hope he might change his mind. I wouldn't say that we were friends exactly, but a mutual respect, a fellowship, grew between us. Through his letters, I learned a bit about the bookselling business and his life here in London and you. He was enormously proud of you, you know."

Fiona nodded, feeling raw emotion welling. "I do know, but thank you for telling me."

"This past year, however, his letters fell off, and I resolved myself to not getting my hands on the Aristotle anytime soon. Beyond the book, I honestly missed our correspondence. When I did hear from him again—"

"He was dying," Fiona finished, eyes misting.

Tobias hesitated. "Yes." He cuddled her closer. "He made me an offer. I could have the Aristotle, provided I purchased the bookshop. The rest you know."

"Thank you." Fiona settled her head on his shoulder. Suddenly it struck her. "I was to have accompanied Da to the auction."

Tobias's head shot up from the pillow. "The Devil you say! Why didn't you?"

Fiona hesitated. But if she'd wanted Tobias's trust, his honesty, it was only fair she respond in kind.

"I only made it so far as Paddington Station. It was the holiday season and the train platform was thronged. Someone shoved against me, just a little push, but it was enough. I lost my footing on the ice and fell. My ankle wasn't only twisted but badly broken. Of course, I had to stay behind."

They stared into one another's eyes for a long, fraught moment. Tobias was the first to speak. "We were to have met five years ago at the auction!"

"It would seem so," Fiona agreed, shivering to think how close they'd come to not meeting at all.

Her dream journey to Christmas Future made sudden sense. What if The Powers That Be, acting through Fern, had arranged to give her and Tobias a second chance at falling in love?

"By the by, I mean to give you the Aristotle, Tobias."

"Thank you." He swallowed hard and added, "I hope you don't think that—"

"Of course not," she broke in, reading his eyes. "Whatever happens between us, the book is yours."

Outside her window, a triple chorus of "Hallelujah" broke out, three female voices singing the praise in unison. Christmas carolers, Fiona wondered? Surely no one in her right mind would venture out at this late hour and in this weather—no one in her right *earthly* mind, that is. Happy, she closed her eyes, snuggled against Tobias and fell into a swift and sugar-plum-fairy-filled sleep.

CHAPTER SEVEN

December 25th, Christmas Day

"RISE AND SHINE, SLEEPY HEAD."

Tobias cracked open an eye to find Fiona's bright countenance bearing down on him, her beautiful unbound hair tickling his chest. Accustomed as he was to sleeping until twilight, waking up to Fiona made mornings something to which he might actually look forward.

"Good morning." He reached up, intending to pull her back down for a kiss. At least he meant to begin with a kiss.

She blessed his lips with a sweet buss before flitting off across the room to the window. "I do believe it has finally stopped snowing, but let us see for ourselves."

"Fiona, don't!"

Humming, she didn't seem to hear him. She pulled back one panel of curtain and let in the light. "Shall we dress and go for a walk in the snow? Perhaps we can build a snow-woman to keep company with the snow-man. He looks lonely out there."

Shielding his face, Tobias felt as though someone had poured acid in his eyes—and slashed a razor through his heart. "Fiona!"

This time she turned back inside. "Tobias?"

"The curtains, Fiona, for the love of—"

"Oh, no!" Whipping about, she grabbed the edge of the drapery and dragged it closed.

Shrouded in shadows once more, Tobias let his hands fall away from his face. Water streamed down his cheeks, not tears, though they might as well be.

Footfalls raced toward the bed. The mattress dipped as Fiona landed beside him. Slender arms wrapped gently about him.

Pillowing his head on one lovely soft breast, she gently wiped the wetness from his cheeks. "Forgive me, Tobias. I didn't think, I—"

"Forgot," he finished for her, wishing he might as easily do so. "There is nothing for which you need apologize, Fiona. Why should you have to keep in mind a malady that isn't yours to bear?"

Her earnest eyes fixed on his. "But it is yours to bear and so therefore it is mine, as well. Hence forth, I will exercise the utmost caution and restraint."

Saddened, Tobias shook his head. He didn't want Fiona to be cautious or, God forbid, restrained any longer. He wished for her to spread her wings and soar, to be carefree and playful and, yes, even silly whenever she wished. Above all, he wanted her to be happy and free, free as he could never be. To inflict himself on her in his present state would be to deprive her not only of daylight walks in the snow but also springtime picnics and summertime jaunts to Brighton Beach. All the trappings of the normal, happy life she so deserved. Fiona was meant to live in the light. Loving her as he owned he did, how could he condemn her to a life in his cloistered shadow world? Barring a cure, a miracle, there was no future for them, not on Christmas Day or any other.

He steeled himself to be cruel in the service of kindness and love. "These days with you have been lovely, Fiona, the happiest of my life, but unless I can find a cure, there's no future for us. Were we to attempt to build a life together in my present state, I would end up making you miserable. In time, you would come to resent not only my affliction but me. Surely you must see that?"

Face falling, Fiona shook her head. "My limp, my fear of crowds… You are the one responsible for making me see that they are obstacles only if I allow them to be. Is your condition truly so different?"

"Yes, my dear, I'm afraid it is. There is no known cure and should the Aristotle fail me—"

"You can still have a full and happy life, and we… we can still have a future together."

Tobias sank both hands into his hair. "Not the life I want. Not the future I want with you." As hard as parting from her was, Fiona's stubbornness was making it that much harder.

Locking her beautiful eyes on his, she shook her head. "You're a fine one to lecture me on seizing freedom and traveling and taking chances when you make a crutch of your condition and use it as an excuse for sending away the people who…care for you."

Tobias had steeled himself for weeping, but Fiona's dry-eyed, unflinching stare and razor-sharp honesty caught him off guard. Unprepared, he retreated into the sanctuary he knew best—scholarship. "Upon what basis beyond emotion do you advance such a weak and unsubstantiated argument? Our situations, our *conditions,* are as unlike as…as night is to day. Mine is a true affliction, a curse of birth, and one which I'm coming to suspect no words in any book can cure."

Fiona's face hardened. Her eyes were as yet quite dry. "That must make it bloody convenient…for hiding behind."

For the space of several successive heartbeats, Tobias stared at her, dumbfounded. By the time he finally found his tongue, rage ripped through him. Like the boiling lava that had erupted to bury ancient Pompeii, he let loose. "How dare you lecture me, Fiona?"

She tipped her face up to his, eyes blazing green-and-blue fire. "I dare, Tobias, because I'm your soul mate, your One True Love, as you are mine. I dare because I love you. I love you with my whole heart, not the little leftover pieces. Beyond loving you, I see you in my dreams and I hear you with my heart."

She reached across to the night table, pulled open the lower drawer and brought out a small volume bound in deep green leather. Watching her carefully unwrap it, Tobias didn't have to look within to know what it was: the Aristotle. The volume had been beneath his very nose all along.

Handing it to him, she said, "I wish you a Merry Christmas, Tobias, and a long and lovely life."

I SEE YOU IN MY DREAMS and I hear you with my heart.

Fiona's declaration haunted Tobias like a ghost's whisper. Still, steeling himself to do the right thing, he departed early that evening for Hungerford, the Aristotle wrapped in cotton wool and tucked in his saddlebag. Despite having had it in his possession for hours, he hadn't so much as cracked the cover.

Halfway to home, he surrendered to the inconvenient yet irrefutable truth. Fiona was his soul's other half, his One True Love, the sun to his moon. Without her, he was but a specter, a shadow of the man he might yet be. He'd known it from the moment he first laid eyes on her in that bookshop doorway, but he'd been too intent on the book to listen to his heart. He could almost believe that the Aristotelian tome might be nothing more than a celestially sent lure to bring Fiona and him together. Its printed pages held wisdom, perhaps, but likely no real magic. The true Christmas miracle, the magic, came from Fiona. His Ghost Girl had given him the book freely and from the bottomless well of her bountifully loving heart.

Fiona hadn't only given him the book. She'd given him her heart, wholly and without condition. What greater Christmas gift or miracle did he require than that?

He turned his horse's head back in the direction from whence he came—London and Fiona.

Morning, December 26th

"YOU DID YOUR BEST. We both did. It simply wasn't going to work," Fiona said aloud to Fern, though to anyone passing her shop's front window it would seem she addressed the two traveling trunks parked by the door. "I'm not going to have my Happily Ever After and that's that. Then again, the witches in fairy tales never do get to go off with the prince. It quite simply isn't done." The night she'd spent in Tobias's arms, first dancing and later making love, had made her feel like a fairy princess indeed. She sighed. "For what it's worth, I'm terribly sorry about your wings. Who knows, perhaps The Powers That Be will assign you a more promising case next century, someone who's better Happily Ever After material than I am."

She stopped talking and listened. There was no reply, of course. Fiona sighed. Tobias appeared to have taken her guardian angel with him. Since his leaving the previous night, there had been no mysteriously appearing clothing or feasts, no choruses of Hallelujah, no magic at all in her life.

And now she was leaving, too.

Peering out the frosted window glass, she saw that the hansom cab she'd bespoken had indeed arrived. She bent and lifted the wicker picnic basket in which she'd sequestered the Grey Ghost.

"It looks as if it's only you and me again, Grey," she said, dashing a gloved hand across suddenly watery eyes.

Christmas might not be the humbug she'd made it out to be, but falling in love was bloody hell.

RIDING THROUGH COVENT Garden, Tobias took stock of the bustling, snow-covered city through goggle-sheathed eyes. London City and its inhabitants seemed to have awakened from their holiday slumber. The sidewalks once more teemed with people, and the streets were clogged with private carriages and hansom cabs and mail coaches. Indeed, everyone seemed to be back to their routine, to daily life.

Everyone but him.

Occasionally a stare or smirk found its way into his awareness, but for the most part he was too intent on reaching the bookshop to pay them much heed. But when he did, he found the windows shuttered and the sign in the bow front window turned over to Closed.

He spotted a boy shoveling a path for the flower shop next door and called out. "You there, do you know the lady who keeps shop here?"

The boy looked up. Predictably his eyes widened and his mouth fell open but after a moment, curiosity must have gotten the better of him. He dug his trowel into the banked snow and ambled over.

Swiping a gloved hand over a red and runny nose, he asked, "The lady with the fat gray cat, do you mean?"

"The very one." Tobias walked his horse over. "Miss MacPherson. Do you know where she's gone?"

The boy's red-cheeked face took on a canny look. "It'll cost you a quid."

Swearing beneath his breath, Tobias dug into his pocket and produced a coin. He held it up.

The boy's eyes popped. "Crikey, that's a guinea!"

Tobias crushed the coin into his fist. "First, tell me her direction."

A cheeky grin replaced the awestruck look. "She's gone to Scotch Land, guv."

Tobias hadn't expected that. "Are you quite certain?" He tossed the coin.

The boy caught it between his mittens. Pocketing it, he bobbed his head. "She left a half hour or so ago for the station, arsked Mum to look after the place until the new owner arrived."

"Do you know where in Scotland she went?"

The question was met with a shrug. "Dunno."

Tobias took off his hat and raked hard fingers through his hair, his fingers catching on the blasted goggles' leather band. He recalled Fiona bringing up The Lowlands—something to do with whiskey stills and Scotch—but that was all he remembered. The Lowlands narrowed his search but barely. The region was certain to be chock-full of MacPhersons. Searching for a tall redhead, even one with one blue and one green eye might well turn into a lifelong quest. What *was* the name of that blasted hamlet?

Dinwiddie Diddle, you goose of a man. A woman's lilting voice, soft but decidedly annoyed, tickled the tip of his ear. Tobias had no time to stop and search for an explanation, rational or otherwise.

Dinwiddie Diddle was indeed it. If his memory served him, the northbound line leading into Scotland left from King's Cross. Praying he caught up with Fiona before her train pulled out, he shoved his hat back on and set his course for the station.

FINGERS CLENCHED ABOUT THE handle of the hamper holding the Grey Ghost, Fiona stood barricaded behind her two traveling trunks. Freezing on the rails had delayed her train, thickening the throng and making her trip a true test of courage.

The platform teemed with people either wishing to enter London or leave it. Standing as far back from the tracks as she could, still she found herself bumped and jostled, elbowed and shoved. A harried young mother rushing for her train nearly ran the wheel of her baby's pram atop Fiona's foot. A trio of boys with mischief plainly written on their faces passed a ball back and forth, striking Fiona and others more than once, their smirking apologies less than convincing. A portly gentleman pushed past, inadvertently poking Fiona in the foot with the point of his cane. She jumped back from his path, her big toe smarting, just as her train pulled in.

Uniformed porters rushed about, some pushing carts stacked with luggage to be stowed. Catching the eye of one whose cart was empty, Fiona beckoned him over. "Sir, sir, *here!*"

But the train's whistle covered her calling out. He turned away and hurried over to help another passenger. Fiona tried again, pitching her voice higher and waving her free hand more vigorously. It was no use. She stood too far away to be within earshot. She hated to leave her baggage unattended, but there was no help for it. If she didn't find someone to load it, she would miss her train and have to spend the next hour awaiting another. Holding on to Grey's basket, she stepped around her trunks. The cat's weight threw her off. Her feet tangled and her weak ankle folded. Panicked, she tumbled forward. It was five years all over again, only this time there would be no Da and, it seemed, no Fern to pick her back up.

Strong arms bolstered her. Grey's basket was whisked away and set safely down. Tucked against a hard male chest, the stiff tweed grazing her cheek, Fiona inhaled the now familiar scent of bay rum and old books. Half-afraid to believe, she lifted her gaze to her rescuer. The top hat and goggles hid much of his pale, handsome face from view but she would know him anywhere.

Tobias.

He'd saved her precisely when she'd needed saving the most.

"THANK YOU." REACHING UP a shaky hand to right her bonnet, Fiona stepped back.

Tobias dropped his arms to his sides, hating how empty they suddenly felt. "You're welcome."

Two large weathered trunks stood at her feet. Sitting beside them was an enormous picnic hamper. The hamper stirred, seesawing. A husky meow announced that the Grey Ghost was within and clearly none too happy about his confinement.

Tobias swallowed hard. "You're embarking on a bit of an adventure, it seems."

"I suppose I am." She hesitated. "For years, I've listened to my father's stories of Scotland, I've read travel journals of Scotland, but never have I *seen* Scotland. I decided it was time I changed that."

"When do you return?" he asked, dreading her answer. That Fiona had brought her cat didn't bode well for her trip being only a holiday.

She bit her bottom lip. "I have no plans to do so."

The confirmation sent his heart sinking. He shuffled his feet and stared down at his boot tops and struggled to find the magic or perhaps not so magic words that might persuade her to stay. Words, he'd always put such stock in them, but just when a grand declaration should have been forthcoming, he couldn't think of a bloody thing to say.

She dropped her gaze to her gloves. "There is little to keep me here. Being in the Lowlands, Dinwiddie Diddle isn't so very far away. Besides, the bookshop belongs to you now."

"I don't want it." *I want you.*

She sent him a gentle smile. "Whether you want it or not, it is yours." She lifted her lovely eyes to his face. "You've made me want to step outside the tomb, to live in the light. I thank you for that."

Tobias didn't want her paltry thanks. Nor did he want their Christmas together to be only a beautiful memory, an ending. He wanted it to be a beginning, the first chapter in a long and happy life.

"But what are *you* doing here, Tobias? I thought you'd be home by now."

"I was. Only I realized I left something behind, something most dear to me."

"The Aristotle?" she asked in a small voice.

"No, you." Tobias shook his head fiercely. "I don't want you to go to Scotland. I don't want you to go away at all. I don't want you to go anywhere. Not without me."

Fiona's mouth formed a shocked circle. "All…all right," she finally said.

"All right?" he repeated.

She nodded. "Yes."

Joy and relief flooded Tobias. He caught her up in his arms. "I'm in love with you, Fiona. So very in love. For the first time in my life, I feel as though my heart is whole and my flesh fits."

Too impatient to wait, he covered her startled mouth with kisses. At the first touch of their lips, heat radiated from Tobias's heart outward to his limbs. Deepening the kiss, he felt his entire body thrum with an intensely pleasurable warmth.

Fiona reached up to touch his face but drew back. "Tobias, your spectacles!"

He followed her horrified gaze to the ground. The leather band on the goggles had broken but the lenses and frames appeared unharmed. He stooped to retrieve the eyewear, but Fiona got there first.

Straightening, she handed the special spectacles to him. "Thank goodness they don't seem to have suffered any damage."

Tobias held the goggles at arm's length and stared.

Fiona nudged him. "Do put them on, darling, before you burn your eyes."

Swallowing his fear, Tobias lifted his head and directed his naked gaze up to the train shed's cantilevered ceiling. Iron girders supported curved panels of clear glass through which sunshine streamed. The brightness should have burned and blinded him. Only, it did neither.

Could he be...cured? If so, the Christmas miracle hadn't to do with any book. The true Christmas miracle was the dazzling woman standing before him. All these years, he'd hidden himself away in order to search for a cure. Instead he should have been searching for the missing half of his soul, his Ghost Girl, Fiona. She wasn't only his One True Love, his soul mate. She was his soul's other half.

He found his voice at last. "On the contrary, Fi, it does not seem that I must wear them at all."

Looking beyond her, Tobias could clearly see the

other passengers on the platform, down to the wart on one old woman's nose. He turned back to Fiona, her bemused, freckled face the most beautiful he'd ever beheld.

She stared at him as though she saw a ghost indeed. "Tobias, your face… It's positively…*glowing.*"

Tobias could wait no longer. He tossed the goggles aside and pulled Fiona into his arms. They kissed again, joyously, freely, uncaring of the giggles and frowns thrown their way. From somewhere nearby a bell rang, the sound's crystalline purity cresting above the commotion.

Breaking away, Fiona lifted her face skyward and smiled. "You know what they say, darling? An angel has just gotten her wings."

Tobias smiled, too, though the only angel he saw was Fiona, her lovely mismatched gaze meeting his. Framing the pale oval of her face between his blood-warmed and fast-darkening hands, he felt as if his heart, joined with hers, might overflow with the flood of love he felt.

"Whatever manner of miracle brought about my cure owes nothing to any book. It owes to you, Fiona. My cure, my miracle, owes to destiny, and my destiny, my darling, is you."

* * * * *

HARLEQUIN® A *Romance* FOR EVERY MOOD™

CLASSICS

Quintessential, modern love stories
that are romance at its finest.

Harlequin Presents®

Glamorous international settings…
unforgettable men…passionate
romances—Harlequin Presents
promises you the world!

Harlequin Presents® Extra

Meet more of your favorite Presents
heroes and travel to glamorous
international locations in our regular
monthly themed collections.

Harlequin® Romance

The anticipation, the thrill of the chase
and the sheer rush of falling in love!

Look for these and many other Harlequin and Silhouette
romance books wherever books are sold, including most
bookstores, supermarkets, drugstores and discount stores.

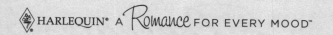

HARLEQUIN® A *Romance* FOR EVERY MOOD™

HARLEQUIN
RECOMMENDED READS
PROGRAM

LOOKING FOR A NEW READ?

**Pick up the latest Harlequin Presents® book
from *USA TODAY* bestselling author
Lynne Graham**

THE PREGNANCY SHOCK

Available in November

Here's what readers have to say about this
Harlequin Presents® fan-favorite author

"If you want spark and a heart-thumping read,
pick up any of Lynne's books....
I can never get enough of her intense stories."

**—eHarlequin Community Member Katherine
on *The Greek Tycoon's Defiant Bride***

AVAILABLE WHEREVER BOOKS ARE SOLD

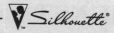

SPECIAL EDITION

USA TODAY BESTSELLING AUTHOR

MARIE FERRARELLA

BRINGS YOU ANOTHER
HEARTWARMING STORY FROM

When Lilli McCall disappeared on him
after he proposed, Kullen Manetti swore
never to fall in love again. Eight years later
Lilli is back in his life, threatening to break
down all the walls he's put up to
safeguard his heart.

UNWRAPPING
THE PLAYBOY

*Available December
wherever books are sold.*

REQUEST YOUR FREE BOOKS!

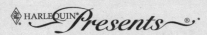

2 FREE NOVELS PLUS
2 FREE GIFTS!

YES! Please send me 2 FREE Harlequin Presents® novels and my 2 FREE gifts (gifts are worth about $10). After receiving them, if I don't wish to receive any more books, I can return the shipping statement marked "cancel." If I don't cancel, I will receive 6 brand-new novels every month and be billed just $4.05 per book in the U.S. or $4.74 per book in Canada. That's a saving of at least 15% off the cover price! It's quite a bargain! Shipping and handling is just 50¢ per book.* I understand that accepting the 2 free books and gifts places me under no obligation to buy anything. I can always return a shipment and cancel at any time. Even if I never buy another book, the two free books and gifts are mine to keep forever.

106/306 HDN E5M4

Name	(PLEASE PRINT)	
Address		Apt. #
City	State/Prov.	Zip/Postal Code

Signature (if under 18, a parent or guardian must sign)

Mail to the Harlequin Reader Service:
IN U.S.A.: P.O. Box 1867, Buffalo, NY 14240-1867
IN CANADA: P.O. Box 609, Fort Erie, Ontario L2A 5X3

Not valid for current subscribers to Harlequin Presents books.

Are you a current subscriber to Harlequin Presents books and want to receive the larger-print edition? Call 1-800-873-8635 today!

* Terms and prices subject to change without notice. Prices do not include applicable taxes. N.Y. residents add applicable sales tax. Canadian residents will be charged applicable provincial taxes and GST. Offer not valid in Quebec. This offer is limited to one order per household. All orders subject to approval. Credit or debit balances in a customer's account(s) may be offset by any other outstanding balance owed by or to the customer. Please allow 4 to 6 weeks for delivery. Offer available while quantities last.

Your Privacy: Harlequin Books is committed to protecting your privacy. Our Privacy Policy is available online at www.eHarlequin.com or upon request from the Reader Service. From time to time we make our lists of customers available to reputable third parties who may have a product or service of interest to you. If you would prefer we not share your name and address, please check here. ☐

Help us get it right—We strive for accurate, respectful and relevant communications. To clarify or modify your communication preferences, visit us at www.ReaderService.com/consumerschoice.

HP10R

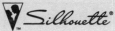

Sparked by Danger, Fueled by Passion.

RACHEL LEE

A Soldier's Redemption

When the Witness Protection Program fails at keeping Cory Farland out of harm's way, ex-marine Wade Kendrick steps in. As Cory's new bodyguard, Wade has a plan for protecting her—however falling in love was not part of his plan.

Available in December
wherever books are sold.